THE
CURE

By
JG Faherty

This is a work of fiction. All of the characters, names, incidents, organizations, and dialogue in this novel are either the products of the author's imagination or are used fictitiously.

2nd Printing 2017

1st Printing 2015 by Samhain Publishing

ISBN-13: 978-1543156522
ISBN-10: 1543156525

Cover Art: Kanaxa

"Faherty's The Cure is a terrifically written novel. I think of it as a wild elevator ride where every floor is a new level within the story, and when the door opens on some of those levels, I wanted to peek my head out of the door, have a quick look, shut it, and get the hell away from there. The Cure takes you in directions that are unexpected and masterfully realized from Faherty's imagination. It's a wild read with many unexpected turns. Faherty's got a flair for this stuff." – Matt Molgaard, Horror Novel Reviews.com

"The overall premise of the power to heal an ailing body and discharge the harmful, negative energy unto another is a highly fascinating theme and redefines the supernatural/paranormal genre. In a sea of over saturated story lines and ideas, Faherty manages to pique the interest of all readers new and perhaps even the most jaded of horror aficionados. Faherty's ability to conceal the most pivotal of heightened climaxes is unprecedented in contemporary genre writing. He keeps us guessing until the very end. Seemingly when we think we have everything figured out, he changes the questions at the last moment, making him a certifiable well-seasoned author for the ages." – Dave Gammon, HorrorNews.net

"The Cure is fast-paced and original. As I have to come to expect with JG Faherty's expertly crafted stories, this was a riveting story, full of twists and turns, strong characters and a compulsive plot. I empathised with Leah. I suffered with her. Just when I thought she might make it, along came another enemy. I genuinely had no idea how the story would resolve and the ending fitted perfectly. Thoroughly recommended. Suspenseful, thrilling horror." – Catherine Cavendish, author of THE PENDLE CURSE

"The Cure is a fast paced story that really keeps you on the edge of your seat." – Chantal Noordeloos, author of ANGEL MANOR and COYOTE: OUTLANDER

ACKNOWLEDGEMENTS

For Andrea, who, like me, hates how the furry ones we cherish never get enough time with us in this world.

Thank you's go out to the usual suspects: family and friends, always. Rena, Patrick, Erinn, Peter, Chantal, Stephen – for sharp eyes, sound advice, and a helping hand, you guys rock! As always, you make me so much better.

To Don D'Auria for his edits and Kanaxa for the great cover art – thank you!

And to all the animal owners out there. Love and enjoy them while you can, and treat them like family. Adopt from shelters. And support the organizations that strive to put an end to cruelty and abandonment.

To Mom and Dad, for everything they've done.

Part One
In the Beginning

Today is the first day of the rest of your life.
—Anonymous

Chapter One

Fifteen minutes before she saved a man's life, committed murder and started a chain reaction of events she could never have imagined even in her worst nightmares, the only thing on Leah DeGarmo's mind was a hamburger and French fries.

It had been years since she last ventured into a McDonald's—or any other fast-food restaurant—and after a particularly bad morning at work, her cravings had reached the point where she couldn't ignore them any longer.

"I'm taking lunch," she said to Chastity Summers, as she hung up her white lab coat and headed for the front door of her veterinary clinic. "I'll be back in an hour."

"Okay, Doctor D." Chastity waved, never looking up from her computer screen. She was busy entering the data on the last patient of the morning, a twenty-year-old beagle in remarkably perfect health. At one time Smokey Two had suffered from cataracts and liver disease, but he'd managed to beat them both. His owner, Tanya Weston, always told people Smokey Two was a walking advertisement for Leah's skills as a veterinarian.

Opening the door to her three-year-old Toyota, Leah felt a pang of sadness in her heart. Smokey Two couldn't keep it up much longer. Dogs rarely lived past twenty. She wiped tears from suddenly damp eyes. It would break Tanya's heart when her beloved pup finally passed away.

She glanced in the rearview mirror to make sure she hadn't smudged her makeup. People always said her eyes were like windows to her emotions, changing from hazel to brighter green when she was happy or excited, and to a murky brownish green when she felt sad or depressed.

Today there was almost no green at all, and the dark color looked odd against the glowing backdrop of blonde hair flowing down to her shoulders in waves that were always on the verge of turning unmanageable. Even her face looked pale beneath the deep summer tan.

"Get a grip on yourself," she told her reflection. "It's too nice a day to wallow in regrets."

The warm September day helped push her melancholy away, and Leah decided to treat herself to a greasy cheeseburger and fries. A determined smile on her face, she pulled out of the parking lot and headed toward McDonald's.

Leah opened the heavy glass door and entered a different world, one where the air dripped with oil, steam and fat-laden odors that simultaneously repulsed and excited her.

There's something about a McDonald's that reminds you of being a kid. Not to mention the dopamine spikes triggered by the smell and taste of hot grease and fried meats.

Why is it the foods that are the worst for you are always the ones that taste the best?

The lunch-hour crowd filled the space in front of the counter. As she waited her turn in line, Leah struggled to read all the choices on the menu board.

I've never even seen half those meals before. Guess that's what happens when you make an effort to eat healthy. I didn't think McDonald's could change so much in three years!

Luckily, the basics still held their places on the menu, and when her turn came Leah ordered a Quarter Pounder with cheese, large fries and large Diet Coke. While she waited for her food, she went to the condiments bar and gathered napkins, ketchup and a straw. Her one task completed, she let her vision roam around the crowded room. She couldn't help noticing the police officer standing a few people behind her in line.

He doesn't look like he eats here any more often than I do. Leah admired his tall, wiry frame and the way his brown hair fell across his forehead. With his dark, intelligent eyes and bright-white smile, he looked more like a politician or maybe a banker than a cop.

Smile? Oh shit, he's smiling at me! *He saw me staring at him.* Leah turned away, feeling her face grow hot. The counter girl returned with her order and

Leah grabbed the tray, nearly spilling the contents onto the floor as she hurried off to a table before the man could say anything to her.

"Christ, I can't believe I did that," she whispered to herself. "Get a grip, Leah. You're not fifteen anymore."

She took a long sip of her soda, hoping the cold liquid would drive the heat from her cheeks. Still, she couldn't help thinking about the cute, half-quizzical, half-admiring smile the cop had shown her, and she peeked to the side to watch him pump ketchup into a little white corrugated cup.

Straw still in her mouth, she tried to push away the particularly graphic thoughts all the pumping and squirting created in her head.

I guess it really has been too long. She followed her rueful thought with a quick duck of her head as the object of her fantasy glanced in her direction.

"Shut up or I start shooting!"

The shouted words made Leah look up again just as people started screaming.

A man at the counter had a gun aimed at one of the cashiers, who was crying and holding her trembling hands in the air.

"Hurry up!" The gunman's order acted like a signal for everyone to move. People fell to the ground or ran for the doors, and one of the other cashiers, a man in his thirties, darted back into the kitchen.

The would-be thief grabbed a nearby woman and pulled her tight against his cracked and aging black motorcycle jacket, his crazed eyes darting back and forth. His hostage tried to struggle, but he clamped a hand over her mouth and put the large, evil-looking handgun to her head.

"Gimme the goddamn money now, or you're gonna have brains all over your counter!" he told the two remaining cashiers in a voice as frenzied as his motions. The two teenage girls clung to each other, eyes shut, crying uncontrollably.

Leah dropped her cheeseburger, the sudden spastic opening of her fingers the only movement she seemed capable of making. *He's going to shoot that woman.* She knew it as surely as she knew that he was high on drugs, or that the two girls would never get past their fear and give him the money. *Ohmigod, he's gonna...*

A quick movement interrupted her thought as the police officer threw his tray of food in the direction of the gunman. The tray clattered on the floor and soda sprayed everywhere, distracting the man from his robbery attempt.

"Police! Drop the gun!" the cop shouted, no longer smiling. He squinted down the barrel of his service pistol at the heavily bearded robber, his dark eyes cold and dangerous.

"I'll kill her, man."

"If you do, you'll die right after her," the young officer said. Sweat stains bloomed in the armpits of his previously immaculate uniform, but neither his gun nor his voice wavered.

"Not if I kill you first." Without letting go of his hostage, the man turned the gun and fired two shots. The twin reports broke the spell that held the remaining patrons captive, and once more the air filled with screams as the remaining customers rushed for the exits.

The officer let out a cry of pain and fell backwards into the condiment counter. A wet, red smear followed him as he slowly slid down the white plastic to the floor.

"No!" Leah jumped up and ran to the officer, insanely hoping it was just ketchup dripping onto the floor, too familiar with violent wounds to be fooled into thinking it was anything but blood.

"Get the fuck away from him!" the shooter said to her, but she ignored him, already placing her hands on either side of the crimson flower blooming in the center of the man's shirt.

Amazingly, the officer—*Officer Carrera,* she read on his tag as she ripped open his shirt—opened his eyes and looked at her. "Get out of here," he tried to say, but the words disappeared in a wet hiss, informing Leah that one of his lungs had collapsed. From the amount of blood pooling around the body, it seemed likely at least one major blood vessel, probably the vena cava, was ruptured as well.

"You're gonna be okay," she told him, pressing her hands against the wound. "Lie still." The familiar warmth surged through her, followed by a sharp pain as if she'd touched a live wire. Even though she was prepared for the shock, it still made her twitch. Under her hands, the officer's body bucked as if jolted by a defibrillator. Leah started to tell him again that he'd be all right, but just then a rough hand grabbed her by the back of her shirt and pulled her away, nearly choking her in the process.

"Are you deaf, bitch? I told you to stay the fuck away." She looked up and saw the gunman aiming his pistol at her. "Now you can die alongside your boyfriend."

Without thinking, Leah grabbed the man's leg, sliding her hand up under his pants to touch his skin. Another spark, but this one brought relief, a coolness, as if a poison had been sucked out of her body.

His eyes wide and surprised, the man opened his mouth to yell but it turned into a choking gasp. Blood filled his mouth and ran over his lips. He stumbled away and his finger twitched on the trigger as he collapsed, sending a bullet whining past Leah's head to chip the tile floor before ricocheting away.

He landed hard, his eyes already blank and lifeless, a red stain spreading on the front of his shirt.

Oh shit, Leah, you've really done it this time. The thought forced her into action.

"Hurry, move him over to the counter," she ordered Officer Carrera. She grabbed one of the gunman's arms and pulled him towards the small island holding the ketchup and napkins.

Carrera rose unsteadily to his feet, then put out a hand to stop her. "What the hell happened?"

"We have to make it look like he got shot over here. Now help me!"

Carrera stood there for a moment, fingering the hole in his uniform. Then he grabbed the man's other arm and helped her slide the body over until it was roughly in the center of the blood and ketchup already staining the floor.

"Lady, will you tell me what's going on? I was shot, and now I'm fine and we've got a dead gunman."

Sirens sounded outside, reminding Leah they didn't have time to talk.

"I'll explain everything later," she promised him. "Please, just trust me." She sat down on the floor a few feet away, preparing herself to play the part of the terrified witness.

I won't have to pretend too hard, but what am I more scared of? Almost being shot or having my secret exposed?

Crouched behind a nearby garbage can, Emilio Suarez watched the events unfold in front of him like some bizzaro drug-induced hallucination. Only this was no trip or flashback. He'd really seen the young woman cure the cop, good as new after taking at least one to the chest. *Strange shit indeed.*

But that didn't compare to what happened next. She'd touched the shooter, and, next thing you know, he's lying dead on the floor. Emilio considered sticking around to see how everything played out, but decided the smart thing to do leave before the place was swarming with cops.

And to think, he'd left Manhattan because he thought he'd be safer hitting houses in the suburbs than apartments in the city. *Go figure.*

While the woman and the cop moved the dead body, Emilio lowered himself to the ground and crawled to the back exit by the restrooms, where he pulled open the door and ghosted out before anyone could see him.

He had a feeling he knew someone who would pay major *dinero* for this story.

By the time Leah finished giving her statement and returned to the animal hospital, her body was awhirl in a weird mixture of exhaustion and excitement. She'd already called Chastity and explained the situation, telling her to reschedule her remaining appointments until later that afternoon or to another day.

She pushed through the double doors into the cool reception area, where she found three patients waiting for her: Tim Damara with his five-year-old poodle, Sammy, June Watson and her ancient Pekinese named Muffins, and a young girl she didn't recognize with what looked like a small tabby cat in a carry box.

"Jesus, I guess it was too much to hope for that I could come back and catch my breath," Leah whispered to Chastity, as she went behind the glass-fronted counter and pulled on her white lab coat.

"You should have seen it before. I think you'll need the rest of the week to catch up," the vet tech said, rolling her eyes. Her frazzled expression and mussed hair testified to how busy the clinic had been. "I rescheduled seven or eight appointments. The rest of them said today was the *only* day they could see you." Chastity handed her the first chart.

"Of course." Leah closed her eyes and took a deep breath.

"Leah, are you sure you're all right? You just saw someone get shot, for God's sake. Maybe you should go home."

"No, I'll be fine. Let's not keep them waiting." Opening the door between the reception area and the hallway, Leah called out, "Mister Damara? You can bring Sammy to exam room one."

"Good night, Leah."

Leah looked up from her paperwork. Chastity stood at the office door, pocketbook in hand.

"What time is it?"

Chastity laughed. "Nine-thirty. Go home. Get some sleep. Your first appointment isn't until ten tomorrow."

"Thanks, Chas. You were a huge help today. I couldn't have done it without you." She meant it too. The young woman had skipped lunch and stayed late so that Leah could concentrate on her patients.

Chastity waved a goodbye. "I'll remember that when it's time for my Christmas bonus!" she called out as she walked away.

Leah returned to her files. She should go home and get some sleep; God knew she was exhausted. But the files had to be updated just right in order to ensure everything looked normal. Tim Damara's poodle had been no problem. It had chewed some shoes and had a ball of leather lodged in the large intestine, just above the anus. She'd administered an enema and told him to watch the dog carefully over the next six hours. If the mass didn't exit on its own, the dog would require some minor surgery.

June Watson's Pekinese was another story. The dog was already eighteen years old. Leah had nursed it through liver disease and two bouts of cancer. Now it had some type of tumor on its spine, too embedded to operate on. She'd been tempted to Cure it anyway; after what she'd been through that day, the thought of anything dying brought a sick feeling to her stomach.

But the dog really deserved to exit life gracefully. Besides, how much longer could she keep it alive and healthy without someone, especially Mrs. Watson, becoming suspicious?

In the end, it was the kitten that decided her. The little tabby was weak and disoriented, its breathing labored and crackling. Worse, the young girl who'd brought it in was near tears, asking the whole time if Leah could "make Snuggles better".

She couldn't Cure them both; she had nowhere to pass the darkness to at the moment. Mrs. Watson had two more dogs at home, one of which she'd bought last year when Muffins developed the previous set of tumors. She was prepared for her dog to pass on.

Still, Leah was practically in tears herself when she broke the news to Mrs. Watson.

"I'm sorry, June," she'd said, after passing the cat's illness to Muffins. "Here are some painkillers for Muffins. Take her home and make her comfortable. I don't think she's got more than a day or two."

The old woman had nodded. "I thought so. It came on so fast. Thank you, Dr. DeGarmo."

Now, looking at Snuggles's chart, Leah tried to figure out what to write. The symptoms were already listed, typed in when Chastity set up the chart.

What else presents like this?

Coming up with a diagnosis after a Cure was always the hardest part. It had to sound believable. You couldn't explain a tumor away as a cut or bruise; you couldn't pretend the symptoms of rabies or feline leukemia were simply a case of stomach upset. Since opening her practice ten years ago, Leah had become an expert at dissembling on charts. And to her patients.

A large mass on the body? No, it's not a tumor, just a swelling from a bee sting.

Vomiting and bleeding from the mouth? Food poisoning.

Hit by a car? Multiple organ damage, broken bones? Don't worry, it's worse than it looks. He'll be fine in no time.

Her favorite was the time someone had brought in a yellow Lab who'd gotten its leg caught in a car door. There'd been no hiding the greenstick fracture—the bone had protruded almost an inch from the torn flesh, and the dog had been howling like a banshee.

Luckily, she'd been alone in the office at the time and she'd rushed the dog into the room she used for surgeries, telling the owner to stay in the waiting room.

After healing the wound, she'd put a quick cast on the good-as-new leg and told the owner to keep it on for six weeks and then bring the dog back. The poor dog had probably been uncomfortable in its cast, but that was better than having an arthritic leg the rest of its life.

"Snuggles, I think we're going to put you down as stomach upset and fever of unknown origin." She closed the folder and tossed it into the *To Be Filed* box for Chastity to take care of in the morning.

"Time to go home. I need a hot bath and a glass of wine, not necessarily in that order."

Two minutes later she was pulling out of the parking lot.

Emilio Suarez put down his binoculars and started his car while he watched Dr. Leah DeGarmo lock the door to the veterinary office. As he'd expected, Tal Nova had been very interested in his phone call. He'd also been pissed off that Emilio hadn't gotten the woman's name, but that had easily been rectified by watching the evening news. They'd flashed her name across the bottom of the screen while showing some reporter cornering her for a comment in front of the McDonald's. Once he had that, he'd looked her up online and found her work address, Leah DeGarmo Veterinary Services. A little more searching had turned up her home address and phone number as well.

Nova's instructions had been explicit: "Follow her. I want to know everything she does, everyone she sees. Send me a report every day, and contact me immediately if anything else unusual occurs."

Unusual? That was a mild way of putting it, Emilio thought as he paced DeGarmo's Toyota from two car lengths behind. *The fuckin' broad cured a bullet wound to the chest just by touching the guy.* She was like some modern Jesus, a thought that made Emilio more than a little nervous. A talent like that would sure come in handy, especially for someone like Nova, whose business sometimes dipped into dangerous territory. But the talent also went against the teachings of the Church, and that was dangerous too.

The only problem was how to stay close enough to see if she cured anyone else, without being seen himself. For all he knew, it might have been a one-time fluke.

If that was the case, Nova would be very unhappy with him.

And you didn't want to make Tal Nova unhappy.

Chapter Two

The light on Leah's answering machine—the same one she'd had since college—was blinking a rapid, irregular pattern when she walked through the door, indicating she had multiple messages. She pressed the button, hoping it wasn't more requests from the press for interviews. They'd called the office five times while she'd been tending to her patients.

BEEP.

"You have six messages. Message one."

"Hello, Leah DeGarmo? This is Don Oberfeld from Channel 9 News, and—"

Leah hit the Delete button. The next two calls were from other television stations. The fourth one, however, caught her attention.

"Leah? It's John Carrera. Wow, I didn't realize anyone still used answering machines. Um, I looked up your number in the book. I didn't want to call you at work. You said you'd explain everything. I'd really like to get that explanation. Call me, I'll be up late."

"Shit." In all the craziness after she returned to work, she'd forgotten about her promise to the police officer she'd Cured. She glanced at the small clock in the machine's window. Almost ten-thirty. The last thing she wanted to do was spend several hours trying to explain something she didn't even understand herself.

I can't leave him hanging, though.

She played the message again to get his number and then dialed. She half hoped she'd get his voice mail, but he answered on the second ring.

"Hello?"

A shiver ran through her at the sound of his voice. She hadn't expected a return of the feelings she'd had when she'd seen him in line.

He sounds as good as he looks. He—

"Hello? Who is this?"

"Uh, sorry. It's Leah, Leah DeGarmo. I, um, I got your message and, um..." She froze as she realized she was starting to sound like an idiot. Luckily, he rescued her before the pause grew too obvious.

"Leah? Christ, I've been waiting all night for you to call!"

"Sorry. I went back to work after...you know. And it was a madhouse. I just got home."

"You went back to work after being involved in a shooting? Jesus. Even cops have to take time off after something like what we went through today."

"Well, I'm a doctor, not a cop. Sick animals don't care if I've had a bad day. They need me."

"A bad day?" He laughed a deep chuckle that was somehow masculine and sensual at the same time. "That's putting it mildly. Listen, can we meet somewhere? I've been going crazy here. I need to know how—"

"Not tonight," she interrupted. "I'm tired, and cranky, and desperate for a shower."

"Okay. I'm sorry I pushed you. It's just...well, you can imagine how I'm feeling. How about tomorrow after work? There's a diner near my house. We can meet for coffee or something."

A public meeting was the worst possible idea. She'd never told anyone what she could do, not even her parents, although she suspected they'd figured out at least some of it. Especially after...

"Leah?"

John's voice brought her back to the present. A diner was out. There was no way to tell how he'd react. Or who might overhear.

"I've got a better idea. Come to my office tomorrow evening. Around eight. Everyone will be gone by then."

"I'll be there. And thanks."

"I'll see you tomorrow." She hung up before he could say anything else.

Christ, what do I do now? Her stomach was in knots.

She decided to forego the wine and head directly for the shower. *Hopefully that will relax me so I can think about this with a clear head. Maybe*

I can even come up with some kind of story without revealing what really happened.

As the hot water beat down on her neck and shoulders, she knew she was only deluding herself by thinking she could hide the truth.

After more than twenty-five years, someone had finally discovered her secret.

Crouched behind the neighbor's bushes, Emilio Suarez had a perfect view of the DeGarmo woman's house. He'd watched while she checked the machine and then made a call. Whomever she'd been talking to, she hadn't looked happy.

Too bad she has the damn air-conditioning on. If the windows were open I could've heard.

When he saw the bathroom light go on, he decided a little closer inspection was in order. He crept across the dark lawn until he was right by the window ledge. She had the curtains drawn, but there was a small gap in the middle, just enough for him to get a few glimpses when she emerged from the shower and toweled off.

Not bad for her age, he thought with a smile. He'd already found out she was thirty-six and single. Never married. Now he knew she was a natural blonde as well. *Keeps herself in mighty fine shape.*

He admired her toned, athletic body while she blew dry her hair and brushed her teeth. Then the lights went out and he stepped away from the house again.

A moment later the bedroom lights came on but his view was blocked by the drawn shades. He waited until the window went dark again, signaling she'd gone to bed for the night, and then stuck around another ten minutes— just to be sure—before leaving to make his first report to Tal Nova.

On his way to his car, he thought about God and healing powers.

And sin.

Chapter Three

"It's another beautiful day, with temperatures expected to reach eighty-five. The tanning index is seven, so grab that sunscreen if you're heading to the park or the beach. Now here's the latest song by—"

With a groan, Leah reached out and shut off the alarm. In her exhaustion the night before she'd forgotten she didn't have to be at the office until ten. She considered going back to sleep for another hour, then decided to use the time to exercise instead.

After a quick trip to the bathroom, she pulled on her jogging shorts, sports bra, and sneakers, and tied her hair into a pony tail. She had to pause for a moment at the front door while her eyes adjusted to the bright light, and then she started off down the street.

A brisk one-mile jog brought her to Elvio's Deli, where she got a cup of coffee and a low-fat bran muffin to go. By the time she got back home she was drenched in sweat and starving. She took a quick shower, got dressed and then tossed some ice cubes in her coffee.

Chilled drink and muffin in hand, she went outside to the back deck and sat down to read the paper.

She nearly spit out her iced coffee when she saw the front page.

"Murder and Mayhem in Downtown Rocky Point!"

Oh no.

Her appetite gone, Leah scanned the article to see if it mentioned her name. Sure enough, there it was, halfway down column two.

"One witness, Leah DeGarmo, came to the aid of Officer John Carrera after he'd been shot by the gunman. DeGarmo, a veterinarian in Rocky Point, administered first aid to the downed officer before being accosted by Hibbert."

Hibbert? She glanced back up the page. Douglas Hibbert, age forty-two. *So that was his name.* She continued reading.

"Hibbert turned his gun on Dr. DeGarmo, but Officer Carrera, who'd been saved from serious injury by his vest, wrestled the gun away from the assailant and fired at least one shot. Hibbert died on his way to the hospital. Police Chief..."

Leah put the paper down, relief flooding her system faster than the caffeine from her coffee.

Somehow John had managed to convince everyone he'd had his vest on. *Thank God.* But her name was still in the papers, and most likely on the news. She'd have to call her parents before they saw it on television. Luckily, they'd retired to Las Vegas instead of Florida, so they probably weren't even awake yet.

Still, it wasn't all good news. Any half-decent investigation would show holes in the story: fingerprints, bullet trajectories, DNA...

And then the real problems would start.

Leah's day ended up being a relatively easy one, a relief after the craziness of the previous afternoon and night. She'd only had to Cure one animal, a two-year-old husky with pancreatic cancer. The disease had been obvious as soon as the owner walked the dog in, visible to her as a bilious green glow on the poor animal's abdomen. After sending the pup home healthy and happy, she'd passed the cancer along to an aged, dying cat whose owner had brought it in to have it put down.

By the time John knocked on the door at ten to eight, she'd already finished her paperwork and reviewed her schedule for the next day.

Leah tried not to stare as she let him in. It was the first time she'd seen him out of uniform, and the muscles of his arms and legs were displayed to good advantage by his plain blue T-shirt and jeans. It was the physique of a long-distance runner or bicyclist, rather than a body builder, but the hard chest and corded arms gave evidence of some type of cross-training, perhaps swimming or boxing.

His smile was just as charming and inviting as it had been yesterday, only today it seemed warmer, perhaps because he was out of uniform, or perhaps because of the way his left eyebrow arched up when he smiled, lending a boyish air to him.

"Thanks for meeting me here," she said. "I just didn't feel comfortable discussing this in public."

"Don't thank me. You're the one doing me the favor. I should still be thanking you for saving my life, however you did it."

"Yeah, about that." She sat down in one of the waiting-room chairs. Her office was too small and cluttered for a second chair, so she always spoke to her patients either in the waiting area or one of the examining rooms. "It's not easy to explain."

He took a seat across from her. "It's not easy to understand, either. Maybe I should start, tell you what I felt."

"That'd be great."

"After I was shot, all I can remember is a crushing pain in my chest." He looked down at his hands, as if unable to meet her gaze while retelling the story. "I could see the ceiling over me, but it was all blurred. There were noises, voices, but I couldn't make out what anyone was saying. Then I felt it."

She knew what was coming. "An electric shock through your body."

He glanced up, his eyes excited. "Exactly! Like someone had touched a live wire to my chest. Then all the pain went away and I could breathe again. I saw you looking at me. I was going to say something, but that guy grabbed you, aimed his gun at you. I thought he was going to kill you right there, and then all of a sudden he just fell over."

"What did you say to the police when they came?" This was the most important thing. She had to know; if their stories didn't match, sooner or later the authorities would be back to question her again.

He gave her a rueful grin. "I didn't know what to say, but I remembered something my grandfather used to tell me. 'If you ain't sure of your words, keep your trap shut.' So I told them I was okay, I had my vest on, to take care of you and the shooter. While they were talking to you, I said I needed to go get some air, clear my head."

"They let you leave?" She'd never even noticed. Three officers had cornered her and kept firing questions at her.

"Sure. I know them all, remember? I ducked into my car and put my vest on really fast. It was stupid of me not to be wearing it, but it was so damn hot yesterday. Anyhow, when it came time to write up my report, I put down that I'd been knocked unconscious for a few moments when the bullet hit me, and when I woke up you were tearing open my shirt to see if I'd been hurt."

"But what about the gunman being shot?"

John shrugged, adding to the boyish look he wore so well. "I told them he and I struggled for his gun, it went off, and he fell over."

"And the blood on your shirt?"

He smiled. "The gunman's."

Leah shook her head. "No, the blood types won't match. And there was the bullet in the wall—"

"He fired and missed."

"And there's going to be a hole in his chest with no bullet in it."

Another shrug. "I can't explain that. That's the coroner's job."

"You really think everyone's just going to let it go at that?"

John's grin grew wider. "Leah, this is a small town, not New York City. A guy tried to rob the place. He fired at a cop. He got shot. He's dead. End of story. The blood will never be tested for DNA. That would be a waste of money. The witnesses won't get called in for more questioning because there won't be a trial. I'll get a medal and some time off, the department will get some great press, and the coroner, who happens to be the police chief's brother-in-law, will hardly glance twice at the autopsy results because everyone will want the case closed and done with."

"So no one's going to be questioning me about what I did?" She couldn't believe she'd be so lucky.

He shook his head. "I seriously doubt it. The guy was a repeat offender with no immediate family. No one's going to call for an investigation."

Leah sat back in her chair and allowed herself a sigh. All of the tension she'd been feeling seemed to drain away, leaving her as limp as if she'd just gotten a massage.

"You can't imagine how good that is to hear."

One of John's eyebrows went up. She was beginning to realize he was a man of many facial expressions and body movements. His hands were always in motion, adding emphasis to his words. And his face was a neon sign for his feelings, switching from anxious to happy to confused as he spoke.

"As good as it was to hear that I wasn't hurt by a bullet to the chest?"

She took the hint. "Okay, my turn." She took a deep breath and blurted out the words she'd never said before, not even to her parents. "I did heal you. I can do that."

His eyes grew wide. "Holy shit. For real?"

"Yes. I've been able to do it since I was a child. The first time it happened, I was nine. I was in the woods behind my house and I found this bird. It was hurt. Just lying on the ground, gasping for air. I picked it up and...it was like getting struck by lightning. The bird flew away, leaving me with a weird feeling all the way up my arms. I went home, but I didn't tell anyone what happened. I started to feel sick later that night, so my parents called the doctor. I was on the couch, and my cat, Mrs. Puff, jumped onto me. I put my hands on her and there was another shock, and then I felt all better."

Leah paused and took a breath. Even after so many years—twenty-seven, to be exact—thinking about Mrs. Puff still had the power to bring tears.

"That's fantastic."

"No, it's not. The next day, Mrs. Puff died."

"What?" John's eyes grew wide.

"The vet said it was old age. But she was only twelve. That's not old for a cat."

John shook his head. "I'm not sure I under—"

Leah spoke over him, continuing her story. She knew if she didn't get it all out now, she might never have the courage to do it.

"I forgot all about the incident, the way little kids will. A year later, my mom...my mother had a cancer scare. A lump in her breast. They did an x-ray, and when the report came back the doctor told her she had to come in for a biopsy. I was still just a kid, so I didn't understand. But she was scared. I could see that. My parents arranged for me to spend the weekend at a friend's house. Right before we left, I went to hug my mom and there was this glow, a weird green glow, around the left side of her chest. It made me feel sick and afraid just to look at it. I don't know why, but I reached out and put my hand on her breast."

"And got a shock," John said.

"Yes. But it was worse for my mother. It's always worse for the...for whoever I touch. Everyone was in a hurry, though, so my dad got us in the car and we left. They dropped me off at my friend's and went to the hospital."

"What happened then?"

Leah looked away. She didn't want to see his eyes when he figured it out. "My friend's dog died of cancer and my mom was fine."

John frowned. "I don't understand."

"I played with the dog while I was there. A day later, it was dead." She watched his eyes, but the relevance of her statement didn't register in them.

"You've been able to do this since you were nine and no one's ever found out? How'd you keep it a secret?"

Leah shrugged. "If I'd known what was happening then, I probably wouldn't have. It's only looking back I've realized that's when weird things started happening. The first time I actually knew I'd Cured someone was when I was sixteen. My dad cut his arm really bad in the garage. On the way to the hospital my mom asked me to hold the bandage on it while she drove."

Leah paused, the memories of that day rushing back as if it had only been weeks ago instead of twenty years. "There was that same nasty green glow, and then that same electric shock. By the time we got to the hospital, my dad's arm was healed, but we didn't know it until later, when the ER nurse removed the bandage and there was nothing there but a thin cut."

John reached out and took her hands. "That's the most amazing thing I've ever heard. You're like a miracle worker."

She pulled away, shaking her head. "No I'm not. I'm more like a death bringer."

His eyebrows furrowed in confusion. "What do you mean?"

This was the part she'd been dreading, trying to explain the dark side of her Power. "You haven't been listening. The dead cat. The dead dog. I didn't realize it then, either. We were still in the emergency room. The nurse was mad at my father for not being as badly hurt as he'd said he was. She made him fill out all these papers. While I was waiting, my arm started to ache. A little at first, and then really bad. I pulled my sleeve up and there was a red line running from my elbow to my wrist."

"The same place your father had been cut?"

Leah nodded. He was finally getting it. "I was going to say something, but just then the man sitting next to me started yelling at his kid to sit still, really chewing the kid out. It made me angry, and suddenly I had this feeling, this compulsion, to touch him. So I did. And all my pain went away."

"Leah, don't tell me..." John's face registered his fear of where the story was going.

"He screamed and grabbed his arm. Luckily, no one had seen me touch him. His skin split open and blood started gushing all over the place. He fell off his chair. People were shouting; nurses came running to help him. In the confusion no one, not even him, realized that I had anything to do with it."

"But *you* knew."

"Everything hit me all at once, one of those light bulbs that just goes off sometimes and you have perfect understanding. I could Cure people, but I had to pass the sickness on to someone else or suffer it myself."

John sat there for a moment, not saying anything, just staring at her with his chocolate-colored eyes. She tried to read his expression. Fear? Sympathy? Or maybe just trying to process the information?

Finally, he spoke. "So, when the gunman fell down, it was because you...?"

"I touched him when he grabbed me. I passed your fatal wound to him."

There was another moment of silence before John spoke again. "What happened with your father?"

It took Leah a moment to adjust to the change in topic. "Um...my parents were confused, but they didn't say anything. After that, I saw them looking at me funny a few times, and more than once over the years it seemed like they stopped talking when I came into the room, but they never asked me about it. And I made sure I never Cured anyone or anything around them or anyone else again."

"Why? Wouldn't they have understood?"

"I don't know. Maybe. But no sixteen-year-old girl wants to be different. It's hard enough having braces or wearing the wrong style clothes. Can you imagine people knowing I could heal with a touch? I'd have been the class freak. Maybe even gotten locked away in some government lab. So I practiced on my own whenever I could, on injured wild animals. I learned how to control the Power, rather than just have it happen every time I touched someone or something."

John moved his chair closer to hers and looked straight into her eyes. "You realize you were the real hero yesterday, don't you?"

"What?" His words caught her by surprise.

"By killing that man, you not only saved me and yourself, but all the other people in there he might have shot, or the police he might have fired on when they arrived."

"I never thought of that. I was just afraid he'd hurt me."

"You did good, Leah DeGarmo. And your secret is safe with me. I owe you my life. It's the least I can do."

Leah felt tears come to her eyes. Something about the man made her feel like she could trust him. And it wasn't just that he was a police officer. There was a warmth to him, a sincerity that touched her heart. She wanted to throw her arms around him, but she settled for giving his hand a squeeze before reluctantly pulling away.

"Thank you. I'm still so paranoid about it. That's why I could never work in a clinic with other vets. I couldn't let anyone know."

"You're a smart girl, Leah. Even if the government didn't try to turn you into some kind of science project, there are a lot of shady characters out there who'd love to get their hands on a weapon like you."

Leah jerked back in her chair. "Weapon? Me?"

He nodded, his soulful eyes—bedroom eyes, her grandmother would have called them—very serious. "You've only been thinking about the healing part. But there's the other side of the coin. You could kill or injure people without anyone knowing. The perfect murder: touch someone today and next week they die of cancer."

A chill ran through her body that had nothing to do with the air-conditioning. "I never... I wouldn't do that."

John shrugged. "You can't say what you'd do if someone had a gun to your head or was holding your family hostage. If anything, I'd think twice about ever using your powers again, for any reason."

His warning barely registered on her brain; she was still reeling from the idea of being used as an unwilling assassin.

"You're right," she whispered. "I'll try not to use it."

But in her heart she knew it was impossible. There was no way she could let animals die when they didn't need to.

From the way John was looking at her, she knew he didn't believe her any more than she believed herself.

Chapter Four

Emilio Suarez ducked down below the window sill as the two people in the veterinary clinic stood up. He hadn't been able to hear more than a few words, but as far as he was concerned it didn't matter. He had his proof. Why else would the lady vet and the cop from the shooting be meeting if it not to talk about how she'd healed him?

From the snatches of conversation that he'd caught, it wasn't the first time she'd done something like this. Now he finally had something positive to tell Nova.

Maybe he'd even get a bonus.

And if not, well, there were other people who'd be interested in this as well. People who might have a different idea of what to do with Dr. DeGarmo.

Staying in a crouch, he moved around to the back of the building so he could use his cell phone without being heard.

"It's me." He knew better than to use names. "I heard her telling that cop what she did. It's for real, man. I think she's 'splaining to him how it works, but I can't hear nuthin' through the glass. What you want me to do?"

Secretly, he was hoping Nova would tell him to grab the girl and force the information out of her. Questioning her would have some serious side benefits. He'd never seen a vet that fine when he was growing up in Brooklyn; in his opinion she should have been dancing on a pole instead of sticking thermometers up dogs' asses.

So it was a disappointment when Nova instructed him to do nothing.

"Continue to watch her. If it looks like she's going to talk to someone from the press, make the person disappear, but under no circumstances reveal yourself to the doctor or harm her in any way."

"You got it." No matter what his feelings, he knew better than to disobey Tal Nova. No one did that.

Not if they wanted to live.

Still staying below eye level, he returned to his car to wait for the lady vet to leave.

As he watched her through his binoculars, he slowly rubbed his crotch with his free hand and wondered how she'd look nailed to a cross.

Leonard Marsh leaned back in his oversized leather chair and looked out the window. The wide, bullet- and sound-proof glass panes of his twenty-fifth floor office offered a panoramic view of the Hudson River from Eightieth Street to Fifty-Sixth. In the last rays of the setting sun, the river resembled a fresh watercolor on a heavy canvas, the pastel reds, oranges, purples and golds melting together at the edges, each ripple frozen in mid-crest by the artist's brush.

"So, what do you want to do with her?" Tal Nova's deep voice broke the silence.

Marsh swiveled the chair around so he was facing the other occupant in his office. Tal Nova stood six feet four and weighed just over two hundred forty pounds. Looking at him, it wasn't hard to believe he'd been a star football player in college. What would be difficult to understand was why he'd turned down a career with the Arizona Cardinals after being drafted in the first round.

Leonard Marsh was one of only four people in the world who'd ever found out the answer to that question; he was one of only two still alive.

"You know me well, my friend," Marsh said to his Vice President of Business Affairs.

"Well enough to know you don't sit back and watch things happen." Tal took a seat on the other side of Marsh's wide mahogany desk and opened a fresh stick of cinnamon gum. Since quitting smoking three years earlier, he'd become as addicted to the sharp burn of the gum as he'd been to the bitter taste of the tobacco.

Marsh allowed himself a chuckle. "Quite right. You don't get anywhere in life by watching the world go by. You've got to grab what you want and make it yours." He punctuated his words by snatching an imaginary prize from the air. "My father taught me that."

"And you had him killed."

"He just happened to be in the way of what I wanted." Marsh spread his arms, indicating the expansive office. "What can I say? I learned my lessons well."

"So what do you want this time?" Tal asked, the bemused expression on his dark-as-night face evidence that his question was a rhetorical one. His smooth-shaved head reflected the soft lights in the room as he leaned forward.

"I want the girl, obviously," Marsh said. "But I can't take the word of a low-level thief. I need hard evidence before I act."

"I presume that's where I come in."

Marsh pointed a finger at his associate. "Right again. It's your job to provide me with facts. I want to see this 'miracle worker' in action before I get my hopes up."

Tal stood up, his wide, muscular frame impressive and threatening, even in the custom-tailored charcoal suit he wore like a second skin, as comfortable in the expensive clothes as he'd ever been in a football uniform.

"No problem, boss. I'll take care of it." With a flick of his fingers he tossed his empty gum wrapper into the small garbage can next to the minibar and exited through the door that led to his adjoining office.

Leonard Marsh returned to his contemplation of the evening view. White and green lights moved up the river as a private yacht returned from its travels farther up the Hudson. On the far side of the water, the lights of New Jersey sparkled like captured stars.

He caught a glimpse of himself in the window and frowned. Even the semitransparent reflection couldn't hide the growing signs of his illness: the sallow complexion, the dark smudges and baggy flesh under his eyes. In the two months since being diagnosed, it looked like he'd aged ten years beyond his previously healthy sixty.

And what his reflection revealed was just the tip of the iceberg; deep inside him even more radical changes were occurring as his body succumbed to the onslaught of the invading cells.

Hepatocellular carcinoma. He could still hear the doctor's words, delivered so matter-of-factly. He'd gone to the specialist after his internist had diagnosed his sore back as an inflamed liver.

"What's the treatment?" he'd asked the oncologist, who'd hemmed and hawed a bit before answering, which told him all he really needed to know.

"The cancer is already very advanced. Too advanced for surgery. Chemotherapy can slow the progression, but..."

Cold fingers had clutched at his belly when the doctor's voice trailed off. *"But what? How long have I got?"*

"Six months, maybe eight. I'm sorry, Mr. Marsh."

Six to eight months. Which probably meant four to six before being totally bedridden. And who knew if the oncologist was right? The man had admitted things could change if the cancer spread to his lymph system or to his other organs.

Months to live. How the hell did you prepare yourself for something like that? It wasn't fair! He'd spent the first week in a raging tantrum, breaking things, shouting at people, even firing an attendant in the parking garage who'd been late in bringing his car around.

Then he'd come to his senses and realized this was just another problem to be solved, the same way he'd approach a hostile takeover or a declining stock market.

He'd done his research. Hepatocellular carcinoma was usually 90 percent fatal; that meant a 10 percent chance his chemo would work. Not great odds, but he'd taken chances on worse. However, it wasn't in his nature to toss all his eggs in one basket, be it finances or his life. He'd put the vast resources of his business empire to work on finding a cure. Research and development labs were ordered to drop everything and look into liver cancers. Pharmaceutical firms were instructed to go through their enormous files of botanicals and other natural substances.

And the word had been put out to look for any unusual cases of spontaneous cures or "miracle" healings.

Over the past six weeks he'd subjected himself not only to the exhausting effects of the chemotherapy treatments, but also to the salves, lotions and hands of supposed faith healers, voodoo practitioners and saints-in-waiting.

He'd traveled to remote villages to dip himself into healing pools and stand shoulder to shoulder with terminally ill, stinking, Third World refugees at special Masses.

None of it had helped.

But now fate had delivered this veterinarian, Leah DeGarmo, into his sights; she could very well hold the key to his continued life in her pretty little hands.

And if she did, there was no way anyone or anything was going to keep her from him.

Chapter Five

Leah started her car and rolled down the windows, but didn't take it out of Park. She didn't trust herself to drive just yet.

Not after what John had asked just before leaving her clinic.

She'd assumed they were done talking, so she'd stood up to say good night. Not that she wanted him to leave, but now that she'd explained her Power to him, she figured she'd never see him again.

"Leah, there's something I want to ask you. Actually, I would have asked you yesterday, but the shooting and the dying kind of got in the way."

"What's that?" Even as he smiled at her, she had no clue.

He took a deep breath. "Would you like to go out with me sometime? Maybe dinner? Or even just coffee."

Her mouth had opened but no words came out. *Did he really just ask me on a date?* An embarrassed look came into his eyes, and she'd realized she'd left him hanging.

"I shouldn't have asked. I—"

"No, no! It's okay, really. I just didn't expect it. I thought...I thought you weren't interested," she finished lamely.

"You thought wrong. But you still haven't answered my question."

"Oh! Yes, I'd love to go to dinner. How about Friday?"

"Friday it is. I'll pick you up at seven. Good night." He'd gave her another of his bright-white smiles and then walked out the doors, waving to her through the windows as he headed for his car.

Now, sitting with her hands on the Avalon's steering wheel, she smiled to herself. *I've got a date.*

Her first one in years.

Oh God. I don't even remember how to date. What should I wear? Do women still offer to pay?

I'll have to corner Chastity tomorrow. She's got like three guys she sees.

Not caring that she still had a goofy grin plastered across her face, Leah pulled out of the parking lot and headed home.

I've got a date!

She never noticed the brown pickup truck that exited the parking lot next door and stayed two cars behind her all the way across town.

Chapter Six

Tal Nova leaned back in his chair, a smaller version of Leonard Marsh's leather throne, and checked the door before pulling his cell phone from his pocket. Having an adjoining office to the head of the company held both advantages and disadvantages. On the one hand, even though he only carried the title of Vice President, his status as Marsh's right-hand man was well-known throughout Marsh Enterprises, providing him with a multitude of perks he never would have enjoyed in any other job, even as a star NFL tight end.

On the other hand, he was expected to be at the boss's beck and call every minute of every day, unless he was traveling on business. And even the lowliest of cubicle drones had more privacy—Tal never knew when Marsh would walk through the door. And God help him if the big man found him with his feet on the desk or his television turned to something other than the news.

On top of that, Tal was pretty certain his office was under surveillance. Marsh hadn't gotten to be one of the world's richest businessmen by staying within the legal lines. Tal had planned enough "extracurricular" operations over the past six years to know exactly what lengths Marsh would go to.

It would be foolish to think that just because they were confidants of a sort, Marsh wouldn't still have eyes and ears on Nova all the time.

So Tal made it a point to never conduct any personal business in his office. More importantly, he made sure to never use his office for any business of any kind that might be used against him later in a court of law. That's why, after finishing his conversation with Marsh, he'd used his personal cell to send an innocuous text. *Meet for coffee?* Now, ten minutes later, he had an equally bland message waiting.

Corner of Ninth and Fifty-Fifth. Fifteen minutes.

Perfect.

As he left his office, Janice, his secretary, asked him where he was going.

"To take care of something for Mr. Marsh," he replied. "I'll be back in an hour."

Janice nodded and returned to her typing. She'd been handpicked for him by Marsh, and he trusted her about as much as he trusted the security of his office phone.

In the back of his limo, Tal had time to consider his place in the grand scheme of things at Marsh Enterprises. His innocuous title was as much of a cover as any used by the CIA or FBI. In reality, Tal's job description was simple: to take care of anything that Marsh couldn't accomplish through regular, or legal, means. Corporate espionage, blackmail, even physical violence—they'd all been carried out on Tal's orders.

And he wasn't afraid to get his hands dirty, either, when the situation called for it. That was how he'd earned the position in the first place.

He remembered that night like it was yesterday; he'd barely gotten back to the apartment and gotten out of his bloody clothes when the phone had rung.

"Tal Nova?" The voice on the other end was filled with jovial good humor.

"Yes?"

"This is Leonard Marsh. It's come to my attention you were involved in an unfortunate incident earlier this evening."

"What?" Tal nearly dropped the phone. How the hell had anyone found out already? It had only been an hour since the accident. The fact that it was the owner of Marsh Enterprises, where Tal was presently working as an intern, was even more unbelievable.

"Come now, Mr. Nova. Don't play stupid. You did a piss-poor job of covering up your involvement in the hit-and-run. You left your fingerprints on the body, and no doubt there is DNA evidence on your car which would link you to the crime if the police were to do even a cursory investigation."

"What do you want?" He knew blackmail when he heard it.

"I'd like to offer you a business proposition. Say yes and you'll have my guarantee your name will never be brought up in connection with any police investigation. Say no and one carefully placed call will have you behind bars before the sun rises."

Tal knew he was helpless to say no, but he asked his next question anyway. "What kind of business proposition?"

Marsh's laughter echoed in Tal's ear. "My dear boy, you don't get to know that until you answer. That's the whole point."

The decision was easy. "Fine. I accept."

"Excellent. Come to my office tomorrow and I'll explain everything. Welcome to the team."

That was the end of Tal's old life, and the beginning of his new one. A week after graduation he turned down the offer from the Cardinals and accepted the position of Security Manager with Marsh Enterprises. Marsh arranged for him to attend an intense twelve-week school in corporate espionage that included classes in firearms, self-defense and computer hacking.

He surprised himself by not only showing an aptitude for the science of security operations, but also enjoying it, which lessened the disappointment of not fulfilling his dream of playing in the NFL. His rise to Vice President was rapid, and along the way he picked up several other useful talents.

There were times when Tal worried that Marsh might have stashed away evidence that could point a legal finger at who really ran over that traffic cop six years ago. But then he'd think about all the dirt he had on Marsh, names and phone numbers and even photographs, all stored away in safe deposit boxes scattered around the city under false names.

And, of course, he was the only one who knew Marsh was dying besides the old man's doctors.

It would be interesting to see how things played out with the DeGarmo woman. If she was the real deal, there was a lot more the company could do with her besides keep Leonard Marsh healthy.

She could make Tal's life a lot easier.

"Stop here," he told the driver as they approached Ninth Avenue. He exited the car and walked the final block out of habit, keeping an eye out for anyone who might be watching him.

Del McCormick waited by the newsstand, their usual meeting spot. As always, Tal marveled at the man's ability to blend in anywhere. Unless you were specifically looking for him, there was nothing about him to catch the eye, nothing that would stick in a witness's memory.

McCormick was average everything. Not too tall or short, plain brown hair, plain brown eyes, and a face that would never be called ugly or handsome. A medium-sized nose, lips perhaps a shade on the thin side but not obviously so, and just enough color to his skin that you wouldn't call him pale. His frame looked slender, but Tal knew the man's slightly baggy clothes hid a body kept in excellent shape through intense martial arts training.

"What's up?" Del asked, as the two men sauntered down the sidewalk. His eyes darted back and forth, watching everyone and everything around them.

Tal stuck a piece of gum in his mouth. "Got a strange one for you. Highest priority. I want you to take care of it personally."

"Hush-hush?" Del kept his eyes forward, but Tal heard the change in inflection, indicating he was interested.

"You, me and the big man makes three," Tal said. "And it has to stay that way."

"No problem. Are we talking interaction?"

Tal shook his head, knowing the other man was asking if there'd be violence involved. "Not that kind. But you will have to meet the subject in person. She's a vet."

One of Del's eyebrows went up. "Army? Navy?"

"No, a veterinarian. I need you to pay her an official visit. She lives up north in the burbs."

Del frowned. "Got no pets. Travel too much."

"Don't worry, I'll supply the pet. Meet me at this address tomorrow afternoon at five." Tal passed him a piece of paper. "Wear something you don't mind getting blood on, and that you can hide a videocam in. You'll be playing the role of desperate pet owner."

Pulling a battered Yankees cap from his back pocket, Del chuckled, a rare event for him. "Now I'm really interested. Later, my friend." He adjusted the hat on his head and walked away.

In less than twenty steps he was lost in the afternoon crowd.

I swear he's part chameleon, Tal thought, as he headed back to the limo. But McCormick was perfect for the job. An hour after talking to him, DeGarmo wouldn't even remember what he looked like.

As the car wove its way through the streets of Manhattan, Tal dialed Marsh's direct line.

"It's me. I should have what you need tomorrow night."

Chapter Seven

"Jesus Christ, what the fuck did you do to it?"

Del McCormick looked around the parking lot to make sure the dog's pitiful cries weren't drawing any witnesses. In the city a howling dog might not be noticed, but in a boondocks town like Rocky Point some Good Samaritan might decide to check out what was going on.

The dog's broken limbs twitched and jerked, and Del could see jagged pieces of bone sticking through the bloody fur.

"Getting squeamish?" Tal Nova lifted the animal from his trunk and placed it in the late model Volkswagen Jetta Del had stolen for the job.

"No, just a little surprised. You could have warned me." He had no intention of telling the hulking man that he had a soft spot for dogs, especially little brown mutts like the one he'd had growing up.

Like the one now dying in his backseat.

One thing you never displayed in front of men like Tal Nova was weakness. They were like lions, always watching the herd to cull out the sick or vulnerable.

Tal wiped the blood off his oversized hands. "That would've taken all the fun out of it. You got the camera ready?"

Del patted the breast pocket of his denim jacket. "Fiber optics. Transmits to a receiver in the car. Wide angle, so I can get almost a whole room."

"Good. Here's what you do. You go into the clinic with the dog in your arms, screaming how someone ran over your poor puppy. Then you make sure you stay with the doctor the whole time. When she's done, you bring me the video. I'll be waiting right here."

"That's it?"

The taller man leaned forward, his blocky features tightened into a menacing scowl. "That's it. You come right to me. You don't eat, piss or make a phone call. You don't pass Go. You don't do anything before I get that video, understand?"

"Hey, no problem. I'll call you when I'm out."

Del jumped into his stolen car and exited the parking lot.

Driving to the clinic, Del couldn't help but think about what kind of play Tal was working. *Something big's going on. I've never seen him like that.*

For the first time in all his dealings with Tal Nova, Del wondered if maybe he'd gotten himself into something he was going to regret.

He turned the radio up, trying to ignore the heartbreaking whines from the backseat.

Leah jumped up from her desk at the sound of the man's voice from the waiting room.

"Help me! Is there anyone here? My dog's been hurt."

She ran out of her office and found herself facing a middle-aged man holding a bleeding, crying dog with obvious compound fractures.

"Oh my God! Come this way. What happened?" she asked as she led the man to the first exam room.

"He got hit by a car. I didn't even know he'd gotten out of the yard. I was in the house and I heard him howling. When I got outside, the car was already driving away."

Leah had the man hold the dog down on the steel table while she looked it over. Besides the jagged bones sticking through the skin, there were several bloody cuts on the dog's sides and back.

Worse, her talent revealed the presence of multiple internal injuries, visible to her as glowing spots on the dog's abdomen.

She knew instantly that even with emergency surgery the dog had a fifty-fifty chance, at best.

"Go wait in the other room," she instructed the man. "Your dog needs multiple operations right away, but I can save him."

"No, I have to stay with him," the man insisted.

She shook her head. "I'm sorry, that's impossible. I'll come get you as soon as I'm finished." She pushed him gently but firmly out into the waiting room, and then shut the door. As soon as she was sure he wouldn't try to get back in, she placed both hands on the dog and concentrated on making its injuries disappear.

Immediately her hands grew warm and the dog stopped crying. Leah closed her eyes and braced herself for what was to come next.

The dog cried out, a sharp, surprised bark, and twitched under her hands at the same time as the electric shock ran through her body.

When she opened her eyes again, the dog was healed, its legs straight and whole, new fur already filling in the patches where the skin had been abraded away in the accident.

The dog looked up at her, panting and smiling a doggy grin.

"Hey, boy, feel better now?" she asked, rubbing her hand under its chin. It lifted its head and licked her fingers.

"C'mon, let's take you in the back and wrap you up, and then you can have a nice meal and take a nap."

Leah carried her patient down a back hallway and into the room that served as a combination library and surgical recovery area. The trick was going to be making the dog look like it had undergone an operation.

She gave it a small bowl of canned dog food laced with a strong sedative. Once the dog was suitably groggy, she shaved the back legs and wrapped them in plaster casts. She also shaved a few patches of fur on the body and put iodine on the bare skin, then taped gauze over the areas. After that, she wiped the dried, crusted blood away from the rest of its fur.

After leaving the dog sleeping in a recovery cage, she checked her watch. Only forty-five minutes had passed since she'd ushered the owner into the waiting room.

Still too soon to pretend I'm done. She thought about going to her office and catching up on paperwork, but there was no way to get from the recovery room to her office without passing the waiting area.

Resigned to wasting the next couple of hours, she turned on the computer and visited some of her favorite online shoe stores.

And tried to ignore the growing ache in her legs.

Del McCormick waited ten minutes until he was sure the lady vet wasn't coming back out. Then he slipped out the front door and made his way around the building, checking each window to see if he could get a glimpse of what she was up to.

That she was hiding something was a given. There was no other reason for Tal to want her videotaped. The question was, what could a veterinarian be doing that was so important?

He was just about to move on to the next window when he saw movement in the room. Dr. DeGarmo came in, the mutt cradled in her arms. She set it down on the floor, which seemed odd until the dog followed her across the room.

"Holy shit," he whispered as he pulled the fiber-optic camera from his pocket and aimed it through the glass.

He watched in growing amazement as she gave the dog something to make it sleep, and then proceeded to shave and bandage it. When she was done, she placed it in a cage and sat down at her computer.

Del hurried back to the waiting area and sat down, unsure of when DeGarmo would come get him. He held a magazine in his lap like he was reading, but his mind was trying to make sense of what he'd seen.

That dog was dying when I brought it here, he thought. *I'm no vet, but even I could see that. Now there's not a damn thing wrong with it.*

She healed it.

It seemed impossible, but he had the evidence in his pocket. Then another thought came to him.

Tal suspected this. That's why he arranged this whole thing. A vision of Tal Nova finding a stray or adopting the dog from a shelter someplace and then running it over with his car—or worse, beating it with a pipe or bat—ran through his head. He'd set up the doctor with a patient that couldn't be saved the normal way, forced her to use whatever powers she had to cure it.

But how? If only the examining room had had a window, he could've seen the whole thing. As it was, he had to hope he'd gotten enough to earn his money.

Footsteps on tile alerted him to DeGarmo's return before she came through the doorway.

"Is he all right?" Del asked, putting as much concern as he could into his voice.

"Yes," she said with a happy smile. "It was touch and go for a while, but your dog's going to be just fine. Come with me and you can see him now."

She waited until he'd put his magazine down, and then led him down a hallway to the same room he'd seen her in earlier. Her movements were stiff, as if she'd been sitting too long in the same position. The dog was still asleep in its cage, its bandaged legs sticking out as it lay on its side.

"He's really okay?"

"Yes."

He could see how it would be easy for her to make pet owners feel at ease. She had a genuine smile full of warmth and compassion. Nothing like the cool, clinical expressions so many doctors used on their patients.

"I was so afraid. I thought... Well, when I saw his legs, I didn't think he'd ever walk again." It was no lie; Del hadn't expected the damn thing to make it out of the clinic alive. "We just got him a few weeks ago, but the whole family loves him."

"There were some broken bones, but animals heal better than people do," DeGarmo explained. "Luckily there were no internal injuries, so I didn't have to do surgery. Everything else was just bruises and cuts."

Something about the way she said "internal injuries" made him look at her. She was staring at the sleeping dog, and her face had gone very serious and sad.

She's lying! That dog did *have internal injuries. She cured them as well.*

"How long before the bandages come off?" he asked.

"What? Oh, I'd say three to four weeks. I'll want you to bring him back in two weeks, so I can take another x-ray and see how the bones are healing."

"Can he walk like that?"

She smiled again, but this time he could tell it was at some private joke, rather than for his sake. "He'll have some trouble at first, but don't worry about it. Let him decide how much weight to put on his legs, and don't let him run or climb stairs."

Del wondered what she'd do if he just leaned over and rapped on the casts, exposing her secret. The idea was tempting, if only to force her to explain everything to him. But it would undoubtedly piss Tal off. If he'd wanted the full secret, he'd have told Del to get it.

"Can I take him home tonight?"

"Sure. As soon as he wakes up. But in the meantime, can you come out front with me? I need you to fill out some paperwork. And then there's the bill…" Her voice trailed off as if she expected him to object to paying.

"Don't worry," he said. "I've got money."

Thirty minutes later he was back in his car, the still-drowsy dog resting in the passenger seat and the video playing on his tablet. Everything was there, just like he'd seen it.

This could be worth millions. Now he knew why Tal didn't want him to talk to anyone.

Which brought up the ugly possibility of what would happen after he delivered his information. Exactly how far would Tal go to keep this a secret?

Thank God for Boy Scouts. Always be prepared, indeed. He opened his leather case and took out a flash drive, inserted it into the USB port on the pad.

While the video copied, he pulled out his cell phone and hit the prearranged contact number. "It's done. I'll be there in ten minutes."

Chapter Eight

Leah tossed her bloodstained scrubs into the dirty-laundry bin and returned to her office. Another set of files to doctor. The injured mixed breed had been one of the worst cases she'd seen in months.

Good thing he brought it in while I was alone. If Chastity had been here I might not have been able to Cure it.

She opened the file and Mr. Johnson's paperwork. He hadn't offered much information on the dog, had said he'd just adopted it recently from a shelter and didn't even know how old it was. He'd said the dog's name was Nova. *Funny name for a dog.* He'd paid in cash too, another oddity. Three hundred fifty dollars. Most people put something like that on their credit card.

Now came the hard part.

Description of injuries or symptoms:

After thinking for a moment, she wrote: *Multiple contusions from hit-and-run accident. Fractures to left and right fibulas.*

There. No mention of compound fractures and no one would be surprised at rapid weight bearing from a broken fibula, the smaller of the two lower-leg bones.

Treatment: Resetting and casting of injuries. Prescription for mild painkillers. Follow up in two weeks.

Patient History:

The animal was recently adopted, so the owner had nothing to tell her.

However, there was a way to find out. She'd made sure to jot down the ID tattoo in the dog's left ear. All the shelters in the area made it a habit of tagging their animals in case they ever got lost or stolen. It wasn't as effective as an electronic subdermal tag, but then most shelters couldn't afford the electronic tags.

She looked up the shelter in her list and found it was a place in New Jersey.

"Sure, he was one of ours. Cute little thing," the woman who answered the phone told Leah. "Adopted just today by a man named David Smith. You said it was hit by a car? Poor thing. I'm glad to hear he's okay."

Leah hung up the phone and stared at the file.

Adopted today? David Smith? The name on the forms said "Larry Johnson," and the man had specifically said he'd had the dog for a few weeks.

Something wasn't right.

She thought about calling John, but just then sharp pains ran up and down both her legs. At the same time, a sick feeling came alive in her stomach.

Damn, I waited too long.

She groaned as she struggled out of her chair. The dog's injuries had been severe; she still had a few hours before her life was in danger, but they would be hours filled with agony if she didn't do something about it right now.

Each step down to the basement was an effort and she had to hang on to the railing with both hands. From their cages, four dogs stared at her with ancient, sad eyes as she fumbled with the lights. Doing her best to control the shaking in her hands, she prepared a syringe of sodium pentobarbital and then approached one of the cages.

"Sorry, Trixie, but I don't have a choice. Don't worry, you won't feel a thing."

The elderly cocker spaniel lifted its head and thumped its tail weakly as Leah opened the cage door. It made no resistance when she injected the lethal compound into a leg vein. Leah waited for a count of ten, watching as the dog's eyes closed and its breathing grew shallower. Then she placed her hands on it and let the blackness and pain flow out of her. She felt the usual shock of transference, but beneath her hands the dying dog didn't react at all, its nervous system already deadened by the injection.

As the dog took a final breath, the skin on its legs split open and blood poured out from around the broken bones.

Leah fell over on her side, her body suddenly weak from the cessation of pain. She stroked the dead dog's side and let the tears spill out.

Damn it, DAMN IT! I hate this. Why couldn't there be another way?

It was the same thought she had each time she had to come down here and serve as executioner. It didn't matter that the animals in this room had already been scheduled for euthanasia; the fact that she had to injure them in any way before they died, even if they didn't feel it, was just so goddamned *wrong!*

One of the other dogs, a Rottweiler dying of congestive heart failure, whimpered softly.

Don't let it suffer. You don't need it.

All the animals in the basement had been brought in by local kennels; Leah had a standing arrangement that once an animal had an incurable disease, she'd take them from the kennel and make their last days comfortable. If the animal was young enough, she'd Cure it and then find a home for it. Otherwise, she'd keep it around as long as possible, in case a situation arose like this evening.

But she'd never let an animal suffer needlessly.

Crying even harder than before, she prepared a second syringe.

Tal Nova took Leonard Marsh's private elevator up from the garage so no one would see him. Later, he'd use the computer in his office to erase himself from the security tapes. The healed dog cowered at the end of its leash, staying as far from Tal as possible.

Maybe he remembers what I did to him. I know I'd never forget someone who gave me that kind of beating.

In Tal's pocket were two flash drives, one of them containing the video Del McCormick had taken. Before paying him, he'd made sure Del had deleted the file from the pad.

The elevator took him right to Marsh's office, where Marsh was waiting for him.

"Show me what you've got," he said to Tal.

Tal nodded and put the first drive into the computer. "This is the dog before Del brought it to DeGarmo's clinic," Tal narrated. On the extra-wide screen, the dog's brutal injuries looked even more grotesque than they had in real life. The camera zoomed in on each leg, showing in graphic detail the jagged bones protruding through the skin and fur.

"Jesus Christ," whispered Marsh. In the light of the computer monitor, his skin looked greener and paler than it had in the afternoon.

Tal removed the memory stick and put in the second one containing the video shot by Del McCormick. The two men watched in silence as Leah DeGarmo, her face taut with shock and horror, rushed the dog away and shut the door.

When the view switched to the room where the dog was walking on unmarked, perfectly healed legs, Marsh gasped and leaned forward, but didn't say anything.

The video ended with Del following the now-happy dog's progress out to the car.

Marsh slapped a hand on his desk as Tal removed the drive from the video player.

"Goddammit! Why didn't he stay in the room with her?"

Tal placed the two memory sticks on the desk. "She wouldn't let him. My guess is she's done this before and doesn't want anyone else to know what she can do. If Del had insisted on staying, she probably would have operated on the dog the normal way, maybe even let it die, rather than expose herself."

"But this doesn't prove anything." Marsh's voice was angry and bitter. "That could have been another dog."

"That's why I brought the dog back," Tal said. "You can see for yourself." He lifted the dog onto a chair and took a pair of heavy metal-cutting scissors from his pocket. Holding the dog still with one massive hand, he snipped the casts away from both legs.

"See? She shaved the legs so if the bandages slipped a little it would look like she'd treated the wounds. That's why she told Del that by the time the fur grew back, the dog's legs would be better."

"I still don't have actual proof of her doing the healing," Marsh insisted.

Tal settled himself into his usual chair across from his boss and popped a stick of gum in his mouth. The sharp bite of the cinnamon burned away the stale taste of too much coffee.

"Pardon me for saying so, but you don't need it."

"What?"

"You're not trying to convince anyone else. This isn't a story for the newspapers or a way to get funding for research. It's just for you. We know she can do it, so why not just bring her in?"

Marsh stared at him with wide eyes, and for a moment Tal thought the old man might be getting ready to launch into one of his increasingly frequent tirades. Then his pale lips widened into a smile and he started laughing.

"And that's why I hired you. You have a knack for seeing right to the heart of something and not worrying about the extraneous details. So, how do you propose we get her here?"

"We just grab her. Nice and simple."

"No, no. Nothing illegal. I want her to help me of her own free will. Otherwise, there's no guarantee it will work."

Tal rubbed his hand across his smooth-shaven scalp, a habit he had whenever he was concentrating. "There's always money."

"Perfect! I'm sure running that clinic is expensive. Tell her I've got a business proposition for her, that I'd like to donate some money to fund an expansion or purchase new equipment. A philanthropic gesture. Arrange a time for her to come here and meet with me. Then, once she's here, we lay out the specifics of the deal."

Tal stood up. "I'll take care of it right away."

"Excellent." Marsh picked up the chips and stared at them as if he could see the video on the opalescent plastic. "These are the only copies?"

"Of course."

"Good. And there's one more thing," he added as Tal started for the exit.

"Yes?"

"The dog." He waved a hand at the mutt, which was now curled up on the floor. "Have one of our labs do a complete autopsy on it. Before I let this woman touch me, I want to make sure there's nothing...*different*...about that animal."

With a brief nod, Tal grabbed the dog's leash and led it out of the office.

At his own desk, Tal arranged to personally bring the dog to one of Marsh Enterprises' pharmaceutical research centers in New Jersey, one that already performed extensive animal testing.

Only after he was home for the night and locked in a room he knew was completely secure did he remove his own copy of the video from a secret pocket in his jacket and watch it on a laptop that wasn't connected to the Internet.

Like Marsh said, I have a knack for seeing to the heart of the matter.

Chapter Nine

Emilio Suarez waited until the lights went off in Tal Nova's brownstone before starting his truck and driving down the block. He pulled into the next empty spot he found—no easy task on Riverside Drive—and turned on the overhead light.

He'd had a busy night so far, and it wasn't over. He'd been watching the DeGarmo broad like Tal ordered, and he'd made careful notes about who visited the office.

So he'd had a perfect view of the guy who'd brought in the dog after regular visiting hours. The guy'd been carrying the howling mutt in his arms when he entered the clinic, and two hours later it had come out walking on its own, even if it was bandaged. Knowing what the lady vet could do with her hands, he thought it might be a good idea to follow the dog owner and maybe snatch the dog for Tal Nova. It could be the proof he needed to show the vet could really heal things.

So it was something of a shock to find out the guy was delivering the friggin' mutt right to Nova himself.

That's when Emilio decided to follow Tal. A little bit of information about what was going on could end up bringing him a lot of money, either by blackmailing the big man and his billionaire boss or by bringing it to the other party he knew would have an interest in DeGarmo and her powers.

A very different sort of interest.

Tal had driven back into Manhattan, taking the dog to the Marsh Enterprises building on the West Side. An hour later he'd come back out and headed down to Jersey, finally stopping at one of Marsh's pharmaceutical plants just outside of Newark. He'd gone inside, dragging the dog with him, and then come out alone.

That's one dog that'll never chase another ball, Emilio thought with a grin as he followed Tal back to the city. *But they're looking in the wrong place. God don't leave clues.*

That was something his grandmother had said once when he'd asked her how she could believe in the faith healers on TV.

"Abuela, *those people, they look cured, but afterwards no doctors can prove there was ever anything wrong wit' them in the first place. Maybe it's all fake.*"

"*Don't be* estupido, Emilio. The sanadors *don't use no* medicinas, *no fancy 'quipment. They don't need 'em. And God don't leave clues.*"

Of course, back then he hadn't believed in the *sanadors*, the healers. He'd thought his abuela was just throwing away her ten dollars a week.

But now that he knew at least one really existed, it made sense that she'd leave no clues. What was there to leave? She didn't use no chemicals, no stitches. Just the power of her hands.

The power of God.

He wrote the words in his notepad.

The real question was, did God's power reside in the lady, or in the lady's hands?

And if it was in the hands, did they need to be attached to the lady?

Chapter Ten

"I hope you like Italian," John said as he opened the car door for her. "Leone's isn't much to look at from the outside, but they have the best food in town."

"Right now I'm so hungry I could eat a horse," Leah responded as she climbed into the long, black Cadillac Seville. She had to wait until John got behind the wheel before he answered.

"A horse? That's pretty rude, coming from a vet."

She smiled. "Fine. A pound of pasta, then. Just stick some food in me." As if to emphasize her statement, her stomach gave a loud rumble.

"Whoa!" John laughed and started the engine. "I'd better hurry and get you there before I start looking like an appetizer."

She patted her stomach and gave her lips an exaggerated lick, hiding her embarrassment at her body's loud complaints. As usual, she'd gotten busy at work and hadn't had time for lunch. All she'd eaten the entire day was a couple of chocolates she'd grabbed from the stash Chastity kept in the reception area.

"Don't mention appetizers," she said as her stomach gave another groan.

"Maybe I should turn on my siren," he teased.

"Maybe you should."

He laughed again and reached for the dashboard. For a terrifying moment she thought he'd taken her seriously, but he only flicked on the radio. Mellow blues filled the cavernous interior of the car.

"This isn't what I pictured you driving," she said.

"Because it doesn't look like a cop's car, or because you know what small-town cops earn?"

"Neither. I had you pegged as more of a BMW or Volvo kind of guy."

"Please don't say I look like some kind of metrosexual." He raised one eyebrow, taking the sting out of his words.

"No! But you've got sort of a conservative look, like you'd be more at home selling insurance than stopping a robbery."

John shrugged as he guided the car into the parking lot. "You're not far off," he admitted. "I worked for the county as a tax auditor for two years before entering the academy. Working in an office was just too boring for me. But the goal is the same—do my time and get out young so I can enjoy my retirement, maybe get myself a little winter home somewhere."

"That sounds nice."

He nodded. "Yeah. And if it wasn't for you and your magic touch, my early retirement would've been a hole in the ground."

"John, we said—"

"I know. No talking about it. And I won't. I just wanted to say thank you one last time. There. Now we can move on to something else."

True to his word, he changed subjects and chatted about the different states he'd considered retiring to. Leah's nervousness about the evening faded away as his voice relaxed her into believing he really didn't have ulterior motives, like blackmailing her to keep her secret.

The inside of Leone's wasn't anything like she'd expected. The décor was simple yet elegant, far different than the plain wood shingles and small neon sign outside. Photographs of Italy were arranged in purposely random fashion on the walls. Large electric candles in wrought-iron sconces sat between the pictures, providing most of the light in the room. The flatware on the tables was an eclectic mix of colors and shapes, as if the owner had shuffled three or four different sets together.

"Hi, there," the short, perky waitress greeted them as she placed menus on the table. "My name's Angie. Can I get you a drink?"

"Leah?" John asked.

"Um, I guess a glass of red wine would be good."

"Bring us a bottle of the house Chianti," John said to the waitress. "And some bruschetta while we're deciding."

"Sure thing." Angie hustled off.

"So what's good here?" Leah flipped open her menu. The variety of choices stunned her; the pasta list alone took up a full page. And then there were the veal, chicken, beef and seafood selections.

"I can't believe you've lived in town all your life and you've never eaten here," John said. "The place is practically an institution."

Leah shrugged. "I don't get out much. I'm too busy during the day, and by the time work is over I'm usually too exhausted to do more than go home, water the plants and collapse on the couch with a glass of wine, a medical journal and a warm blanket. Some nights I don't even make it to bed; I just fall asleep on the couch."

John put down his menu and looked at her. His dark eyes met her gaze and she found she couldn't turn away. "What about weekends? Don't you have any hobbies or friends to go out with?"

She recognized the subtle undertones of the question: *Are you seeing anyone?*

"No." She forced herself to look back down at her menu. His penetrating stare made her uncomfortable, as if he could see right through her happy façade to the lonely, sad person beneath the shell. "I don't have time. My only day off is Sunday, and even then I'm on emergency call. I just started my practice a few years ago and trying to run it by myself has turned out to be a lot harder than I thought it would be."

"So why not get a partner?"

Leah shook her head. "I can't take the chance of someone finding out what I can do."

"Hmm. I can see that." He paused while the waitress set down the plate of bruschetta and poured the wine.

"Are you ready to order?" Angie asked.

John glanced at Leah. She still had no idea what to get. Hell, she didn't even know what half the items on the menu were.

"Umm..."

"Tell you what. Do you trust me to order for both of us?"

She jumped at the offer. "Sure. Just don't get anything with mushrooms."

He nodded and then looked up at the waitress. "We'll start with two orders of pasta fagioli. She'll have the eggplant Bolognese over linguini, and I'll have the veal saltimbocca with a side of ziti."

"Comin' right up." The girl took their menus and hurried away.

Leah leaned close so the patrons at the other tables wouldn't hear her. "Okay, so what did you order for me? The only thing I recognized was eggplant."

He smiled and patted her hand. "Nothing too exotic. Macaroni and bean soup, followed by diced eggplant in a red meat sauce over pasta."

She returned his smile. "I can handle that."

John raised his wineglass to her. The ruby liquid seemed exotic in the flickering candlelight. "A toast." He waited until she picked up her glass, before continuing. "To a relaxing, enjoyable evening."

"Oh, I'll drink to that," she said and then took a healthy sip of her wine. The Chianti flowed over her tongue, breaking apart into different bursts of flavor. Essences of grape, cherry and strawberry filled her mouth, with just a hint of spice and alcohol burn.

"Oh, that's good. I don't usually drink red wines. I'm more of a white Zinfandel person."

"If you're going to have a hearty sauce, you need a stronger wine to compete with it."

"So you're a wine connoisseur too?" she asked, hoping to hide her returning embarrassment behind playful banter. She was suddenly having second thoughts about agreeing to the date. She knew she wasn't knowledgeable about a lot of things. Fine food and wine had never interested her while she'd been in college or vet school, and her vacations had usually been spent either with her family or volunteering at local veterinary offices.

But she'd never realized until now how uninformed she was. Being with John made her feel like she'd just stepped off the bus from Buttmunch, Idaho, for her first trip to the big city.

"A connoisseur? Hardly." He let out a short, self-deprecating laugh. "I just know what I like. Plus I have a friend who owns a liquor store, and he has monthly wine-tasting parties. I'll bring you to the next one; they're a lot of fun."

"Maybe." She put down her glass, deciding it was better to be honest right away. "I feel like I just crawled out from under a rock. I don't know what to order, I've probably only been to three restaurants in the last five years, and I'll be lucky if I use the right fork for my salad."

"Hey, don't worry about that. This isn't school. There's no test later."

He leaned toward her, his face radiating sincerity. "Your problem is you need to get out more. At the risk of ruining the mood, I have to ask. Have you ever had a steady relationship?"

The question cut too close to the truth, and she found herself overreacting. "Of course! I haven't lived in a bubble, you know."

John held his hands up in mock surrender. "Hey, don't get upset. I didn't think you'd *never* dated, but didn't any of your boyfriends ever take you anyplace nice?"

Damn him! "Is that something they teach you at the academy?"

"What?"

"How to figure out just the right question to ask. How to get past a person's defenses."

"I think it's just more of a talent of mine," he answered with a sheepish grin.

Angie arrived just then with two steaming cups of soup.

"Everything okay?"

John nodded and she left them alone again. Leah took another sip of wine to calm herself before answering his question. "To be honest, I've only had one serious relationship. I met him my senior year in veterinary school, and I thought my whole life was falling into place. A man who seemed to love me, my career getting ready to start, what more could a girl want?"

"What happened?"

She looked down at her plate, not wanting to see his expression when she told him. "He died two years after we started dating. We were talking about getting engaged."

"I'm sorry." He sounded sincere, but still she refused to look at him. It was always same when it came time to tell the story, the expressions of sorrow followed by supposed understanding.

"It was a brain aneurysm," she went on. "He was supposed to come over to my apartment, but he said he had a headache and wanted to go to bed instead. I figured I'd just get some extra studying done and see him the next day. In the morning, he didn't answer his phone so I went over there. I found him... I called 9-1-1 but it was too late. The doctor at the hospital said there was nothing anyone could have done."

She stopped there, waiting for the response she always heard.

This time it didn't come.

"But you could've, if you'd known." John's voice was matter-of-fact. No recrimination, but no hiding from the truth, either.

She looked up and saw that he was staring back at her, complete understanding in his eyes.

For the first time, she was able to get the rest of the story, her feelings, out.

"Yes! It would have been so easy. But he said it was just a headache. If...if I'd been there, I would have known something was wrong. I can see where the sickness is, but only after it gets serious. That's why I didn't notice it before."

"You never told him what you can do?"

"No." She finished her wine and he poured another glass for both of them. "I didn't think he'd understand. Hank was a great guy, but not exactly educated. He'd gone to work as a plumber right after high school. His idea of a big night out was TGI Fridays."

"Don't do that."

The coldness in his voice caught her by surprise.

"Do what?"

"Blame this on him. He wouldn't have needed a college degree to understand what you can do. The truth is, you never told him because you were afraid. Afraid he'd think you were a freak. Afraid he'd leave you."

Leah wanted to shout at him, throw her wine in his face, storm out of the restaurant. His words twisted her insides, filling her with pain and guilt.

Because he was right.

She felt a tear run down her cheek and quickly dabbed her eyes with her napkin before her makeup could smudge. John reached across and took her hands in his warm, rough ones.

"It's okay. You didn't do anything wrong. Maybe in time you would have trusted him. Maybe not. Maybe you were right not to tell him because he would have left you or spilled your secret to the world. But there's one thing you should know."

"What's that?" she asked, sniffing back more tears.

"You have nothing to feel guilty about."

"That's sweet. But you don't know what it's like, knowing you could've saved someone but you didn't."

"That's where you're wrong. I know exactly what it's like. Every cop does."

"What?"

"Sure. Take what happened in McDonald's the other day. What if that guy had shot his hostage, or you? It would have been my fault for not handling the situation right. That's a reality we face every time we respond to a call, that someone will get hurt or killed because of something we do, or don't do. But the fact is, sometimes you simply can't control what happens. And it's nobody's fault, except maybe Fate's."

"I never thought of it that way," she said. The few occasions the possibility had crossed her mind, her guilt had immediately reacted, telling her she was wrong, she should have done something. *This whole time, maybe all I needed was someone else to absolve me.* Something shifted inside her, as if the two-ton weight of her guilt had lifted just a little bit off her soul.

"You should." He let go of her hands and picked up his spoon. "Now eat your soup before it gets cold. And for the rest of dinner, I propose a rule: No talking about powers, death or guilt. Deal?"

She couldn't help but smile. "Deal."

Leah tasted her soup, but even though the thick, tomato-based broth was delicious, she couldn't properly enjoy it.

She was too busy thinking how nice John's hands had felt wrapped around hers.

Chapter Eleven

"I had a great time tonight," Leah said, leaning against her front door. She had too, which was something of a surprise to her.

The rest of the evening had been filled with pleasant, ordinary conversation. She'd told John about her childhood in Rocky Point, and he'd told her stories about growing up in Queens. He'd also casually provided information on his past loves, nothing too detailed, just enough to let her know he'd had some relationships that didn't work out but he wasn't bitter over them.

Most incredibly, they'd laughed a lot, something she rarely got to do anymore.

"I did too," he said, his smile wide and white in the light of the tiny porch bulb.

She should have expected it, but when he leaned in and kissed her, it took her completely off guard. At first she didn't respond; the act of kissing was almost unfamiliar to her. Then her body took over and she felt herself melting into him, pressing tight against his muscular body as she wrapped her arms around his back.

By the time he ended the kiss and stepped away, her face was unusually warm and she was short of breath.

"Wow." It was all she could think of.

John laughed. "I'll take that as a compliment."

"You should."

"Does that mean we can do this again?"

She smiled. "You mean kiss? I hope so."

"Actually, I meant go out, but if you want to skip the date and get right to the kissing, that's okay by me."

Leah reached out and touched his cheek. "Tell you what. We'll compromise. Wednesday is a short day for me, no evening hours. I'll cook dinner, you bring the wine."

One of his eyebrows went up, an expression she was beginning to realize was almost a habit with him. "I thought you only made frozen dinners. I'm not sure I know what wine goes with tater tots."

She punched him on the arm. "Very funny. I can cook. I just don't, normally. In fact, I might even make something that doesn't require the microwave."

"It's a date," he said, leaning down and kissing her cheek. "Call me during the week and let me know what time."

He turned and walked back to his car, waving once as he got in. Leah stayed on the small porch until his taillights were well down the street. Then she unlocked the door and went inside.

The voice spoke to her before she had a chance to turn on the living-room lights.

"Hello, Doctor DeGarmo. Please don't be alarmed. I'm not here to hurt you in any way."

Leah gasped and dropped her keys. She fumbled for the light switch. The sudden brightness of the track lights revealed a tall, heavyset black man sitting on her love seat. His shoulders seemed as wide as the couch, and even in his expensive-looking pinstripe suit, he looked mean and dangerous.

"Please don't be afraid." The stranger held his hands out to the sides, indicating he had no weapons.

At least none that he's showing. Oh my God, what does he want? Her heart felt like it would jump out of her chest, and she had to squeeze her legs together to keep from peeing herself.

"I'm here to deliver an invitation," he told her. He leaned forward and tapped a finger on an envelope sitting on the cocktail table. "I apologize for entering without your permission, but I wanted to make sure you got this, and I found your back door unlocked. You really should be more careful about that."

"I will," she said, finally finding her voice. "Who are you?"

He shook his head and gave her a friendly smile, but his eyes betrayed him. They had the same look as some of the cats her clients brought in, the ones that waited patiently until you unlocked their cages, and then they sprang at you, claws out and fangs ready to draw blood.

"It would be kind of silly to tell you that, after I just admitted to entering your house illegally. But if you accept the invitation..." he tapped the envelope again, "...I'll not only tell you my name, but I'll be handing you a very large check as I say it. Very, *very* large."

He stood up, and for a moment she thought his head would keep rising until it hit the ceiling. Definitely way over six feet.

"I'll let myself out the same way I came in." He started toward the kitchen, then stopped. "We'll be expecting your response by tomorrow. Have a good night." He nodded his head and exited out the back door.

For a moment Leah stood motionless, terrified he might return, that his polite exit was just a ploy. Then her legs gave out and she fell to her knees, collapsed into a fetal position.

She screamed, and it was as if the sound opened a dam of emotions. All at once she was crying and sobbing and holding herself, images of being raped or beaten or murdered flashing through her head like the morbid opening scenes of a police drama on television.

After a few moments she started to get control of her fear, and she pulled herself up onto the couch.

Got to call the police. Even without a name, they'll find him. His fingerprints were all over.

As she was reaching for the phone, she caught a glimpse of the writing on the invitation.

Fancy, calligraphy-style script spelled out *Marsh Enterprises.*

What the hell? Why would one of the largest companies in the world send a criminal to deliver an invitation to a small-town veterinarian? One that involved a lot of money?

Oh no. There was only one thing she could think of.

There's no way. How could they have found out? She knew the last thing she should be doing was touching the envelope, but she had to see what was inside. Holding it between her fingernails to avoid smudging any fingerprints that might be on the paper, she carefully tore the embossed seal keeping the flap closed.

She slid the folded piece of paper out and read the handwritten note.

Dear Doctor DeGarmo:

It has come to my attention that you may be able to help me with a special problem that has come up. I would be willing to pay you most handsomely for your one-time services. I'd like to have the opportunity to discuss this business venture with you in person. Please contact me at any time of the day or night with your answer.

At the risk of being melodramatic, this is a matter of life and death, and there is very little time to spare.

Kindest regards,

Leonard Marsh

Beneath Marsh's signature was a telephone number.

Shit! She crumpled the note and threw it onto the table. He'd found out somehow. That meant other people knew as well, the ones who'd told him. And the ones he'd told.

How many people knew about her now?

For a brief instant John's face appeared, but she dismissed him as Marsh's source. He didn't seem the type to break a promise.

That meant someone else had seen her use her Power, either at the clinic or during the robbery at McDonald's.

She thought about calling John, but what could he do? He couldn't investigate on his own, and if she got the police involved, sooner or later her secret would be revealed and she'd have a lot more to worry about than Leonard Marsh.

What do I do?

She went into the kitchen and poured a glass of wine, downed it in three gulps. The sweet-sour flavor of the white Zinfandel made her mouth pucker, and it immediately started a war in her stomach with the mellow Chianti, hearty sauce, and rich tiramisu she'd had at dinner.

Thoughts of dinner led to John Carrera again. He was a cop. Surely he'd have some advice.

Yeah. He'll tell me to call the police. Or a lawyer. The very things I can't do.

She slammed the glass down on the counter and went back into the living room. Unfolding the note, she read it again.

Calling him would be stupid. But then, not calling might be just as bad. The man owns several newspapers. He could expose me to the world. On the other hand, just because he wants something doesn't mean I have to say yes. If I don't want to get involved, I can always call John afterwards.

As she dialed the number with a shaking finger, she tried to rationalize that she was only being logical and protecting herself from public exposure.

Leonard Marsh closed his cell phone and leaned his forehead against the cool glass of his office window.

Tal had done it again. Somehow he'd convinced the DeGarmo woman to agree to a meeting, without any threat of violence and without bringing up her abilities.

Now it was a matter of waiting. She'd said her first available night was Wednesday. He'd offered to come into town and meet with her before that, but she insisted her schedule at the clinic wouldn't allow it.

"Four more days," he whispered to his reflection.

The corpse-like face in the glass stared back, a deadly reminder of how important this woman was to him.

He couldn't take any chances. Opening the phone again, he punched in Tal's number.

"She's agreed to meet," he said as soon as the other man answered. "Wednesday. You'll pick her up in one of the company cars. Make sure everything looks aboveboard. But in the meantime, I want a twenty-four hour surveillance on her."

He hung up before Tal could respond.

Four more days. Then he could *live* again.

Chapter Twelve

The next four days passed by in agonizingly slow fashion for Leah. She tried to keep busy at work, but all she could think about was what Leonard Marsh wanted her to do.

That she'd have to Cure something, or someone, was a given. The question was, could she trust him to keep her secret safe, or was he planning to blackmail her? Worse, what if it was all just a trick and he intended to kidnap her so he could turn her into some kind of human guinea pig?

More than once she nearly broke down and called John, but each time she talked herself out of it. There was no point in getting him involved unless she had proof Marsh was up to no good.

Then again, she kept telling herself, maybe it was a point in Marsh's favor that he seemed to be going out of his way to not leave any clues as to her ability. Nothing was in writing, and the giant black man who'd snuck into her home had never said a word. It showed he knew how to keep a secret.

Of course, it also showed he was a criminal.

So she kept quiet, and did her best to act like nothing was wrong. On Tuesday, Chastity did ask if anything was bothering her, but Leah brushed off her concern.

"I'm fine, really," she said. "I've had a headache the past couple of days, that's all. Maybe I need a vacation."

"Hell, I've been telling you that for over a year." The bubbly vet tech laughed. "You need to get away for a few days, forget this place."

Leah did her best to smile. "We'll see. Easier said than done."

Chastity flashed a naughty grin. "If I were you, I'd pick up that phone, get myself a hotel in Atlantic City for a few days and invite Mr. Hunky Policeman to join me."

"Enough about John! I should never have told you he took me out."

"Leah, it was your first date in, like, two years. Now it's time for the next step. You and him, alone in a room. Some wine, some music, some—"

"Oh crap." Leah nearly dropped the clipboard she was holding.

"What? I didn't mean—"

"No, not that. I just remembered something. I have to make a phone call." She rushed out of the reception area and into her office.

In her confusion about whether or not to tell John about Marsh, she'd forgotten to call him and cancel for Wednesday. Now she'd be canceling only a day before, something she hated to do because it bothered her so much when people did it to her.

What if he asked why she was canceling? She had no excuse ready.

And I know I'm a damn poor liar.

She decided the best thing would be to leave a message on his machine at home. She dialed his number, praying he was at work.

After four rings she got the hoped-for sound of his voice mail picking up. "Hello, you've reached John Carrera. I'm not available right now, so please leave your name and number, and I'll get back to you as soon as I get your message. Have a nice day."

Leah chewed a nail as she waited for the beep.

"John? It's Leah. Listen, something's come up for tomorrow. I have to go into Manhattan for the evening, so I'm afraid we'll have to postpone dinner. How about over the weekend? I'm really sorry. I'll call you on Thursday. Bye!"

She hung up and then leaned back in her chair, staring at the phone. *Did I sound normal? Was I too chatty? Maybe I should've let him know where I was going, in case something happens.*

Taking a deep breath, she tried to quell the voices in her head. *Nothing's going to happen. Marsh may know your secret, he might even try to blackmail you, but he's not going to hurt you. After all, if he did that, how could you work a Cure for him?*

Still, the anxious feeling wouldn't go away.

The long, black limousine pulled up in front of her house at exactly 5:30 p.m., just as Marsh had told her it would. A large man stepped out, and Leah realized it was the same person who'd been waiting inside her home. Before he could take more than a few steps she hurried out of the house and down to the car.

The last thing she wanted was for the man to go inside and see the note she'd left on the counter for John. Just a little insurance in case Marsh didn't let her go. At least John and the police would know what was going on when they went to the house to investigate her disappearance.

"Good afternoon, Dr. DeGarmo. My name is Tal Nova," the black man said, holding the limo door for her. "Please make yourself comfortable. It will take us about an hour to get to Mr. Marsh's office at this time of day."

Leah ducked and entered the car, which was filled with the spicy scent of cinnamon gum. She slid across the soft leather seat, keeping as much distance as she could from Nova. He seemed to sense her nervousness, and he sat down across and at an angle from her.

"Would you care for a drink?" His rich baritone and cultured words filled the confines of the vehicle, even though he hadn't raised his voice. When he spoke, it reminded her of James Earl Jones reading a commercial.

"No, thank you," she said, figuring she might as well remain polite, as long as he did. "What can you—"

Nova held up one finger. "I'm sorry, but I'm not allowed to discuss anything with you. Please don't bother to ask me any questions."

"But I just—"

He leaned forward, and any traces of pleasantness disappeared from his face, leaving behind a cold, hard expression devoid of warmth. "I said no questions."

The man leaned back and turned his head away, staring out the window at the scenery passing by as the limousine glided down the Palisades Parkway toward Manhattan. His only movements were to occasionally open a stick of Big Red gum and pop it into his mouth. As each new piece went in, he'd take out the old, chewed piece and add it to the small pile growing in the ashtray next to him.

Leah copied him, looking out her window and hoping it wasn't the last time she'd be able to do so. After a while she closed her eyes, focusing on breathing deeply and staying calm.

"Hey, Dr. DeGarmo."

Someone touched her. She opened her eyes and realized she'd dozed off. Glancing out the window, she could see they were just getting off the George Washington Bridge. A quick look at her watch told her she'd been asleep for over half an hour.

"We'll be there in a few minutes. Sure you don't want that drink?"

She started to say no, but the dry, sticky feeling in her mouth changed her mind. "Do you have water?"

"Certainly." Nova removed a bottle of spring water from a small cooler built into the bottom of the seat. "Here you go. I'll let you open it. That way you know it's safe." He smiled, but there was no humor in it.

"Thank you." She took a long swallow, letting the cold water wash away the cotton mouth caused by her anxiety.

"You're welcome."

After that he was silent again until the car pulled into the underground parking garage at Marsh Enterprises' worldwide headquarters on Riverside and Seventy-Seventh. The afternoon sunlight turned the reflective steel-and-glass tower into gold, while its modernistic design of interlocking towers set it apart from the older, mostly brick-and-stone buildings around it.

The car stopped in front of a private elevator. Nova exited and then held his hand out to help Leah from the car. "I'll take to you Mr. Marsh," he said, swiping a plastic card to open the elevator doors.

Leah moved to the back wall as Nova pressed the Up button. Even in her apprehensive state she was able to wonder at the opulence of the elevator's interior. Thick carpet covered the floor, and the walls were all real-wood paneling, varnished until they shined like a dining-room table. Soft, wordless music trickled down from a hidden speaker, and it took her a moment to recognize the tune as Bruce Springsteen's "Dancing in the Dark".

What's the world coming to, she wondered, *when the Boss becomes elevator music?*

The elevator came to a smooth stop. The doors parted and Leah found herself staring at the largest office she'd ever seen. Just as the building itself was a monument to pretentiousness, the inside was just as overdone.

From the floor-to-ceiling windows that stretched the entire length of one wall, to the entertainment center and wet bar opposite the extra-large desk in front of the windows, and the paintings and sculptures decorating the office, the entire room screamed "excess" to someone who'd grown up in a middle-class, suburban neighborhood where vacations were taken at the Jersey Shore rather than on islands in the Caribbean, and "making it" meant purchasing a new car instead of a secondhand vehicle.

She'd seen Marsh's name in countless newspaper articles and television stories, had understood he was wealthy, but until now she'd never realized he was Donald Trump wealthy. Maybe Bill Gates wealthy.

John was right, she told herself. *I've had my head in the sand for too long. And look what that's led to.*

"Hello, Dr. DeGarmo."

Behind the desk the tall, black leather chair swiveled around and she had her first look at Leonard Marsh.

He's seriously ill.

It was obvious from his pale color and gaunt features, and the stiff, slow movements of his hands, arms and neck as he rolled his chair up to the desk.

"Hello." She tried to keep her voice neutral.

"Please have a seat." He waved a hand at the chairs placed in front of his desk.

As she moved closer, she saw that his flesh had a distinct yellowish tint to it. A quick glance at her own hands as she sat down told her it wasn't from the room's fluorescent lighting.

He's jaundiced. Some kind of liver disease, perhaps?

"I won't beat around the bush, Dr. DeGarmo. I'm dying. Hepatocellular carcinoma."

Liver cancer. "I'm sorry to hear that." She waited, knowing what was coming next.

He leaned forward, his gaunt face corpse-like. When he spoke again, a faint foul odor reached her.

Sick breath, we used to call it in school. It doesn't matter if it's an animal or a person, you can smell the death in them.

"It's come to my attention that you have certain...abilities that might be able to accomplish what chemotherapy has not."

"Your information is wrong. I'm a veterinarian. There's nothing I can do for you."

Marsh laughed a sudden, barking sound that sent more foul breath her way. "Come now, Doctor. Do you think I'm stupid? Please look at the TV." He pointed past her.

Leah turned and watched as Tal Nova, who'd remained standing by the closed office door, went to the entertainment center and did something with a remote control. The flat-screen television came to life, and she was startled to see herself on the screen.

Next to her was the dog she'd Cured the previous week, the one with the broken legs.

The tape continued to show her shaving the dog's legs and wrapping them in unnecessary bandages.

Still hoping to convince him she was an ordinary person, Leah tried to argue. "I don't see what this proves. I was taking care of a dog. That's what I do."

"Yes, but this is what the dog looked like before Tal had it brought to your clinic."

Tal pushed another button, and the video changed to show the injured animal lying in the backseat of a car, its legs twisted and broken, blood all over its body.

Leah turned back to face Marsh, but couldn't find any words to say. They had her. She couldn't deny it, but she didn't want to admit it, either. Not out loud.

"Now, I'm a reasonable man," Marsh continued, leaning back in his chair. "I don't expect you to do this for free. So I'm prepared to make you a generous offer. One hundred thousand dollars, donated to your clinic, for you to use any way you see fit."

One hundred thousand dollars? Leah knew the shock must be evident on her face. With that kind of money she could buy new equipment, hire a second assistant, maybe even offer discounts or free services to people who couldn't afford to pay for their pets' care. All for something she could do with just a touch.

Then reality returned.

"No, I...I can't. You don't understand." She felt close to tears, heard the frustration in her voice.

"Can't, or won't?"

"I can't!" Frustration bubbled up but she didn't try to control it. "You think you know everything, but you don't. I don't just wave a magic wand over a dog and, presto, it's Cured. What I do is more like surgery. I remove the sickness, the injury. But then..." She paused for breath.

"Yes?" Marsh was staring intently at her.

"It doesn't disappear. I have to put it somewhere else. Put it in *something* else." She waited to see if he'd understand.

He did. His eyes went wide as he made the connection.

"The gunman at the McDonald's. He wasn't shot."

Leah shook her head. "No. I just transferred the injuries from J...from the police officer to the man who was threatening me. That's how it always works. For the animals, I keep terminal, aged strays from the shelter at my clinic. When I need to Cure someone's pet, I transfer the sickness to the animal that's already dying, one I can't Cure because too many people already know it's on its deathbed. I do it at the same time I administer the euthanasia. That's the part your cameraman missed."

She sat back in her chair, exhausted from her admission. "That's why I can't Cure you. I have to complete the circle within a few hours, or whatever I've taken inside me becomes a permanent part of me."

Tal Nova spoke up for the first time, startling her. She'd forgotten he was there. "You mean, if you cure Mr. Marsh, but you don't touch someone else, you'll end up with the liver cancer?"

"Within hours. So unless you have a terminal dog or cat here, I can't help you. If something happened on the way back to the clinic, and we didn't get there in time... " The rest of her statement hung in the air.

"So, that would be the only thing stopping you," Marsh said, his voice slow and thoughtful.

"Well, yes. I mean, if you wanted to come to my clinic tomorrow, after hours—"

"No, I'm afraid that won't do. I have an important meeting tomorrow, and I can't appear ill or it might lead to the board calling for me to step down. It has to be tonight."

Leah shook her head. "I've already explained that I can't. Not tonight."

"Maybe this will change your mind." Tal leaned past her and placed a photograph of John Carrera on the desk. It had been taken from a distance, and showed him unlocking the door to a house that she assumed was his.

"Where did you get this?"

"Doesn't concern you," Tal said. He pointed at the picture. "What should concern you is what will happen to your policeman friend if you don't do what you're told."

"Listen to him, Doctor." Marsh spoke before Leah could think of anything to say. "Mr. Nova is deadly serious. His skills in such matters are exceptional."

Leah looked down at the picture, her heart pounding. Just as she'd feared, she'd gotten herself involved with people a lot worse than white-collar criminals. She wanted to leap from the chair and run out of the office. Scream for help. Anything.

But even if they let her leave the building, which she doubted, they'd hurt John. She couldn't let that happen.

"Fine. I'll do it. But you have to take me to the clinic right after."

"Of course, Dr. DeGarmo. We wouldn't want any harm to come to you. All I want is to be well again, and then you can forget this meeting ever took place. Now, what do I have to do?"

"Just sit there." Leah stood up and walked around the desk. Marsh's lower abdomen, previously hidden behind the desk, glowed a faint green, a glow she knew only she could see.

She reached out and took his hand in hers. Electric fire raced through her, and she felt herself go rigid. Marsh's body spasmed beneath her hands like he'd touched a live wire.

"Aaah!" His voice was a strangled choke, as if his throat had constricted too much to allow air through.

Then the surge of pain was gone, and Leah collapsed to her knees. Her vision faded, and white spots circled in the darkness.

"What the fuck did you do to him?" a distant voice shouted.

The thick carpet cushioned her head as it hit the floor. She struggled to focus on the dark shape before her, and it slowly took form, becoming the angry face of Tal Nova. He held a gun in one hand, pointed at her.

She reached a hand out to him but he stepped back.

"Oh no you don't. You keep your hands to yourself or I'll blow your fuckin' head off. Did you do it?"

Leah nodded, tried to speak. Her mouth still didn't want to work, although her vision had returned to normal. She took a deep breath, then another. Strength crept back into her limbs.

"He's Cured," she whispered.

"She's right, Tal. Look at me."

Marsh stood up, and even from her position on the floor Leah could see the difference. His hollow cheeks had filled in again, and his flesh had a healthy, tanned look. Gone were the circles under his eyes and the lines of pain around his mouth. The bald spots on his head from the chemotherapy had filled in with thick, grayish-brown hair and he looked fifteen years younger. Even his suit seemed to fit better, no longer hanging off skeletal arms and shoulders.

"Amazing," he said, holding his hands out in front of him. "I can't thank you enough. Your payment will be provided via company check, for tax purposes. Tal will take you to the clinic." Turning to Tal, he added, "Come right back here when you're done. We have a lot of work to do tonight."

"Let's go." Tal waved the gun at Leah. "Get up. We're gonna walk nice and slow to the elevator."

Leah used the desk to pull herself to her feet. She kept quiet as she walked toward the door, until Marsh spoke from behind her.

"Dr. DeGarmo?"

She looked back. "What?"

He gave her a brief smile. "Your secret is safe with me."

"Thanks." She was happy that her tone sounded as sarcastic as she'd intended. Marsh shrugged and spun his chair around, putting his back to her.

Still keeping several feet between them, Tal motioned toward the door. "Move it, Doc. We've still got a long ride."

Mention of the car ride reminded her that the seeds of Marsh's cancer were already growing in her body, and she increased her pace.

Suddenly all she wanted to do was get out of the building and back to her old life.

Del McCormick sat up as the limousine containing Tal Nova and the lady vet emerged from the Marsh Enterprises executive garage and headed for the West Side Highway. He pulled out of his parking space and eased into the evening traffic, keeping a few cars between them.

He'd been watching the two of them for a few days now, ever since the episode with the dog. He wasn't the only one, either. A couple of times he'd caught sight of a short, stocky Hispanic who seemed to be keeping tabs on DeGarmo. He figured it was one of Nova's hired help.

The idea of crossing Tal Nova wasn't one he'd considered lightly. The big ex-football player had a reputation for being ruthless and sadistic. That, along with the fact the man was a freaking genius who always covered his tracks perfectly, made him a formidable opponent.

But to get his hands on someone like DeGarmo, Del was willing to take some risks. She was walking gold; he knew there were plenty of people who'd pay him enough for her that he could retire to a beach house for the rest of his life.

The trick was making sure he couldn't be linked to any kidnapping.

He followed the limo onto the West Side Highway North. Odds were it was taking the doctor home again after her meeting with Marsh. But why was Tal along for the ride?

"Only one way to find out," Del whispered to himself as he flicked on the radio.

The drive across the George Washington Bridge and down the Palisades Parkway was as uneventful as the earlier ride had been, when he'd tailed the limo to the doctor's house. As he'd expected, they took the exit for Rocky Point. However, he was almost caught by surprise when the limo headed for the center of town instead of DeGarmo's house.

"Now what are they up to?"

By the time they reached the clinic, Leah's guts were in a knot and she felt weak and feverish. At first she'd thought the stomach pains were simply nervousness, but all too soon she realized it was the cancer blooming. The sickness had come on faster than almost any other time she'd ever used the Cure.

Maybe because Marsh was so close to death? she wondered as the car came to a blessed stop.

"Stay right there," Tal told her. He got out and checked the building, peeking through the doors into the dark waiting area. Then he came around and opened her door.

Leah made sure not to place her hands anywhere near him. His entire demeanor had changed since she'd Cured Marsh going from scary but polite to downright hostile. Unlike the ride into the city, Tal had given her his undivided attention the entire way home, sitting as far away from her as possible and keeping his gun trained on her. The one time she tried to speak, to let him know she wouldn't pass it on to him, he said "shut up" and gave her a look that she deciphered as equal parts fear and hatred.

The kind of look she'd always expected she'd get from people if they ever found out her secret.

A wave of dizziness washed over her and she paused, hanging on to the car door for a moment. She closed her eyes and took several deep breaths, trying to keep her equilibrium.

"Hurry it up," growled Tal.

"Just give me a moment," she said, shocked to hear how weak her voice sounded.

"I'm not helping you inside, so you better have enough strength left to walk in on your own. Unless you want to die right here in the parking lot."

"Fuck you," she whispered. After one more breath, she opened her eyes and walked slowly and carefully to the door. Her hand and arm twitched in time to the cramps racking her body as she unlocked the door and deactivated the alarm system. Once it was off, she stumbled across the waiting area to the basement steps. Clinging to the railing, she hurried down and went to the first of the two occupied cages.

She opened the small door and reached inside. "I'm sorry, Pumpkin," she told the Irish setter. Already dying of its own cancer, it barely lifted its head to look at her. She grabbed one of its paws and immediately felt the electric spark that signaled the release of the sickness inside her. Expelling the illness wasn't nearly as painful as delivering the Cure, but it still hurt.

On the receiving end, Pumpkin jerked and yipped once, then went still.

"Holy shit," Tal said from the bottom of the stairs. "You killed that dog in like one second. You were that sick?"

Leah got to her knees and turned around, all her strength returned as if she'd never been ill.

"Sick? I just Cured a man who was dying of liver cancer. I took it inside me and carried it all the way here. Of course I was that fucking sick!" She didn't mention that part of the reason Pumpkin died so quickly was that his already weak system had been overloaded by the new illness. Screw him. Let him think she could have killed him instantly with a touch. Serves him right to be scared. God knew she'd been frightened enough the last few days.

He raised an eyebrow and his lips curled just a little at one corner. "You sound better now. C'mon, I want to get you home. Your work might be done for the night but mine's not." He waggled the gun, not pointing it directly at her, but reminding her he still held it.

"Not yet. I have to put the body in the freezer. It can't stay here overnight."

Leah grabbed the seventy-pound dog and pulled him out of the cage. "A little help would be nice," she said, glancing at Tal.

He just shook his head.

"Fine. I'll do it myself."

She wrapped Pumpkin in a large towel and dragged him over to a small cold room, where she laid the dog on the floor, still covered. "I'm sorry," she whispered. "I'll be back tomorrow."

"You done?" Tal asked.

"Yes." She shut the door.

"Why did you apologize to the dog? It's dead."

She headed for the stairs, not looking at the man she was coming to despise more and more each second. "Because I had to do what I did without putting him to sleep first. I don't like animals to feel pain because of me. And because I had to leave him there, alone in a cold room, until tomorrow, when normally I'd take the body right away to the funeral home for cremation."

"Lotta work for a dead dog."

His casual tone pushed her over the edge. She turned around to face him, had the pleasure of looking down at him for the first time since he'd shown up in her life, because he was three steps below her. "It's not just a dead dog! It was my patient. I'm a doctor. I care for these animals. People love their pets the same way they love their children. More, sometimes. You—"

She never got to finish the sentence. She reached toward him, one finger pointed at his chest. Faster than her eyes could follow, his free hand came up and slapped at her arm, sending her whole body into the cinder block wall of the stairway. Before she'd even managed to grab the railing he'd jumped up the steps and had a handful of her hair in his fist.

With a powerful twisting motion, he spun her around so that her back was against his chest. He pulled harder on her hair, forcing her head backward until she was staring at the ceiling. At the same time he jammed the gun under her chin.

"Don't you ever do that again, lady. Don't talk to me that way, don't point at me, and don't ever try to touch me. You do, and I'll blow your head off and toss you next to the mutt. Now get moving!"

He pushed her forward. She stumbled and clutched at the rail to steady herself. Her scalp felt like it was on fire, the pain beating in rapid fashion, in time with her heart. She could still feel the cold steel pressed against her skin, smell the sweet cinnamon odor of his breath next to her face.

He's not lying.

She remembered Marsh's words. *"Listen to him, Doctor. His skills in such matters are exceptional."*

Apparently no longer afraid to touch her, Tal held her arm in a tight grip as they walked across the parking lot, and pushed her roughly into the car. He kept a brooding silence on the ride to her house, only speaking when they pulled up in front.

"Go home, Doctor. And if you value your life, or your cop friend's, you won't say a word about tonight to anyone. I'll know if you do."

Leah believed him. It was already obvious he'd been watching her. What else had he done? Tapped her phones? Put more cameras around? "I won't say anything."

He nodded, his lips curled in a malicious smirk. "Good girl. Have a nice life."

She got out and waited until the car drove away before going inside. She managed to make it to the couch before she broke down in a bout of hysterical crying. Curled in a fetal position, her chest heaving, she howled into a pillow until she was gasping for air and the fabric was soaked from her tears.

Gradually her weeping slowed down to whimpering sobs.

She fell asleep with her arms wrapped around her knees and the wet pillow under her cheek, her head filled with visions of her and John lying bloody and dead in the clinic's freezer.

Chapter Thirteen

Del McCormick hadn't been able to see what went on in the veterinary clinic, but, judging from the way Tal kept the doctor at gunpoint and manhandled her into the limousine, it wasn't a friendly chat.

Parked three houses away as the lady vet got dropped off at her own place, Del had to make a split-second decision: continue to follow Tal, or stay and see if DeGarmo went back out.

Ultimately it was the notion that of the two of them, Tal Nova was more likely to lead him to important information he could use.

He put the stolen car in Drive and trailed the limo as it headed for the Parkway entrance.

Christ, I'm getting sick of this drive.

I need to come up with a better plan.

Tal Nova unwrapped a stick of Big Red and popped it into his mouth. The fiery tang of the gum exploded against his taste buds, and a wave of saliva washed over his tongue. He hit a speed dial number on his cell phone.

"Hello?" The new strength in Marsh's voice was evident even through the tiny speaker.

"I just dropped her off. She wasn't lying about having to get rid of it. She was yellow and sweating by the time we got back, barely able to walk. Then she touched one finger to some old mutt, and *bang!* The thing was dead and she was good as new."

"I assumed she was telling the truth. She didn't seem to be a particularly good liar. What about the payment?"

"I've arranged to have it delivered by courier tomorrow. She was real freaked out tonight, so I didn't want to upset her further."

"That's fine. I wouldn't want her to think I reneged on my part of the deal. When you return, come to my office immediately. There's a lot to discuss before tomorrow's meeting."

"Yes, sir." Tal flipped the phone shut. The abrupt way Marsh switched topics was typical of him. Never one to waste words, as soon as one project was completed or one plan finalized, he moved on to the next. In his mind, the subject of Leah DeGarmo was old news, history. Now that he'd been cured, he wouldn't think of her again unless something happened and he needed her services once more.

That's where we differ. Tal could see plenty of opportunities for someone with DeGarmo's talent. *She's the perfect tool. Untraceable. What she can do is something most people would consider impossible. Which means she can operate in plain sight.*

And no one will suspect a thing.

Not even Marsh.

Chapter Fourteen

John Carrera stared at the phone. He'd been doing it on and off since finishing dinner an hour before. Truth to tell, he'd been doing it pretty much since he'd gotten out of bed that morning.

He'd arrived home from work the previous day, only to find a message from Leah postponing dinner and saying that she'd call the following day.

Now here it was, the end of the day, and nothing.

Should I call her or wait? he wondered, while he watched the phone sit there in maddening silence. *Maybe she didn't have as good a time as she said? Did she have second thoughts about dating a cop?*

Stop acting crazy! he told himself. *Something came up. It happens. You're thirty-six, for Chrissakes. Act like it. Either pick up the phone or wait.*

But if I call, maybe I'll sound too needy.

Fuck it.

He picked up the phone, dialed Leah's house. When he got the machine he froze, torn between hanging up and leaving a message. In the end, the idea of acting like a teenage, love-struck loser propelled him into action.

"Hi, Leah. It's John. I guess you're not home. When you get this message could you—"

Something clicked. Leah's voice came on the line. "Hello, John? Are you still there?"

A wave of conflicting feelings washed through him. Relief, annoyance, worry.

"Yeah. I didn't interrupt anything, did I?"

"No." She sounded out of breath. "I was just unlocking the door when I heard the phone ring. It was crazy at work today. Thursdays are always like that, because of Wednesdays being short days."

"I hear you. So, when did you get back?" *Did that sound too pushy?*

"Last night. I would have called you but I was tired and went right to bed."

"Hey, no big deal."

She laughed. "I can hear you pouting. Don't worry, I haven't changed my mind. Dinner, tomorrow night, my place. Seven o'clock. You bring the wine."

Something relaxed inside John's chest, a tightness he hadn't even known was there until it went away. "I'll be there. What are we having?"

"It's a surprise."

Now it was his turn to laugh. "Haven't even gone shopping yet, have you?"

"See you tomorrow, smart-ass." She hung up.

John tossed the phone back onto the table. *What kind of wine should I get?* Knowing the type of person Leah was, she'd probably try to impress him and cook something too hard for her limited skills.

Whatever I get, I'll make sure to get two bottles.

Feeling better than he had in two days, he flipped on SportsChannel and relaxed back on the couch.

Leah took a deep breath after hanging up with John. Once again she'd forgotten to call him, would probably have forgotten tomorrow too, the way her head was spinning. Between work and her anxiety about Marsh knowing her secret, she'd barely been able to make conversation with her patients' owners. Work had always been a refuge for her, a place where she didn't think about anything except helping the sick and injured animals that came through the door each day. But now it was a different place, as if the presence of Tal Nova and the knowledge she'd been spied upon had sullied the building.

"Stop being such a baby," she chided herself as she went into the kitchen and poured some juice. "Why would Marsh need you again? You Cured him. Even if he tells someone, no one will believe it. The video could have been faked."

She caught a glimpse of herself in the kitchen window. Dark smudges made her eyes look sunken, and her pale cheeks and lips didn't help. Her hair had come undone from its clip and hung around her face in wild wisps.

She looked like an escapee from a mental institution.

"And talking to myself doesn't help that comparison," she told the face in the glass.

Suddenly pissed off at herself for being taken advantage of, she turned away from the window, grabbed a pad and pen, and sat down at the kitchen table.

"Time to stop moping. What's done is done." She wrote *Grocery List* at the top of the page. "And John thinks I can't cook? I'll show him. I'll make him the best meal he's ever had."

The knock on the door came just as Leah was adding more milk and butter to the mashed potatoes. The stove was announcing that her roast was ready, in strident, monotonous beeps and, judging by the burnt-toast odor coming from the toaster oven, the garlic bread was getting ready to speed past well done.

"Come in, the door's open!" she shouted, hoping John would hear her. She dipped a greasy finger into the potatoes and scooped up a taste.

Still lumpy.

Jesus, how much milk do these things need?

She was about to pour in another cupful when a strong hand stopped her. "Don't drown them there 'taters, missy."

She turned around and found John standing there, a large paper bag in one hand and a very smug grin on his face.

"Fine. You know potatoes, you take care of them. I'll get the bread."

Embarrassed that he'd walked into a disaster instead of the gourmet meal she'd planned, she rushed across the kitchen and pulled the garlic bread from the toaster oven. It was dark brown, but hadn't achieved charcoal status yet.

She slid it onto a waiting plate and hurried back across the room to the stove, which still filled the kitchen with its robotic beeping.

Carefully lifting a corner of the aluminum foil covering the top of the roasting pan, she eyed the brand-new meat thermometer she'd picked up along with the pan and the roast.

"Do you like your beef rare, medium or deliciously medium well?" she asked, praying he wouldn't say rare.

"I like it on a plate. I'm not picky."

"You've come to the right place, then." Using two oversized serving forks, she lifted the roast onto a carving board. "Make yourself useful and cut this," she said as he scooped potatoes into a bowl. "I'll open the wine."

He handed her the bowl of potatoes and started slicing. "Oh, by the way," he called out over his shoulder, "there's an envelope taped to your front door. Were you expecting something?"

"An envelope?" Leah pulled the cork from the bottle of Cabernet Sauvignon and then went to the door. Sure enough, stuck on the outside was an unmarked white envelope. Slipping one fingernail beneath the flap, she opened it as she came back into the house. Inside was a folded piece of paper and a check.

A one-hundred-thousand-dollar check.

"So, what is— Leah, are you all right?" John hurried across the living room and grabbed her arm.

She let him help her to the couch. She felt as if the world had suddenly tilted around her, leaving her off-balance and numb.

"What is it?" John's voice seemed a mile away.

She handed him the check and the note.

"Holy shit. A hundred thousand?" He opened the note, read it out loud.

Dear Dr. DeGarmo:

Thank you for your assistance with my problem. As I promised, here is a small token of my appreciation. I've made it out to your business so that you do not have to feel guilty about accepting personal payment. Consider it a donation to a worthy cause.

Regards,

Leonard Marsh.

John set the letter and check on the cocktail table. "His problem? You didn't...?"

Leah nodded without looking at him. "I...had to. He was dying."

She wanted to add that they'd threatened his life, but she already felt low enough, dirty enough. Admitting she'd been forced to do it because of her feelings for John would have made things even worse. She'd break down and cry; she could already feel the tears waiting to burst free. Besides, the cop in him might want to file charges of some kind, maybe even investigate.

And she couldn't afford that to happen.

"But how did he know?"

She watched her hands twist and twine together in her lap, physical manifestations of her guilt, fear, and anger. But when she spoke, her voice was dull, lacking in inflection.

Distant.

"He didn't say how he found out. But they set me up. Remember that dog, the one I told you about that was hit by the car?"

"The emergency the other night?"

"Yes. They hid a camera somewhere, filmed the whole thing. That's why I couldn't meet you on Wednesday. They threatened to go public. One of Marsh's men drove me to Manhattan and that's when I found out Marsh was dying. He had liver cancer. So I...I Cured him, and then they took me to the clinic. I barely made it... I..."

The dam burst before she could finish her sentence, all her words washed away by the sobs that burst out from deep inside.

"Hey, it's okay." John put his arms around her. "What's done is done. I just wish you'd called me. You shouldn't have gone off with anyone all alone like that. It could have been dangerous."

His words brought back the memory of Tal Nova pointing his gun at her, and she cried even harder. Deceiving a man she cared about, putting his life in danger, being forced to do something against her will. It was like a kind of rape.

And if she took money for it, what would that make her?

A whore?

Well, at least there was one place she could draw the line.

"I'm not cashing the check," she said through her tears.

"What?" He leaned back. "That's the one thing you *should* do."

Now it was her turn to be surprised. "How can you say that? He blackmailed me. That money's dirty. I don't want it."

One of John's dark eyebrows went up. "It's only dirty if you got it by doing something illegal or you use it for the wrong thing. Think what you could do with a hundred grand. New equipment, more help at the clinic. Think of the animals you could save. The minute you cash that check it goes from dirty to clean, just because of the good it will do."

"No!" Leah knew her vehemence was a result of the secrets she was keeping. But she couldn't tell John the truth. Even if it meant he wouldn't understand her reasons for not cashing the check.

"All right. Do what you want." He held his hands up in surrender. "Let's forget about it for now. Dinner's getting cold and I'm hungry."

He got up and went to the table, poured wine for the two of them. Leah knew he was upset with her.

She sat down and they both tried to pretend nothing had happened, that it was just an ordinary night, but the damage was done. The conversation throughout the meal was strained, and when dessert was done she was relieved when he told her he had to go home and get ready for a midnight shift.

"I'll call you tomorrow," he said as they stood on the front porch.

"Okay." Suddenly she felt bad. She'd used him the way a cat used a scratching post, and it wasn't fair. "I'm sorry I was such a bitch, but the whole thing has me really angry. If I cash his check, then every time I spend some of that money I'll be reminded of how he treated me, how he made me feel."

"I know." John leaned over and kissed her on the cheek. "But this isn't just about you. Maybe you need to put your feelings aside and think about all those people with sick and dying animals. Good night, Leah." He turned and walked away before she could reply.

She was left standing alone on the porch, her cheek warm where his lips had touched, her stomach churning as guilt and frustration did battle inside her.

In the living room, the phone rang.

Two houses down, one of the two men in the unmarked white van turned to the other. "Got a call coming in."

Del McCormick looked away from the darkly tinted window through which he was aiming a parabolic, long-distance microphone. "Put it on speaker and record it."

"Gotcha."

Del watched Leah DeGarmo go inside to answer the phone.

A hundred grand. If I time it right, I could get the girl and *the money...*

Leah's voice, made tinny and small by the speaker mounted in the rack of electronics Del had purchased, filled the van. "Hello?"

"Good evening, Doctor DeGarmo. I take it you received your payment?"

Leah froze at the sound of Tal Nova's baritone voice.

"Ms. DeGarmo?"

Her tongue unlocked. "I'm here. What do you want?"

"Just following up. I had a large sum of money delivered to your home, and I wanted to make sure it arrived safely."

"I got it." She started to say she was going to tear it up, but something stopped her. Hearing Nova's condescending tone, eloquently hidden behind cultured pronunciation, lit a fire inside her, the flames fueled by indignation and rage.

Screw them. They probably expect *me to throw that money away. Serve 'em right if I cash the check.* In the back of her mind she could hear John congratulating her.

"Excellent. Now, I was wondering if you might be available to perform another small favor."

Oh no. Dammit, I knew this *would happen.*

89

She sat down at the kitchen table, a feeling of calm acceptance filling her the way it did before a difficult surgery when she accepted that the animal on the table might not make it, no matter what she tried.

"No."

"I'm sorry?" Nova's voice sounded genuinely surprised.

"I said no. I'm not doing anything for you or Marsh again. Ever. We're through."

"I'm sorry to hear that, Doctor. Maybe you just need a little time to reconsider. After all, some decisions are hard to make, especially when you know what's riding on them. We'll talk again in the morning. Good night."

There was a click as he hung up.

Leah considered dialing John and explaining everything to him, but then remembered he would be getting ready for work.

I'll call him first thing in the morning and tell him the whole story. He'll know what to do. I can't hide it any longer, not when we could both be in danger.

She set her alarm for 9:00 a.m., then got ready for bed even though it wasn't even ten yet. She tossed and turned for an hour before finally giving up and taking two of the muscle relaxers she had left over from the time she'd sprained her back the previous year.

By the time David Letterman began his Top Ten list, she was sound asleep.

Chapter Fifteen

Tal Nova stared at the list of names while he opened another stick of gum. It was a list he kept only on a special personal laptop, the one that he'd never hooked up to the Internet. Totally untraceable, it had never even left Tal's apartment.

Which was exactly the way Tal wanted it because the information in the file represented a potential death sentence if the wrong people—or person—ever found out he had it.

Relaxing against the thick cushions of his suede couch, the apartment dark and quiet around him, Tal considered each name in turn, mentally reviewing the information he had on file for that particular person and how that information could best be turned to his, and Marsh Enterprises', advantage.

While he did plenty of dirty work for Marsh, the company—and the man—primarily conducted business aboveboard. Too many dirty secrets, too many cloak-and-dagger initiatives, and sooner or later something was bound to leak out. That was why Marsh kept them to a minimum, a principle Tal agreed with wholeheartedly.

Or, at least, *had* agreed with. Until Leah DeGarmo came along.

The veterinarian represented an opportunity for Tal to set things in motion that would catapult Marsh Industries past its competitors, and in the process deliver large amounts of money, in the form of stock options and annual bonuses, into Tal's bank account. All with Marsh being none the wiser.

Even if the old man did catch on eventually, it would be too late to take back what was done. And, pragmatist that he was, Marsh would no doubt see that, in retrospect, Tal had made the right choices. And if he didn't?

Well, DeGarmo would be the solution to that problem as well.

A glance at the clock showed it was getting late. He turned off the laptop and returned it to the hidden compartment built into the base of the coffee table. Time to get some sleep.

Tomorrow was going to be a big day.

Chapter Sixteen

Someone was shaking her. Calling her name.

"Doctor DeGarmo? Wake up. It's time to go."

Why is James Earl Jones talking to me?

She opened her eyes, tried to focus on the smiling face hovering over her, illuminated by weak morning sunshine.

Tal Nova.

A strong hand slammed down over her mouth, cutting off her scream before it had a chance to escape. Nova's other arm came down on her chest, pinning her to the bed. She tried to squirm free and in response he pushed harder, until it felt as if her ribs might snap under the pressure.

"If you scream, if you try to run, if you do anything other than what I say, your cop boyfriend dies. Got it?" His lips never stopped smiling, but his voice was cold as winter snow.

Leah stopped struggling, nodded her head.

"Good. Let's hope for both your sakes I can trust you." Nova took his hand away and Leah rolled to her side, gasping for air. Once she had her breathing under control, she lifted her head and looked at him.

"What do you want from me now?"

Nova stood up. "As I said last night, I have need of your services. I am willing to pay you well for those services. However, I am also prepared to inflict a great deal of misery should you decide not to help me. That choice is ultimately yours. The choice to accompany me today is not. You have five minutes to get dressed."

"But I—"

"No questions." Nova pulled a cell phone from his pocket. "Do as I say, silently, or I make a call and your boyfriend starts losing body parts."

Leah sat up, anger and fear battling inside her until she thought she might scream. She would have, too, if she hadn't believed Nova's threat. "Can you at least turn around?"

"No." He moved to the side, simultaneously blocking the door and allowing her access to her dresser. "You have nothing to worry about. I'm not a rapist. I simply don't trust you alone in a room with doors and windows."

"Fine." Leah got out of bed, and immediately her bladder screamed for attention. "I have to pee."

Nova waved a hand toward the master bedroom's bath. "Go ahead. But leave the door open and come back out immediately."

Thankful she'd worn pajamas to bed the previous evening, instead of her usual T-shirt and panties, she crossed the room, aware of his eyes on her the entire time. The feeling reminded her of a pit bull that had been brought to the clinic by the police. They'd captured it during a drug bust; trained for killing, it had watched her from its cage all day with eyes that exuded pure violence and hatred. It was the only time in her life she'd ever been truly afraid of a dog.

Leah considered climbing out the bathroom window. It was already open and she was sure she could knock out the screen and escape before Tal Nova made it across the two rooms. But then there was the two-story drop to the ground. All it would take was a twisted ankle and she'd be right back at his mercy. Even if she did escape, what about John? She pictured Nova dialing a number and giving the order to put a bullet into John's head.

I can't put him in any more danger than he's already in. Unfortunately, that meant doing what Nova asked, and trusting there'd be a way afterwards to let John know the truth about everything.

"Hurry up in there," Nova said from the other room. Leah finished, flushed and took a moment to swish a capful of mouthwash before returning to the bedroom.

"Three minutes." His voice carried no inflection; he could just as easily have been timing an egg as counting down someone's death.

Leah opened a drawer and then paused. "How should I dress?" She hoped that wouldn't violate the no-questions rule.

Nova frowned. "I don't know yet. Wear what you'd normally wear if you were going to the city with a friend. If you need something else, we'll buy it later."

Without responding, Leah selected a bra, some underwear, a plain blue blouse and a pair of jeans. She stared at Nova for a moment, hoping he'd show some courtesy after all, but he simply continued staring at her.

Turning her back while she dressed didn't make her feel any less humiliated, but at least she couldn't see him looking at her while she was naked. After slipping into socks and comfortable sneakers, she turned back around. "I'm ready."

He tapped his watch. "You're almost two minutes over the deadline I gave you."

A cold pit opened in Leah's stomach and threatened to suck her down into its dark depths. But before she could protest, he motioned for her to leave the bedroom. "You're lucky I'm a patient man, Doctor. Next time your lover boy will suffer the consequences."

Leah followed him out to the waiting limousine, knowing that she—and John—had literally dodged a bullet.

There won't be a next time, she promised herself as she climbed into the long, black car.

But even as she thought it, she wondered if she'd ever be free of Tal Nova.

The ride to Manhattan gave Leah an eerie feeling of déjà vu. The only difference was that this time Nova didn't offer her anything to drink. He just sat across from her, his eyes half-closed, looking for all the world like he was dozing while the car crept along in the rush-hour traffic.

Leah didn't trust that look. He was like a cat, wired tightly and ready to pounce. *Probably sleeps with a gun under his pillow, his hand ready to grab the weapon and fire at a second's notice.*

The idea that she'd become involved with people like Tal Nova and Leonard Marsh turned her stomach. *Damn this Power!* Although she'd kept her ability a secret all her life, until now she'd never really wished she didn't have it. Just knowing she could help so many animals had made the associated problems worthwhile.

And then she'd finally found a man who seemed to like her as much as she liked him, a man she could trust, who didn't seem put off by what she could do, who understood her need for secrecy.

Only to have it all torn away by two supposed pillars of society who were no better than common criminals.

Please, God, keep John safe. Just a little longer. Just until I get out of this mess and I can talk to him.

Thinking about telling John the truth scared her almost as much as the hulking man sitting across from her. Leah knew there was the very real chance her admission might drive him away. After all, who'd want to be involved with someone whose very nature put everyone around them in mortal danger? The idea that she might lose him because she hadn't been truthful from the start stabbed at her soul like a dagger.

But I have to tell him. His life is worth more than my happiness.

Tears brimmed in Leah's eyes, and she turned her head toward the window so Nova wouldn't see her crying. Something inside her told her she shouldn't appear weak in front of him. He was like an animal.

And in the animal kingdom, the strong always prey on the weak.

Tal Nova watched the veterinarian look away from him. He'd caught the glimmer of tears, noticed the way she tried to nonchalantly brush them away as if she were just rubbing her eyes.

He kept his face impassive, but inside he smiled. It was good that he had her so scared she was crying. With her abilities, it was important to keep her off-balance and frightened, never let her get the idea in her head to become the aggressor. He knew he'd taken a chance threatening her with the cop's life; after all, there was no way of knowing if she cared more about him than her own safety. She'd only met him a week ago. And who knew what kind of person she was? Thirty-something and not married could very well mean she had a problem with relationships.

But Tal considered himself a good judge of character and he'd taken into account the fact that she'd gone into a field where you needed a lot of compassion. Plus, she'd risked her life to save the cop before she even knew him. That said a lot about her.

It also meant she'd no doubt be very opposed to what Tal wanted her to do. Which was where the cop came in. Without that kind of leverage, there was a very good chance she'd tell him to go fuck himself.

Luckily, he'd had a great teacher in Leonard Marsh. Watching him over the years, Tal had learned all the best ways to manipulate people, to identify and prey on their weaknesses, to exploit any personality faults.

As the sleek limousine worked its way across the George Washington Bridge, Tal guided his thoughts back to the evening's plans.

Soon it would be time to see if he'd played his cards right.

Chapter Seventeen

The warehouse sat in a part of the city Leah had never seen before. Not that she'd made a lot of trips to Manhattan in her life, but she'd been there enough to recognize the major areas: Central Park, Midtown, Little Italy. She knew the West Side from the East Side, knew the difference between Uptown and Downtown.

Today she was completely lost.

At first, she'd thought the limo was taking them to Marsh's building again. They'd been going down the West Side Highway. Then they'd passed the exit she'd expected them to take, continuing on the highway until somewhere between the Village and the new Freedom Towers site, where they'd taken a series of side streets that left her totally confused.

They stopped in front of a dilapidated building that looked the same as all the others on the street. No numbers on the doors, no street sign on the corner. Garbage strewn everywhere, its rancid smell filling the air. Broken windows and graffiti-covered walls gave the place an aura of dangerous disuse. The harsh crunch of crack vials underfoot, as Tal Nova pushed her toward the doors, added to the feelings of violence and despair that emanated from the cold, lifeless buildings.

"Get inside," Nova said. His eyes flicked from left to right and back again, never staying still, as if he was worried they'd been followed. Leah tried to stall their progress, taking slow steps and pretending to stumble once, hoping that maybe a cop would cruise past.

Hell, even a drug dealer would be a welcome sight right now. Any kind of witness would be better than none. But Nova only grabbed her arm and dragged her along with him, and then they were inside the gloomy warehouse while two men shut the heavy doors behind them.

Nova guided her down a dusty hallway to a long room with wide plexiglass windows down one side. The windows looked down onto what had once been either an assembly line or a packaging area, judging from the rusty, broken conveyer system running down the center of the work area twenty feet below. Two cheap wooden chairs were the only furniture in the observation room.

"Sit down." Nova closed the door behind them.

"I think I'll stand," Leah said, feeling anything but defiant, but not wanting to have Nova towering over her.

The big man shrugged. "Suit yourself. Here's the deal. A certain rival of Mr. Marsh is in town. He's been causing some difficulties for us lately, making a big splash in a business area we once had cornered. So, we're going to use those powers of yours to pass a nice fatal disease to this person."

"No. I won't do that. If you need me to Cure someone, that's fine, but I'm not a murderer."

Nova shook his head. "You might want to rethink that. See, if you say no, your boyfriend dies. Either way, you're a murderer. It's just a matter of who you kill."

Leah felt as if she might throw up. "You wouldn't do that." She hoped she was right, that Nova was smart enough to realize he'd lose any leverage with her if he killed John.

"I had a feeling you might say that." He pulled out his cell phone. "Demonstration time."

The sick feeling in Leah's stomach grew worse. "What's going on?"

A thin smile crossed Nova's face. "Watch and learn, Doctor DeGarmo." He tapped a finger on the window.

Leah looked down just in time to see two men drag a kicking and screaming Chastity Summers into the work area. She still wore the clothes she'd had on the previous day. One of the men punched the young blonde girl in the face, knocking her to the floor.

The second man pulled a pistol and aimed it at her.

"NO!" Leah screamed. Down below, Chastity twisted around, holding her hands out as if she could block the bullet. No sound reached the observation room, but Leah knew Chastity was begging for her life.

The man pulled the trigger.

Blood exploded from Chastity's back and she fell over, an irregular red stain already forming on the front of her white blouse.

"Oh God!" Leah ran for the door, but it was locked. She turned to Nova. "Open the door! I can still save her!"

"I know," Nova said. "That's the point. You're going to stand here and watch her die, knowing that if you'd said yes she'd be alive and on her way back home right now."

"You fucking bastard!" Leah ran at him, swung her fists at his chest. Nova caught them before she could make contact, pushed her away while still holding her arms so she couldn't swing or kick at him.

"Picture your cop friend down there, bleeding out onto the floor. Because you'd better believe we have him right here in this building. And if you let him die, there's still your family to think about. Your mother and father live in Las Vegas, don't they? I could be there by tomorrow morning."

Nova let go of her arms, grabbed her by the back of the neck. Pushed her face up to the window. "Look down there. That's your fault. All your fault."

On the cement floor, Chastity no longer moved. A huge pool of blood, more than Leah had ever seen in one place before, continued to grow beneath her.

One of the men bent down and touched fingers to her wrist. Then he looked up at the windows, a wide smile on his face, and gave them a thumbs-down sign.

Tal Nova flipped his phone open again. Down below, the man pressed a finger to the Bluetooth in his ear.

"Get rid of her. No traces, understand? Wash the floor when you're done."

The man nodded. Nova hung up and spoke to Leah, his voice devoid of any emotion. As if he'd just watched someone tie their shoe rather than obliterate a young woman's life.

"So, have you changed your mind, or do we need another demonstration?"

She didn't look at him, her gaze held captive by the horrible sight of the two men dragging Chastity's body away, leaving a wide, red smear behind them. The trail was like a freshly painted arrow pointing to the source of Leah's guilt.

Your fault. All your fault.

"I'll do it." Her whisper was barely audible, even in the silent room.

"Would you mind repeating that? Just so we're all clear."

"I said I'll fucking do it." Leah fought to keep from bursting into tears.

That came later, after they locked her in her cell.

In the dream, everything was normal and happy. Chastity manned the front desk, alive and cheerful as ever. Leah sat in one of the examination rooms, cleaning up after her last patient of the day. No need to use the Cure on this one; just a basic spaying for the dog, a young adult mixed terrier brought in by the local shelter. They routinely spayed or neutered all their charges, and most of the local vets performed the surgeries for free.

The terrier mix, named Whiskers, stared at her from the large cage where it would be spending the night. Thanks to the painkillers she'd given it, it wagged its tail and looked ready for a romp in the park.

"Oh no," she told it, "I know your type. Too much energy to sit still." She made a mental note to dress the dog in a miniature T-shirt after she cleaned up, so it couldn't gnaw at the stitches during the night when they began to itch.

Leah liked to keep the shelter's spays and neuters for a day or two after the operation, just in case they developed an infection or popped a stitch. As much as she loved the work the no-kill shelter did, she knew they weren't set up to care for sick or injured animals.

As she placed her surgical instruments in a bag for autoclaving later, one of her scalpels slipped and sliced the edge of her palm.

"Shit!" The scalpel and retractors fell to the floor as she clutched her hand. A quick glance confirmed the cut was deep enough to require several stitches. Her knees went weak and she grabbed the edge of the examining table to keep from falling. The room spun around her, and everything went gray.

Although she dealt with blood and injured body parts every day without a problem, she'd never dealt with her own before. The sight of it had her stomach doing loops.

Her hand slipped off the metal table and she grabbed it again. A sharp pain ran up her arm, and through her dizziness she felt the first tremors of real fear. Had she cut herself worse than she'd thought? What if there'd been damage to a tendon or nerve? She needed her hands in perfect shape; her whole livelihood depended on it.

Taking a deep breath, she let go and held her hand up again. She had to look twice to realize what she was seeing was real.

A thin, pink line ran down the edge of her hand, the fresh scar smeared with blood but no longer an open wound.

Before she could wonder about what had happened, Whiskers gave a loud yelp. Leah turned and looked at the dog. Fresh blood stained the blanket it lay on.

"I had a feeling you'd pull those stitches," she said to it. "You're too frisky for your own good."

Leah opened her eyes and saw an unfamiliar ceiling above her. For a moment, she had no idea where she was. Then it all came rushing back to her. Kidnapped by Tal Nova. Threatened with blackmail.

Chastity's murder.

Oh God, poor Chastity! The tears came again, the same ones she'd cried throughout the day, dampening the cheap, mildew-stained pillow they'd given her. Once Tal had locked her in the cell, a small room that looked to have once been an office of some kind, she'd been left undisturbed.

And why not? He got what he wanted. In order for John to live, I'll have to do whatever they ask, even if it means passing an illness on to some innocent person.

She'd briefly pondered the idea of suicide, but had given up that line of thought quickly, figuring Nova would still kill John, just to keep him quiet. No, her only chance to get them out of this mess was to stay alive and hope for either a chance to escape or for John's police friends to lead a rescue.

Leah pulled her thin, musty blanket around her shoulders and sat up, leaning against the chilly cement wall. There was a third option, one she wasn't sure she'd have the opportunity to carry out, but had to be ready to put into motion at a moment's notice.

If one of them comes near me while I still have the sickness inside me...

That train of thought led her back to the dream she'd had just before she'd woken up. More of a memory than a dream, actually. The cut on her hand. Whiskers busting his stitches.

At the time, I was too busy closing the dog's wound. And then after that, I got distracted and never really thought about it again, just figured that the Power inside me not only Cured others but also helped me heal faster.

But what if I somehow transferred my cut to the dog?

She mentally shook her head. Her Power required physical contact; it always had, ever since day one. It was just a coincidence that the dog had split its stitches at the same time.

Which meant she'd need to touch Nova or one of his men in order to do any damage to them. And that seemed mighty unlikely since they all knew what she could do and would no doubt stay far away from her anytime she carried something dangerous inside her.

Still, people do make mistakes.

I have to be ready.

Chapter Eighteen

The soft buzz of his cell phone interrupted Del McCormick's lunch. Coffee in hand, he hurried outside of the Starbuck's before answering. "You were supposed to call last night."

"I didn't have a chance," the voice on the other end said. "But I found out what you wanted. Nova's got the girl and the cop locked up in a warehouse way downtown. He's planning on using her as a weapon."

That confused Del until the other man explained what he meant. Del listened closely as his informant described the events of the day before, including the murder of DeGarmo's assistant just to prove a point.

Typical Tal Nova, he thought. *Ruthless.*

What really grabbed his attention, though, was finding out DeGarmo could take an illness or injury from one person and pass it on to another.

Jesus. She really is *a weapon.*

That completely changed the plan he'd had in mind for her.

"Good work. Keep an eye out and let me know what happens next." Del flicked his phone shut and returned to his booth.

This is bigger than I thought.

He'd been hoping to snatch the veterinarian from either her house or office after Nova brought her back, but now that plan was useless. No way Nova was ever letting her return home. Not alive, anyway. Not after witnessing one murder and performing another.

This is going to require a different approach, he thought, finishing the last of his coffee.

And a lot more people.

Leah looked up at the sound of someone unlocking her door.

"Rise and shine." Tal Nova walked in, looking as efficient and confident as ever in his perfectly pressed three-piece suit. "Time to get to work."

"Why do I have to kill someone? Wouldn't it be just as effective to make them ill?"

Ignoring her question, Nova tossed a bag onto her cot. "You'll need these. Our target has a dinner banquet at the Plaza today. He'll be arriving around five. All you have to do is bump into him on the street, give him the touch and keep going."

"I—" Leah began, then stopped as Nova pulled out a wicked-looking gun and pointed it at her.

"No more questions. No more talking, period. Got that? I can't kill you 'cause I need you. But a bullet in your leg won't be fatal; it'll just hurt like hell. Besides," he said, narrowing his eyes, "there are a lot of things I can do to your boyfriend, too, that won't kill him. But he'll wish he was dead."

Nova put the gun away and popped a stick of cinnamon gum into his mouth. "I'll be right outside. You've got five minutes to get dressed and comb your hair."

He exited the room, shutting and locking the door behind him. Leah clenched her jaw to keep from screaming. Counted to twenty. Counted another twenty before she had enough control to open the bag without flinging it across the room. Opening it, she recognized the contents immediately.

They were hers. Which meant someone had broken into her house. Again.

A brush and comb. Her makeup kit. Clean underwear. Socks.

She ignored the clothes and focused on fixing her hair and covering the circles under her eyes, knowing five minutes wasn't enough to do more than that. At the same time, she did her best to ignore the rumbling in her stomach. A guard had brought her a sandwich hours ago, but she hadn't eaten it, afraid it might be drugged. Now she was starving and dying for a cup of coffee.

Poor choice of words, she thought, remembering she was about to commit murder.

"Time's up," came Nova's voice from the other side of the door.

"I'm ready." Leah ran her fingers through her hair one last time, took a deep breath and tried to calm her nerves by reminding herself to stay focused and ready.

Focused and ready.

I'm not the pushover you think I am, Mr. Nova.

Nova led her down a different hallway than they'd used the previous day. A series of doors lined both sides, their windows covered in thick sheets of plywood. All except one door that had two men standing guard outside. Nova grabbed Leah by the arm and pushed her toward the glass.

"Take a look."

Leah glanced inside and her heart froze.

"John!"

John Carrera sat on a bed similar to Leah's. A thick chain ran from his leg to a ring bolted into the cement floor. He stared at the wall, giving no evidence he'd heard Leah's shout.

"He can't hear you," Nova confirmed. "But don't worry, you'll be able to speak with him soon enough."

Something caught Leah's eye and she looked closer. *Oh God, no.* A ghostly, pale green glow surrounded John's body, pulsing in time to his heartbeat.

Leah turned to Tal Nova. "What did you do to him?"

"How can you tell we did anything?" Nova's normally impassive face showed a new expression: curiosity.

"I can see the sickness, dammit! It's all through him. What is it?"

Nova laughed. "You never cease to amaze me. It's clostridium poisoning. A fatal dose delivered in his coffee. He doesn't know. You're going to cure him, and then pass it on to the target."

Even though she knew she had no choice, something inside Leah made her object. "No, I can't."

"In about twenty minutes he'll start to experience the first signs. Nausea. Cramps. Vomiting. After that—"

"Stop it!" He was talking about John *dying*. "I know what happens next."

Tal nodded. "Go in. Cure him. I'll even give you a few minutes to talk to him."

Leah grabbed the knob. It turned easily in her hand and she rushed into the room.

"John!"

"Leah! You're alive!"

Before he could say anything else, she threw herself into his arms. She touched his neck and the shock of the Cure made them both jump. John tried to push her away, but she clung to him even tighter.

"That shock...what did they do to me?"

"Poison," she whispered into his ear. "They poisoned your food. They want me to pass it on to one of Marsh's business rivals."

"What?" Now John did push her back. "You can't."

She shook her head, crying and sobbing as she tried to explain. "They'll kill you if I don't. Kill me. I...I..."

"Hush." John put a finger to her lips. "I didn't know they'd threatened your life too. If it was just me..."

"No." Leah shook her head.

"It doesn't matter now. Do it. No heroics. We'll find a way out of this."

"But—"

"That's enough, Doctor DeGarmo. Time to go." Nova entered the room.

John rose to his feet. "If you hurt her—"

"No one will get hurt, as long as the doctor here does as she's told."

Letting go of John, Leah lunged forward, reaching for Tal. Faster than her eye could follow, he danced out of reach and brought up his hand, a gun appearing in it as if by magic.

"Not another step farther," he said, his voice cold and hard. "Make a single move toward me or any of my men, and lover boy here will meet a very painful end."

Leah stopped, her fury a solid, whirling entity in her head. She considered doing it anyway, just leaping forward and grabbing him. Then John spoke behind her.

"Don't, Leah."

She looked back and stared at him. He shook his head.

"Life is too important. Don't sacrifice it for nothing."

A hundred arguments perched on the tip of her tongue. John was a police officer. How could he condone her murdering someone? It went against everything he stood for, believed in. Could she have been wrong about him?

And then it hit her.

John *wouldn't* condone murder. He had to have something else in mind. A plan to escape? Or maybe he was trying to send her a message. But what?

She let Nova lead her into the hallway where his men kept a safe distance until she was past, and then shut and locked John's door. She managed one last look back, but John was already facing away, his head hanging down as if he'd given up all hope.

Tal Nova and one of his men escorted her down the hall, but she hardly paid attention to them. She kept wondering what kind of message John had been trying to pass to her.

Sacrificing her life. Was that it? Did he want her to try and escape when they were out in public, make a scene, sacrifice herself where everyone could see? That would probably start an investigation, but John had to realize Tal could cover up any traces of what they'd been up to, long before the police found the warehouse.

Sacrifice. Life.

That's it!

Just because she was passing the poison on to someone didn't mean they had to *die*.

Not if the person knew they'd been poisoned.

A wave of relief washed over Leah's thoughts, washing away some of her guilt and anxiety. They were still in a bad position, but at least she wouldn't have to carry the burden of knowing she'd killed an innocent person.

She glanced at Tal Nova.

And felt no guilt at all as she contemplated his murder.

Del McCormick's phone chimed. "Go ahead."

"It's going down right now."

"Give me the address." Del listened, committed the information to his memory and closed his phone.

This should be interesting.

After checking to make sure his digital camcorder was ready to go, he pulled out of his parking spot and headed across town.

Chapter Nineteen

"You're sure you know what he looks like?"

Leah frowned at Tal Nova's question, didn't even bother to look at the photo again. "I'm sure. Just hurry up and get me there. I'm starting to feel sick."

She wasn't lying. Ripples of pain, not as bad as menstrual cramps but getting stronger, had been running through her stomach for the past several blocks, bringing with them a vague feeling of nausea and a cold sweat. She figured she had perhaps fifteen minutes before the poison incapacitated her. She knew Nova wouldn't let that happen; he needed her alive. No, her worry was that she'd be approaching her target and her body would betray her, that a sudden cramp would force her to soil herself right there on the sidewalk in front of everyone. Something like that would surely prevent her from reaching the man she was supposed to kill.

And that would be very bad, for both her and John.

Tal glanced at his watch. "Two more minutes."

"Any more than that and I'm liable to shit my pants right here," she said, gritting her teeth against another painful rumbling in her midsection.

"There he is." One of Tal's men pointed at a group of people exiting the hotel.

"Go," Tal said to Leah.

She opened her door and stepped out, then had to hang on to the door as another cramp dug its nails into her guts. When it passed, she took a deep breath, straightened up, and did her best to act casual as she walked towards the gray-haired man Nova had marked for death. Behind her, the limousine pulled away from the curb.

Making contact turned out to be easier than she'd anticipated. As she passed by, she pretended to lose her balance and clutch at his arm for support. At the same time, she let her hand touch his. The brief contact delivered the usual painful shock.

"Ow!" The man tried to pull his hand away but Leah hung on, pushed herself closer so she was right by his ear.

"Get to a hospital right away. Someone poisoned your food today. You're supposed to die. Tell the doctors it's botulism."

Before he could respond, she let go of his hand and stepped away. "Sorry about that," she said in a loud voice. "I tripped over my own feet." Two of the target's associates approached her, but she gave them a quick smile and kept walking, ignoring their questions and heading for the corner as fast as she could, just as Nova had instructed.

The moment she rounded the corner, she saw the black limousine Nova had said would be waiting for her. She entertained a quick thought of running away, but an image of John, his face battered and his body bleeding from gunshots, prevented her from acting on it. The back door to the car opened, and a man with a gun told her to get in and sit down.

Twenty seconds later the car was pulling into traffic, and the man with the gun was on the phone to Tal Nova.

"She's here. Mission accomplished."

Leah leaned back and closed her eyes.

I did it! John was right. It would have been stupid to sacrifice myself.

Then another thought occurred to her.

But what about next time?

That there would be a next time she had no doubt. Tal Nova had as much as said so, when he'd told her he had a list of people to get rid of.

Which meant she and John had to get free before Nova sent her after his next victim. Or learned that this one hadn't died.

But how? She couldn't see any way for them to break free, not without getting killed in the process.

Hopefully John has something in mind.

Otherwise, someone was going to die. And soon.

Del put down his camcorder after the veterinarian disappeared around the corner. He assumed Tal would have a car waiting for her there. *That's what I would do.*

Instead, he kept his attention on the target. He'd recognized the man right away, a big player in several industries and a major competitor of Leonard Marsh. Del wondered if Marsh knew what Tal was up to. He didn't know Marsh personally, but he had a feeling Nova was operating rogue on this one. A power play? Some behind-the-scenes manipulation to keep the boss on top—or replace him?

"Not that it matters," he whispered as he watched the man's pinstriped posse hustle him into a waiting limo. Something about the way they hurried him, the look on his face...

He knows. Maybe not how or who or why, but he knows something's wrong, that he's in trouble.

Del replayed the events in his mind. DeGarmo pretending to trip. The man catching her. The two of them holding each other for a brief moment, and then letting go...

Holy shit. She told him! He's probably on his way to the hospital right now. And I'll bet Tal doesn't even know.

Chuckling to himself at Nova's sloppiness—*he should never have left before the hit went down*—Del started the car. He now had everything he needed to interest the investors he'd spoken to: the video of the cured dog, plus video demonstrating how easy it was to use DeGarmo as an assassin.

Someone was bound to jump at the chance to acquire her. And with his payment in hand, Del would have no problem assembling the team he needed to steal her away from Tal Nova.

And after I deliver her? Retirement, here I come. Someplace warm, like Mexico or Aruba.

His head filled with visions of bikini-clad girls serving drinks, Del never noticed the battered taxi following him.

Emilio Suarez made sure to keep at least two cars between him and the guy who'd been following Tal Nova all around town the last couple of days.

This was the first time the man had gone in a different direction than Tal or the veterinarian *chica*, and Emilio had made the decision to follow him instead of the doctor lady.

Until he'd spotted Nova's tail, he'd been wondering why he had to keep watching the vet. After all, Tal had her stashed away, never letting her out except when he was with her. What was the point of spying on her? But since Tal hadn't called him to say stop, Emilio had continued following Tal's last order. Although he'd have done so, no matter what, for reasons of his own.

Except now he was purposely disobeying the big man. That could lead to a lot of trouble. Trouble Emilio normally wouldn't want to get involved in.

If it weren't for what the doctor lady could do.

At first, the idea that she could cure people had been amazing to him. He'd figured it would be worth a bundle to someone like Tal Nova, and he'd imagined all that money in his bank account for being the one who found her, so much more than the envelope of cash he'd gotten for spying on her.

But in the course of following her—and Tal—over the past few days, he'd come to a realization. The power to cure or kill by laying hands was something only God should have. Emilio had committed more sins than he could remember, but he still made sure to get to church every Sunday. And he still went to confession as often as possible. That was the great thing about being Catholic. You committed your sins, asked for forgiveness, and a few prayers later you were in the clear.

And since he'd made sure to never commit any of the mortal sins—well, with the exception of stealing, but he figured that couldn't be considered a mortal sin anymore, not when even priests were getting busted dipping into the church funds—he was pretty sure he wouldn't end up in hell.

Sins were one thing. Everyone committed them; it was part of being human. Even murder could be considered a part of human nature, something people had done from the beginning of time. But always with bare hands or weapons.

Not by using some weird supernatural power.

In the end, it was a sermon in church just the other day that had convinced Emilio of what he had to do. The priest had talked about stem cell research and cloning, how man was not meant to play God.

And that's just what the lady doctor is doing, playing God. She isn't using medicine to cure those animals, and she isn't using a weapon to kill people.

She's playing God. And Tal Nova is making the problem even worse.

It had to stop.

After the sermon, Emilio had spoken to several of his *vatos*, friends from the old neighborhood who, like him, still went to church every week, still dropped money into the collection basket even if it was all they had to their names. Even if they had to steal it from someone else.

Friends who believed in God and the Catholic Church.

Emilio spoke, and his friends listened.

In the end, there was only one decision that seemed right.

They sought God's assistance.

Chapter Twenty

Leah sat on her bed and watched as Tal backed away, his gun in hand. "I want to see John," she said.

Nova nodded. "You will. As soon as we need your...special talents...again." He closed the door. A moment later, the distinct sound of the lock clicking into place reached her ears.

Forcing down a scream of frustration, Leah turned her attention to the plate of food and coffee that had been waiting for her when she got back to her cell. A ham sandwich, an apple and a package of Twinkies. The food was cold and stale, the coffee black and bitter, but she wolfed it down anyway, the hunger in her stomach so bad by then that it hurt almost as much as the poison had.

After finishing her food and draining the last drops of the coffee, exhaustion and depression overtook her and she lay down, cradling the skimpy pillow and wondering what John was doing at that moment.

It was only as her eyes closed that she wondered if someone had drugged her food.

By then it was too late.

Tal Nova's intercom rang just as he sat down at his desk.

"We need to talk." Leonard Marsh's voice held no trace of emotion.

Tal frowned. When Marsh's voice grew cold and toneless, it usually meant the old man was royally pissed about something. As he slipped on his jacket and straightened his tie, Tal wondered if Marsh had gotten wind of DeGarmo's kidnapping. Had Marsh tried to contact her, only to find out she was gone? Would that have been enough for him to trace her back to Tal?

There was no doubt that Marsh, with his almost limitless resources, could find the veterinarian within hours if he really wanted to.

Tal headed for the connecting door to Marsh's office. *Only one way to find out. And if he does know, I've got some tricks up my sleeve to pretty much guarantee I walk out of that office a rich man.*

"Sit down." Marsh said as soon as Tal entered.

"Is there a problem?" Tal asked.

Marsh leaned forward in his chair, and once again Tal was amazed by how healthy he looked. There was no way anyone would have thought that just days ago he'd been knocking at death's door.

"I just heard that Edgar Rothstein is in the hospital. Food poisoning, of all things. They're not sure if he'll make it through the night."

"Shit happens," Tal said, keeping to the script he'd written in his head for when this conversation occurred. "I take it that means he won't be moving forward with his acquisition attempt?"

"Yes, luckily for us." Marsh's eyes narrowed as he stared at Tal. "You wouldn't know anything about what happened, would you?"

"No, sir. Food poisoning's not my style."

Marsh continued to stare long enough for Tal to feel the old man might be preparing to call him on his answer. To Tal's relief, Marsh finally leaned back and let out a small sigh. "Good. Much as I'd have hated to lose a company to him, I've always considered Rothstein a worthy opponent. Not many like him around anymore."

"That isn't why you asked me over here." Tal knew there had to be something else. Something that couldn't have been handled over the phone.

Marsh nodded. "I've been thinking about that veterinarian, DeGarmo. She hasn't cashed her check yet. I wonder if we were too hard on her. I want you to pay her another visit."

Tal's stomach did a slow roll. To cover his unease, he took his pack of gum out and popped a stick in his mouth. "Another visit? Why? We don't need her anymore."

"Not right now, no. But the news about Rothstein gave me an idea. What happened to him could just as easily happen to me. A lot of things can go wrong in this world. Car accidents, heart attacks, you name it. I want to put

DeGarmo on retainer. Just in case. She'd be like my personal emergency care physician."

"I got the impression she'd rather not have anything to do with us again."

"Yes, and perhaps that's my fault. In retrospect, maybe I should have handled things more gently. Not that I'm disappointed in the job you did, but someone with a little more compassion, and a lot less intimidating, might have put her more at ease. Made her more open to helping me without being threatened."

For one of the few times in his life, Tal Nova found himself rendered speechless. Had Marsh stood up and announced he'd found God, Tal wouldn't have been more surprised. He'd never heard Leonard Marsh express any type of sentimentality, other than obligatory statements in public that privately they would laugh about. Even when Marsh's wife had died three years ago, the man hadn't missed a day of work, hadn't expressed any sense of loss. He'd skipped the wake and funeral, releasing a statement that he was "too overcome with grief" to attend.

In reality, he'd been locked in his office, working out the details of a new business venture.

Finally finding his voice, Tal asked, "If you think she found me too intimidating, why send me again?"

As soon as the words left his lips, Tal regretted them. What if Marsh agreed and decided to send someone else? Someone who'd end up reporting DeGarmo missing?

"Because I want you to apologize on behalf of both of us," Marsh said.

Tal wanted to sigh with relief, but he kept his control. "If you think that's for the best, then I'll make sure I come across...in a friendlier fashion."

Marsh rolled his eyes. "You couldn't come across friendly if you tried. I just want her to hear you apologize. She'll understand how hard it is for you to do that. Then give her this." Marsh handed Tal an envelope with DeGarmo's name written on it. "That's my apology, plus my request for her to consider a new arrangement."

Pocketing the envelope, Tal stood up. "I'll take care of it tonight." Marsh nodded, and Tal hurried back to his office, eager to escape before his true feelings showed themselves.

Back at his own desk, Tal stared at the envelope and pondered Marsh's odd behavior. Although he'd have never believed the old man capable of such a thing, Tal knew that sometimes people underwent major personality changes following life-threatening or life-changing events. Hardened criminals found God. Millionaires donated their savings to charities. But even if Marsh was going soft, would it happen overnight? It didn't seem likely.

That left two possibilities. One, Marsh was baiting Tal for some reason, setting him up for something. It was possible he'd discovered Tal's dealings with DeGarmo and this was his way of slipping the noose over Tal's head. As much as Tal prayed nothing like that had happened, he almost wanted it to be true, because the only other option was so chilling he got a creepy feeling up his spine just thinking about it.

That DeGarmo had done more than just cure Marsh's cancer when she touched him.

She'd infected him with some of her own goodness.

Chapter Twenty-One

"She's back in her cell."

Del McCormick glanced both ways, making sure no one was near the park bench he occupied, before speaking into his phone.

"How did they do it?" he asked his informant.

"They poisoned the cop. She cured him. The most fucked-up thing I ever saw. She tried to go after Nova, but he was too fast for her."

Pity, thought Del. *That would have made things a lot easier.* "Where's Nova now?"

"Either in his office or home. He already called to say give her dinner and something to make her sleep, but not too much. Says he wants her to be alert in the morning."

"That means he's got another hit planned. Jesus, he's working fast."

"Maybe he wants to off as many people as he can before Marsh finds out."

"Maybe." The reasons didn't matter to Del. What did matter was that if Tal had a busy schedule set up, tonight might be the best time to swipe the girl. "Listen up. The operation is a go. Tonight. Three a.m. No more drugs for her, understand? I want her walking on her own, not holding us back."

"Gotcha. We'll be ready."

Del shut his phone without replying. He knew the team would be ready. If they weren't...well, Tal Nova wasn't the only one who had a ruthless streak.

Leaning back against the bench, Del closed his eyes and ran through the plan again in his head, imagining every possible scenario and developing a counterstrategy. You couldn't be too prepared.

Not when millions of dollars were on the line.

The cell phone's strident ring jarred Tal Nova from a dreamless sleep. Instantly awake, he snatched the phone from his nightstand. "Nova."

"Boss, we just got word that Mason took an earlier flight. He's landing at LaGuardia in five hours."

Tal glanced at his clock and held back a curse. Two a.m. Elmore Mason was the next target on his list. The plan had been for DeGarmo to intercept him at the airport the following afternoon, as he disembarked his plane. Now that schedule was shot to hell. They had to act fast.

"All right. Give the cop his injection. I'll be right in. When I get there, we'll take DeGarmo to him for the cure."

"What if she's still loopy from the sedatives?"

"Pump her full of coffee. Give her a hit of speed. I don't care what you have to do, but I want her awake and walking and full of death when that plane lands, understand?"

"Yes, s—"

Tal shut his phone and headed for the bathroom, already calculating the adjustments the team would need to make in order to bring DeGarmo into contact with the target. The original plan had been based on the event taking place in a crowded airport. But at seven in the morning, the terminal would be a ghost town, occupied only by die-hard business travelers. That meant a different mode of dress for DeGarmo so she'd blend in.

Before he'd even finished relieving himself, Tal was on the phone again, giving terse instructions to his team.

Fifteen minutes later, he was in his car and heading into the city.

The bang of the door opening startled Leah from a nightmare-filled sleep.

"What...? What do you want?" she asked the two guards.

"Let's go," one of them said, grabbing her by the arm. He pushed an armful of clothes at her. "Put these on."

Neither of them gave any indication they would let her dress in private, and their gruff attitudes told Leah she shouldn't ask. Instead, she turned around and quickly slipped into clothes that obviously weren't hers. The slacks and blouse were a size too large and the plain black heels pinched her feet but she kept her complaints to herself.

The moment she was dressed, the men escorted her out of the room and down the hall. She stumbled a bit in the unfamiliar shoes, and the second guard handed her a large container of coffee. "Drink this."

"Why?" The coffee teased Leah's mouth and nose, and made her stomach grumble. But she was afraid of what else might be in the cup.

"Boss wants you wide awake. So either you drink it or I pour it down your throat. Your choice."

Leah did as she was told, wondering how she could enjoy the beverage so much while being marched toward what was undoubtedly another deadly assignment for Tal Nova. The moment she thought about that, a new fear bloomed in her gut.

That means they've probably done something to John again.

Sure enough, they rounded a corner and entered a hallway Leah recognized as the one John was being kept in. Her worry grew worse as they approached the guarded door, and then changed to full-blown terror when she looked through the window and saw the sickly green aura surrounding his body.

They've poisoned him again. Sons of bitches. How many times can they keep doing this to us?

She knew the answer, of course. Nova would continue to use them until he didn't need them anymore. Then they'd end up dead someplace, just two more unsolved murders in a city full of them.

"Tal called," one of John's guards said. "He's on his way. We're supposed to keep the girl out here until he gets here."

"Sorry. We've got other plans." Before Leah knew what was happening, one of the men who'd taken her from her cell pulled out a gun and fired two shots. Blood splattered the walls as John's two guards fell to the floor.

"Let's get the hell out of here." The men grabbed Leah and pulled her away from John's cell.

"Wait!" She tried to break free but they held her tight. "He needs my help! He's dying." She saw John pressed against the glass, pounding on it with both fists.

"Too bad. Our orders are to get you out of here, nobody else."

Leah kicked and screamed as the men dragged her to the end of the hall and out a small side door that opened onto what had once been the loading dock. Three more men waited next to an unmarked gray van, their faces cloaked by the night. It was only when she got close that Leah recognized one of them, an average-sized man with mousy-brown hair.

"You were the one at my clinic that night. With the dog. You work for Tal Nova."

"Not exactly," the man said. "I do jobs for him on occasion; but I work for myself. You might say I'm an independent contractor."

"You have to let me go back inside, there's someone dying in there. I can help him."

The man shook his head. "Believe me, Doctor, I know exactly what you can do. That's why I'm here. You're going to make me a very rich man." He motioned for his men to open the back doors of the van.

Leah muttered a curse as she fought to break free. Did everyone know about her abilities? "If you don't let me go back, I won't help you."

The man held up his hand and everyone stopped moving. "What do you mean?"

"You said you know what I can do. Well, you can't make me do it. I control it."

The man shrugged. "Then maybe a bullet or two in the right places will convince you."

"And what if it doesn't? You'll kill me? I'm no good to you if I'm injured or dead."

For the first time, the man's face showed emotion. His lips grew tight and his eyes narrowed. He stared at Leah for a moment, and then swore. "Goddammit. You did a hit for Nova."

Leah stared back at him. "That's right. Because he injected the man I love with poison. The same man who's going to die soon if I don't get back in there. Without John, I wouldn't have done shit for Nova." She knew she was putting John in danger again, basically moving from one frying pan to another, but at least he'd be alive.

"Damn it to hell." The man signaled his people to move back to the loading dock doors. "Let's go. This isn't finished yet."

"Del, we don't need him. We can find someone else—"

"Quiet." The man named Del pointed at the stocky thug who held Leah. "Keep her here. Don't come in until you get the all clear."

The man nodded and tightened his grip on Leah's arm as the rest of the group headed inside.

Thirty seconds later, the angry sound of gunfire reached them.

"What's going on?" Leah asked, her head filling with visions of the mousy-haired man shooting John.

"Shut up." Her guard maintained his grip, but with his other hand he pulled out a gun and aimed it at the loading-dock doors.

"We have to go in!" Panic rose in Leah's chest.

"I said shut up!" The man gave her a shake, just as Leah tried again to pull free. This time it worked, and she found herself stumbling away. Before the man could do anything, she found her balance and ran for the door.

"Hey! Stop!"

Leah cringed, anticipating a bullet in the back, but didn't stop running. Instead of the explosion of the gun going off, she heard pounding footsteps behind her. She threw open the door and burst into the hallway, just in time to see one of the stranger's men turn in her direction, gun in hand. There was no time to stop or yell; she could only watch helplessly as bright light flared from the front of the gun and a deafening roar filled the air. A split second later, something hot stung her cheek, followed by a buzzing sound in her ear.

"Don't shoot!" the man behind her shouted.

After that, everything seemed to slow down to quarter speed. Images clicked through her head like a slide show.

Someone running past her.

Raising her hand to her cheek.

Staring at her blood-covered palm.

People on the floor.

A white tile smeared in red.

The last picture faded to black, and Leah wondered who'd turned off the projector. *Turn on the lights,* she tried to say, but her mouth refused to move. Something cold hit her face, feeling good against her skin. *How did I get sunburned on one cheek? Who's holding the wet cloth for me?*

Far away, someone called for help. Something about a man being shot.

I can help him, she thought. *That's my job. I Cure the sick with a touch. My name is Jesus.*

Wait. That doesn't sound right.

My name is Leah. I'm here to help someone. Someone named...

"John!" Leah opened her eyes, saw she was lying on the floor next to a dead body.

With a gasp, she pushed herself away and sat up. The memory of being shot came back to her, and she raised a hand to her cheek. No pain now, just smooth, undamaged skin.

No time to worry about that. Have to help John.

She got to her feet, but someone grabbed her leg. Looking down, she saw the mousy-haired man who'd tried to kidnap her.

"Help me," he said, his words coming out in a hoarse gasp. The reason for his pain was obvious; blood poured from a bullet wound in his leg. Based on the flow, Leah figured the bullet had nicked his femoral artery, possibly cut it in two.

"Please. I..." His eyes closed and his head fell back.

Damn! All she wanted to do was save John. But she couldn't let a man bleed to death. Telling herself she was a fool, Leah knelt down and placed her hands over the wound. An electric shock ran through her, and the man's body twitched as if from an epileptic seizure.

The moment the pain passed, Leah pushed herself to her feet and ran for John's door. When she got to it, a sick feeling ran through her. Although he was still standing at the window, watching everything, his face was drawn and pale, and a heavy sheen of sweat covered his skin. Worse, a heavy bilious green glow covered him, a glow she knew no one else could see.

The poison's kicking in. Not much time left. "Hang on!" she shouted.

She grabbed the knob but it wouldn't move. Her fear kicked up another notch. It wasn't fair! She was there to save him, but couldn't get in.

John banged on the glass and pointed past her.

Leah turned and looked. All she saw were dead bodies and a couple of the stranger's men helping him to his feet. Then it hit her.

One of the dead guards had to have the keys.

Leah dropped to the floor and tore through the dead guards' pockets until she located the keys. It took her three tries to find the right key, and even then her hands shook so bad she had trouble inserting the key and turning it. As soon as she unlocked the door, John pushed it open and stumbled out. He went to put his arms around her, and instead ended up clutching at her shoulders as his legs gave out underneath him.

Staggering under his weight, Leah did her best to lower him to the floor without dropping him. He tried to speak, but she put a finger to his lips. "Quiet. You'll be better in a minute."

She focused on John's pallid face, thinking only of Curing him. The moment she put her hands on his cheeks, the pain of the Cure hit her like a heavy fist to the stomach. She cried out and nearly fell over. At the same time, John's body convulsed so hard his shoulders and head left the floor and then crashed down again. Nausea filled Leah's body, and she barely managed to turn her head before her coffee came up in violent fashion. Before she could regain her breath, a second round of vomit exploded out.

After her spasms subsided, she found the nausea had faded to a manageable level. She wiped her mouth on her sleeve and turned back to John, just in time to find him pushing himself to a sitting position.

"Thank God you're all right!" She wanted to throw her arms around him, cradle her head against his chest, but she knew better than to touch him.

It never occurred to her that she'd already touched him after Curing the gunman and nothing had happened.

"No, thank *you*. Again." His voice sounded weak, but the green glow had disappeared and color was already returning to his face. "What about you? Are you okay?"

"I'll be fine. I'm just a little shaky." She stood up. "We should get out of here before Tal's men come back."

"Sorry, you folks aren't going anywhere."

Leah turned, saw the mousy-haired man and one of his men standing nearby, both with guns in their hands. She silently kicked herself; in her frantic hurry to cure John, she'd forgotten about the men who'd tried to kidnap her.

The mousy-haired man's companion stepped forward and took Leah by the arm. "Let's go, little lady."

Before she realized what was happening, the Power surged up inside her, begging for release. Leah grabbed the man's hand and let the sickness flow out of her. This time the electric shock of the transfer was even worse, wrenching a scream of pain from her that the armed man echoed as they both fell to the floor.

"What the...?" For a moment, the mousy-haired man just stood there, his eyes wide, as blood exploded from his partner's leg and vomit spewed from his mouth. But the man's surprise didn't last long. He brought his gun up and around, his expression already changing from shock to anger.

And found John kneeling on the floor, pointing a gun back at him.

"Drop it," John said, his voice no longer weak.

The man's hand twitched ever so slightly, just enough to point the gun at Leah, who was still trying to sit up. "I'll kill her."

Instead of answering, John pulled the trigger. The sound of the gun drowned out the man's cry, but Leah saw the effects as the man dropped his gun and clutched his arm.

"Next time it'll be in the chest." John's hand stayed perfectly still as he spoke. "You've got five seconds to get the hell out of here and never come near us again. One...two..."

Before John reached three, the mousy-haired man turned and ran for the loading-dock door. The moment the door closed, John pulled Leah to her feet. "Let's get out of here before anyone else shows up."

"Why didn't you kill him?" Leah asked as they stepped around the bodies and headed for the door. "He would have killed both of us."

"If I'd thought that, he'd be dead right now. But he was bluffing."

"How could you know that?"

John opened the door an inch, peered outside. "Because you're no use to them dead, and you're no use to them if I'm dead. C'mon, it's clear."

They stepped out onto the loading dock and Leah saw the van was gone. "What do we do now?"

With a tired smile, John pointed at the stairs. "First, we start walking. As soon as we find a phone, we'll get ourselves a ride, and we'll do what you should have done in the first place."

"And that is?"

He gave her a look that was part joking and part serious. "Get the police involved. All of this could have been prevented if you'd just told me the whole story from the beginning."

Leah shook her head. "It would've meant telling the whole world about my secret. I couldn't do that. I still can't. If Tal or those other people get caught, their testimonies, the films, it'll all end up as evidence and get made public."

John took her hand as they walked across the loading-dock parking lot. "Maybe, maybe not. The important thing is that you'll still be alive, and the people who're after you will be behind bars."

"You really think that would be the end of it? Look how much trouble I've caused with only a few people knowing. Now imagine if the whole world knew. How many people would be after me then? How many governments? I'd never be safe."

Leah pulled her hand away and rubbed tears from her eyes. *He doesn't understand. He can't; no one can. I'd rather be dead than live my life on the run or like a lab animal.*

"Leah, I—"

The sound of squealing tires interrupted John as a police car tore around the corner, lights flashing, and then skidded to a stop at the end of the lot. Two Hispanic officers, both of them in plain clothes and NYPD windbreakers, opened their doors and waved. The driver called to them.

"Hurry up, you two. Nova's men are on the way and we want you out of here before the shooting starts. *Rapido!*"

John waved back and then took Leah's hand again. "Let's go. For once, it looks like something's going our way."

Following John, Leah had to admit the sight of the police car was an unexpected comfort. Then thoughts of her secret getting out to the world returned.

We're safe now. But for how long?

Chapter Twenty-Two

Emilio Suarez shut the back door of the police cruiser and silently congratulated himself. He'd come up with the idea for stealing the car after learning that Nova had kidnapped the lady vet's boyfriend, who was a local cop in her hometown.

Who's a cop gonna trust, no questions asked? A fellow cop! he'd thought, and sure enough the *cabrón* had gotten right into the car, smiling and saying thank you all the while. At least the lady had the brains to look nervous, even though she'd followed her boyfriend like a dog on a leash.

As soon as Emilio climbed into the front passenger seat and shut his door, Hector Reyes, the man Emilio had chosen as his driver, put the car in gear and headed away from the warehouse as fast as possible.

One thing Emilio hadn't lied about was wanting to get them out of there before Nova returned. After watching Nova's actions over the past few days, Emilio had decided the man was crazy. Bad enough to play God like the lady vet; Nova had gone past that, playing God and Satan both.

And who's next on his list? Emilio wondered. *Perhaps a man he hired to watch the vet? He's probably forgotten about me for now, but he'll remember soon enough. And when he does...*

It was that thought that finally set Emilio in motion. Not only did he need to keep himself safe from Tal Nova, but he had to make sure Nova would think twice about coming after him at all. And there was only one thing that would scare the crazy mother that bad.

Dr. Leah DeGarmo.

Del McCormick pounded the steering wheel with his fist as he watched DeGarmo and her boyfriend get into the back of the cop car.

How had things gone to shit so fast? Having Tal's men show up was one thing—he'd planned for that possibility, and his men had reacted flawlessly. Getting shot? That was always a chance you took. Being saved by DeGarmo had been a bonus, but then she'd single-handedly fucked everything up, had turned out to be the one wild card he'd never expected. Who'd have thought she'd show such spunk, literally ignore her own safety just to save a guy she'd been dating for, what, a week?

And then the police appeared out of nowhere...

Wait a minute.

Those cops. Something wasn't right...

Del replayed the scene in his mind. The cruiser pulling in, lights flashing. The cop hustling DeGarmo and her boyfriend into the back and then driving off.

Real cops wouldn't have left the scene of a crime, especially not knowing whether DeGarmo and her boyfriend were suspects or victims.

And since when did plainclothes cops ride in cruisers instead of their own unmarked vehicles?

"Shit!" It was a trick. Someone else had snatched the prize from right under his nose.

Nova's men? No, that didn't make sense. A third player? Had to be.

It didn't matter. He had to get them back.

His life depended on it.

Right about the same time Del McCormick put the van in gear, John Carrera's brain finally started working the way he'd trained it to. Up to that point, he'd been running on instinct, first eliminating any threats to their safety and then getting Leah as far away from the warehouse as possible. The police showing up had been an unexpected but added bonus.

Except now it didn't seem that way.

"Excuse me." He leaned forward, placing his face close to the partition between the front and backseat. "What precinct are you from?"

The man in the passenger seat, a swarthy fellow with short hair, turned partway around. "No precinct, man. Special task force. We been watching Tal Nova for many weeks."

"So it was an undercover operation?" John asked. He saw Leah start to say something, and he held up a hand, motioning her to keep quiet. Bless her soul, she did. Another mark in her favor.

"Yeah, undercover." The man nodded, and the driver, an even darker man who had the Dominican flag tattooed on the back of his neck, flashed a grin that contained at least one gold tooth.

"Well, I'm glad you came along. Where are we going?"

"We have a-a safe place. A *casa*."

"A safe house?"

"Yeah. When we get there, you can call a friend or something and get a ride back home."

"Thank you." John leaned back. The man in the passenger seat started scrolling through radio stations, finally settling on salsa music.

Leah rested her head on John's shoulder. "What's going on?" she asked in a soft voice.

"I'm pretty sure they're not cops," he whispered back. "Undercover cops wouldn't be driving a cruiser. And these guys sound more like gangbangers than police officers."

"What are we going to do?"

"We can't do a damn thing until the car stops and they let us out. Just act like nothing's wrong, okay? We don't want to tip them off that we're on to them."

The man in the passenger seat glanced back. "Hey, what's the big secret?"

"Nothing," John said. "Just talking about taking some time off when we get home. It's been a helluva week."

"That's too bad." The man pulled out a gun as the driver guided the car down a narrow alley. "'Cause it's only gonna get worse, Paco. Hands where I can see them."

John silently cursed as he held his hands flat on his lap. He still had the gun he'd taken from one of the shooters in the warehouse, but Leah was leaning against his hip and leg on that side, effectively blocking him from getting to the weapon. The idea crossed his mind of going for it anyway, knowing that if the thug shot him, Leah could cure him afterwards. Except there was always the chance of a fatal wound, one so bad Leah wouldn't have enough time to work her magic.

And what if he decides to shoot Leah? I can't let that happen. Just have to take it slow and see how things develop. We can always go for broke later.

The car stopped in front of a nondescript building. Making sure to keep his gun trained on them at all times, the man in the passenger seat got out and opened Leah's door, motioned for them to exit the car.

"Slowly, *amigos.* We need you alive, but alive and in one piece are two very different things, yes?"

Hands in the air, John followed Leah out of the car. All thoughts of going for his gun were put to rest when the driver came around and did a quick but thorough pat-down. The driver stuck the gun in his pocket and then to the building and opened the door.

"Inside." The gunman motioned for them to walk ahead of him. They entered a warehouse, smaller than the one they'd just left but just as grimy and run-down. Shafts of pale sunlight streamed in from several broken windows on the second floor. The dust kicked up by their footsteps created swirling patterns within the accidental spotlights.

Two chairs sat side by side in an otherwise empty room, informing John that their kidnapping wasn't a random event.

"Sit down. Hands behind you."

With two guns trained on them, John nodded his head at Leah, who looked frightened enough to try something foolish. Being tied up hand and foot wasn't going to make their escape easier, but it was better than being shot.

The driver quickly went to work with some extra-large tie-wraps, tightening them just short of painful, while the other man covered them. Only when they were securely bound did the kidnappers put their guns away and relax.

"Hope you're comfortable," said the man who appeared to be the one in charge. "It's gonna be a long wait."

"A long wait for what?" Leah asked, beating John to the question.

"For your reckoning," the gunman replied.

"I don't understand."

The man moved closer to her. Leah tried to push away from him, but the chair didn't budge.

"If you hurt her, I'll kill you," John said, forgetting one of the first rules of hostage situations—don't antagonize the enemy.

"Hurt her? No, my friend. We are not going to hurt her. We need her alive and well so she can demonstrate her magic for us."

Leah groaned and lowered her head, staring at a point between her feet. John knew what she must be thinking. Once again, her power to Cure things had put them in danger. How they'd learned about her didn't even matter. At this point, her secret wasn't a secret any longer, since it was safe to assume that whoever had kidnapped them—along with whoever had bungled the kidnapping at the other warehouse—had informed people higher up the food chain about Leah's abilities. Add the fact that Marsh and Nova were still probably gunning for them, and it seemed like there wasn't anyone who *didn't* want to use Leah for their own purposes.

Which brought John back to their present situation.

"What do you need Leah's power for? She just wants to be left alone."

The man nodded. "I believe that. However, what she does is an affront to God. Only he has the right to decide if people live or die. Men such as Tal Nova use you like a tool, and we believe that is wrong."

"I haven't killed anyone, except for the man who was going to kill me," Leah said, but her voice carried none of its previous fire. John sensed she was worn out past the point of caring. A defeated attitude like that wouldn't do them any good. He needed to change it, and fast.

"If God didn't want her to cure people or animals, why would he give her that power?"

Their captor shrugged. "Who is to say it is a gift from God? Perhaps it is a curse from the devil. There is a man coming who will tell us the truth of things."

"I used to think it was a curse," Leah whispered to no one particular. "Maybe I was right."

"No." John shook his head. "I can't believe that. Think of all the good you've done, all the animals you've saved that would have died. You saved your mother. You saved me."

Leah looked up at him, and he saw he still wasn't reaching her. Her eyes were dull and lifeless, her face a mask of despair. "None of that will matter if people force me to kill for them."

"Saving someone isn't always the right thing to do," the kidnapper said. "If God has chosen to bring someone to heaven, it is blasphemy to go against his will."

"That's bullshit," John said. "Doctors save people all the time. So do firefighters, and cops, and nurses, and even ordinary people. Are they all going against the will of God?"

"No, but there is a difference. They do not use magic."

John started to argue that there wasn't any difference between magic and using machines and drugs to save a life, but just then someone knocked on the door. Three short knocks followed by two long ones.

Both men listened carefully before the driver went and opened the door.

Three men stood outside, two of them darkly Hispanic and dressed in the same kind of clean but well-worn clothes John remembered from his two years as a patrol officer in Spanish Harlem. These were people who might not have much in life, but what they had, they took care of so it would last a long time.

If their association with criminal activities made no sense, the third man entering the warehouse was as out of place as beer at an AA meeting. Unless his black shirt and white collar was a disguise, the new arrivals had brought a priest with them.

Maybe they mean to perform an exorcism? It made sense in a sick, twisted way. Their kidnapper *had* said someone was coming who could tell them if Leah's power came from God or the devil.

"Hola, Padre," the kidnapper said. "Thank you for coming."

The priest nodded and turned his life-weary face toward Leah. "Is this the one?"

"Sí."

The priest walked over to her, his gait slow and steady, as if he carried a heavy load upon his shoulders. John wondered if that was simply his way, or if years of ministering to congregations of the poor, the illegal, and the downtrodden had simply robbed him of his vitality.

The priest reached out a hand and touched Leah's arm. To her credit, she didn't flinch, although her eyes grew wider. As much as John didn't want to see her frightened, he was glad for the emotion. Anything was better than her previous resignation.

"Please let us go," she said. "I just want to go home."

"That is not for me to decide, my child." The priest stepped back. "Only God can tell us which path to take. I trust in him to show us the way."

Leah didn't answer him, but a tear ran down her cheek. Every inch it traveled was like a knife cutting deeper into John's belly. He understood his guilt was no more sensible than her own, but that didn't make it go away.

Turning to the kidnapper, the priest asked, "Are you sure this will be as you said it would?"

"Yes, Padre. There is no doubt."

"Then show me."

John was still trying to understand what the priest meant when one of the kidnapper's associates pulled out a gun.

A tremendous explosion filled the air, an iron fist hit him in the stomach, and the room flipped around until he was facing the ceiling. In the background, someone screamed over and over.

Then the pain took over, and nothing else mattered.

Chapter Twenty-Three

Lost in her own self-pity, Leah never even saw the man who shot John. The sound of the gunshot brought her eyes open in time to see John tip over in his chair, ending up on his back. Her screams were automatic, tearing out of her throat before her brain finished processing what happened. They grew louder as the blood poured from his stomach and onto the floor.

Then the part of her that she'd trained over the years, the part that let her deal with emergencies quickly and effectively, took over.

"Let me go! There's not much time! That's a stomach wound. His intestines will be spilling bacteria all through his system."

She was afraid her new captors would be like Tal's men, that they'd make John suffer to the point of death before letting her Cure him, but the man who'd kidnapped them motioned with his hand, and two of others immediately ran forward and cut her bindings. Without waiting for permission, she stumbled over to John's body, her wrists and ankles in agony as blood flow returned.

"Hang in there, John. You'll be fine in a minute."

He moaned, but didn't open his eyes.

Bracing herself for the shock, she placed her hands on John's wound.

Except it wasn't a shock, it was a full-out explosion that hit her, a pain so intense it knocked the breath from her lungs and sent her body into convulsions. Somewhere in the distant part of her brain still capable of coherent thought, she understood the reason for her agony. John had been moments from death, worse than the last time he'd been shot, and she'd taken that fatal wound into herself.

This is the end. I'm sorry, John, I...

Then the pain disappeared, and with it, all thoughts.

Leah opened her eyes and saw only white.

Did I die? Is this the white light I've heard about?

She tried to move, but her hands and feet wouldn't obey. Other sensations crept in. Something cold and hard against her back. A familiar pain in her wrists and ankles.

She was alive.

And she'd been tied up again.

The white light resolved itself to a series of fluorescent bulbs overhead. Twisting her body to the side, she saw a dusty cement floor, another clue that she was still in the warehouse.

"Leah?"

John's voice! He was alive.

Relief spread through her, its warmth pushing away the chill from the ground. She rolled her body in the other direction, found John lying a few feet away, his hands and feet also bound.

"John! Are you all right? Did I...?"

His smile was the most welcome sight in the world, even if it was just a ghost of its regular self. "I'm fine. You cured me. Again. This is getting to be a regular habit."

"How long...?" The last thing she remembered was a terrible pain after laying her hands on John. But other than some aches and pains, and the rubbed-raw feeling from her bindings, she didn't hurt at all, which meant not too much time could have passed. Otherwise she'd be feeling the effects of taking in John's wound.

John's smile faded, and something changed in his eyes, and she knew bad news was coming.

"You've been unconscious for at least an hour, maybe longer. Apparently you passed out after curing me, and..." His voice trailed off, like a child admitting a wrongdoing to a parent.

It didn't matter. She had a pretty good idea of what must have happened. "Don't tell me. Someone touched me."

He nodded. "Yeah. I don't know if you were even awake, or if it happened while you were still unconscious. I woke up after...after it was all over."

"Who died?" She had to know. Another black mark on her soul. This time someone who probably didn't even deserve it.

That's not true. One of them shot John. And they're holding you against your will.

All true, but it didn't do anything to ease her guilt.

"One of the men who came in with the priest. It sounds like it was an accident. I only caught a few bits of conversation before they tied us up again and left."

"They left?" Leah tried to look around, but it hurt her neck too much. "We're alone?"

"No." John motioned with his head, but she couldn't figure out what direction he was indicating. "They went into another room. I heard the door shut. My guess is they're trying to decide what to do with us and they didn't want us to hear."

That can't be good. She didn't bother voicing her concern out loud. One look at John's face told her he felt the same.

Leah desperately wanted to feel John's touch. If they only had minutes to live, she wanted whatever comfort she could take. Ignoring the stinging of her ankles and wrists, she squirmed towards him. As soon as she started moving, he copied her, inching his body in her direction.

When they met, all they could do was lean against each other, but it got them close enough to share a long, soulful kiss. Neither passionate nor sad, it was an expression of love, more than sexual heat or despondent acceptance of their situation. And for one brief moment, Leah felt nothing but happiness.

Then a door slammed and footsteps sounded on the hard concrete. They drew closer, each one a stab in Leah's heart as thoughts of execution went through her head. She wondered if it was the same feeling criminals felt on death row as the guards approached the cell for the last time, or the way prisoners felt back in the days of firing squads or hangings, waiting, blindfolded and bound, for their death sentence to be carried out.

Or worse, the way shelter animals felt when the person with the needle came down the hall. Did the dying cats and dogs in her clinic basement feel that resignation when she came down the stairs? Did they wonder if it was their time? And if they did, were they glad their suffering was coming to an end or were they like many people, desperate to hold on to every last second of life, afraid of what lay beyond?

Faces appeared above her. The kidnapper and one of his men.

"The decision has been made."

More faces appeared, and then strong hands gripped her arms, pulled her to her feet. Next to her, two men hauled John up as well. They were guided to chairs and told to sit.

"Don't keep us in suspense," John said.

The priest stepped forward. When he spoke, his eyes mirrored the pity in his voice, lending it credence. That pity scared Leah more than anything, because it meant bad news was on the way. Again.

"I saw the power within you," he said to her. "Perhaps it is God who gave it to you, perhaps the devil. It no longer matters. What I have seen is that you have no control over this thing inside you."

"That's not true!" Leah felt herself growing angry again. How was it that everyone thought they could speak for what she was, who she was? "I've controlled it for years, until all you people forced me into these situations."

"I believe that. However, I also believe you are refusing to admit the truth. That things have changed. I watched a man touch you and die."

"That's different. I was unconscious."

The priest nodded. "Yes. And what if it had been a stranger who found you that way? Or someone in your family? What happens if you are in a crowd of people, and you touch someone who is ill, and then someone touches you? Or..." he narrowed his eyes and his voice grew colder, "...what if someone like Tal Nova kidnaps you again and forces you to do his bidding? You've killed people to save this man's life. How many more times would you do it before you refuse?"

Leah opened her mouth to argue, and then paused. In truth, she didn't have the control she'd thought she had. Sure, in a safe environment like her office, she was fine. But in the real world, the world where violence and evil were as much a part of things as kindness and good intentions? What lengths would she go to in order to keep John alive and healthy? Or herself, for that matter?

What if she touched the wrong person at the wrong time? When you thought about it, it was something of a miracle that an accident hadn't happened already.

"Leah..." John said, clearly a warning not to listen to the priest's words.

But how could she not? He was right.

"So you're going to kill me?" she asked.

Another nod. "I am afraid there is no other way. Either you are a tool of Satan or you have strayed too far from God's path. Either way, you pose too great a threat to the world."

"Then can I ask a favor?" She was surprised at her own calm. "Spare him." She tilted her head towards John. "He's got nothing to do with...what I am."

"Of course." The priest's words carried truth and compassion. "We are not murderers. He will be released after this is over."

"You might as well kill me too," John said, his voice as hard and cold as Leah had ever heard him. "Because I promise I will hunt you down and kill every one of you if you don't."

The priest shrugged. "That is between you and God. I do not control the future. My job is simply to follow the path God has laid out for me."

He placed his hand on Leah's forehead and began reciting words in Spanish. Even though it had been many years—too many to count—since she'd last been in church, and her knowledge of Spanish was limited to a few words, she recognized it as a prayer.

Is he reading me the Last Rites? Asking God to spare my soul? Or maybe asking that his own be spared, considering he was a priest ready to commit— or at least condone—murder.

She turned to John to say goodbye, wishing her last memory of him weren't the terrible sadness and anger etched across his face. She opened her mouth, not knowing what she would say. There were so many things, and not enough time. John's eyes grew wide, and she knew her time must be up, that someone was pointing a gun at her head.

"John, I—"

The world exploded around her, stealing away her last words. For a brief moment she felt like she was flying, her weightless body sailing through the air on invisible wings.

I thought dying would be more painful...

And then there was only darkness.

Chapter Twenty-Four

"Leah? Leah? Leah?"

Yes, that's my name. Now let me go back to sleep.

Leah wished God would leave her alone. Heaven had started out so wonderful—just empty space, no light, no sound, no body. It was beautiful in its emptiness because it provided the one thing she craved: relaxation. She could finally just lie still and do nothing. Be nothing. Forget all the worries of her earthly life, the constant tensions that came with trying to keep her Power a secret from the whole world. And then she'd failed at that, which had only made life even harder. She'd been afraid of death, but it had turned out to be the best thing for her. Just a long sleep, as if God had taken that perfect time between midnight on Saturday night and 10:00 a.m. on Sunday and extended it forever.

In between stretches of nothing, she'd had some random thoughts about her old life. She'd miss her parents, and John, of course. She'd miss working with the animals she loved so much. She hoped they'd all learn how to get along without her and not spend too much time bemoaning her loss. But mostly those were just wisps that moved in and around her consciousness, the opposite of dream fragments in earthbound sleep. And just like she'd always enjoyed doing when she woke too early on a Sunday morning, Leah mentally brushed the fragments away each time they appeared and let herself drift back into blissful sleep.

All was fine until God began saying her name. At least she thought it was God. Maybe it wasn't. After all, wouldn't God know her name? And why would he want to wake her up after creating her own private heaven for her? So perhaps it wasn't God. Who then? An angel? A fellow resident of heaven?

"Leah. Leah. Can you hear me?"

Someone or something knew it was her. Wanted her awake. She didn't want to wake up, though. Waking might mean never recapturing Nirvana, might mean having to think again, make decisions again. Lose the perfect solitude she'd craved for so long and never even realized she needed until it miraculously fell into her lap.

And now they wanted to rip heaven away from her? Why? Who would be so cruel?

"Leah. Leah!"

Damn them!

Leah relinquished the darkness. More than she'd ever hated exiting dreamland on a Sunday morning, more than she'd ever hated waking up when all she wanted to do was sleep after a grueling week, she acquiesced to the inevitable—they weren't going to go away—and opened her eyes.

"Leah! Thank God!"

"John?" His features were fuzzy around the edges but there was no mistaking the person looking down at her, relief branded across his face.

"Oh, John, I'm so sorry they lied to you. I didn't want this to happen." The priest had promised not to kill him; now John was dead because of her. Well, at least they could be together in heaven.

"What? Why... Never mind. There's no time to talk now. We've got to get out of here while we can." His strong hands grabbed her arms and pulled.

She resisted. Why would he want to leave heaven? Maybe he didn't realize where they were.

"No. I'm happy here. This is my place, what I've been searching for. You can stay here too."

"You're not making sense. I think you have a concussion. I'll get you to a doctor as soon as we're safe. Can you walk?" He tugged at her again, and for the first time she noticed that her head hurt. So did one shoulder. That didn't make sense. How could you feel pain after you died?

"C'mon!"

This time she allowed John to help her to her feet. A rush of dizziness swept through her and her legs went weak. She gripped John's arms to steady herself while the gray clouds rotated around her. The dizziness brought with it nausea, a feeling like her stomach was doing circles in time with the clouds.

At that moment, she hated John. Whatever he'd done by waking her had ruined everything. Her body ached, her headache was growing in intensity, and the air stunk of dust and fire. It was like…

Hell.

"No!" She tried to pull away and he kept hold of her as her legs buckled again. "No! I don't want to be here! This isn't fair!" She'd sacrificed her life. Wasn't that enough?

"Stay close. We're leaving. I promise."

With no strength to resist him, Leah did her best to walk as John half dragged, half guided her through the clouds of brimstone. Along the way, she caught glimpses of the nightmare world around her. Body parts scattered across the ground. Pools of blood. Smoldering pieces of rock. In the distance, anguished voices cried out for relief.

Please, God, let this end. Get me out of here.

Ahead of them, glowing symbols shined red-hot amid the smoke. Leah tried to focus on them but they remained blurred. Eyes? A face? She pulled away but John hauled her toward them. She tried to shout at him and lost her words to a fit of coughing as more fire-tinged air attacked her lungs. What was he doing? Was he in league with the evil forces?

A wall loomed up out of the gray and John threw himself at it. She expected him to fall or bounce back. Instead, the stone gave way and a blinding light struck her. Hands pushed her forward.

Suddenly, she could breathe again. She gulped at the cool, clean air. Wiped away the tears in her eyes.

And saw they were in an alley.

"How…?" Leah rubbed her eyes again, trying to clear the blurriness. A street? She looked behind her. A building. Gray bricks. Smoke pouring from shattered windows and an open door they'd just emerged from.

A building?

Not hell.

Something much worse.

John took her hand. "It's okay. We're safe now. Let's go." He led her down the alley, unaware that all she wanted to do was lie down and cry.

No heaven. No hell.

Just the terrible fact that she was still alive.

Chapter Twenty-Five

By the time they found a cab willing to take them from Manhattan to Rocky Point, Leah had gotten enough control of herself so that she wouldn't break down and cry or scream. John fussed over her in the back of the cab, dabbing blood away from her nose and ears, talking about how, as soon as they were home, they were getting her to a doctor.

She let him talk, responding with the occasional monosyllabic answer when she could muster the strength. Mostly, though, she stared at the passing scenery and felt herself grow cold inside. Not her temperature, but her emotions. Each passing mile seemed to erase a little more sadness, a little more fear, a little more anger, until all that remained was reluctant acceptance.

She was alive. Bad people were still after her. And good people would continue to die because of her.

Unless she did something to change it all.

The idea of suicide was an obvious one, but she quickly put that out of her mind. Although she no longer feared dying, enough of her Catholic upbringing remained in her that she was still pretty sure suicide meant going to hell. Which left only one other option.

Disappearing.

How hard could it be? You packed a bag, drained the cash from your bank account, dyed your hair and went "off the grid," as people liked to say. She'd work odd jobs for cash. Stay at shelters. A hard life, for sure. But better than the alternative.

There'd be no one to abuse her, threaten her. And no guilt about putting other people's lives in mortal danger.

It made perfect sense when you just stopped and thought about it.

Of course, she couldn't tell anybody. Not John, not her parents. That would be hard. But in the end, worth it to keep them safe. And being alone wouldn't be so bad. Hell, with the exception of her parents and Chastity, she'd really had no friends or social life before John anyhow.

Something dripped onto her hand, and she looked down. A drop of blood. Her nose was bleeding again. She dabbed at it with one of the napkins John had gotten from the taxi driver.

He was right. She probably had a concussion. It made sense. There'd been an explosion. More violence, someone attacking the religious men who'd kidnapped her. That was too bad. They'd been right, she probably should die. Maybe she would too. Living on the streets was dangerous, and it was obvious she couldn't heal herself anymore. Otherwise her nose wouldn't be bleeding. And her body wouldn't hurt.

Did the explosion do something to me? More than a concussion? Wouldn't that be something if hitting her head had taken away her Power? Then she could really be free. If she could just tell people that... Of course, no one would believe her. They'd try to torture her into performing miracles, maybe even torture the people she cared about. No, running away, disappearing, that was still the only option.

As soon as her head stopped pounding.

"We're here."

Leah looked up at the sound of John's voice. She hadn't noticed the cab had stopped. Hadn't noticed her eyes were closed. How long? It didn't matter. She was home.

The door next to her opened and a hand reached for her. Who... John? How had he gotten over there? He helped her out, holding her steady.

The walkway to her steps...why was it slanted? Stairs...one...two...three...

The couch. So soft. She loved her couch. Was going to miss it. Why was she on the couch? Who was spinning the couch around?

"Turn off the lights," she said, but no one listened.

So tired. Why wouldn't they let her sleep?

Then the lights faded away and everything was good again.

"She's resting now," Jim Fogerty said, joining John in Leah's kitchen. "Probably sleep 'til tomorrow."

"She's okay, though?" John asked. He needed it to be so. Not just because he didn't want anything to happen to Leah, but because if it was something serious, that would mean a hospital trip.

He'd called in a major favor to get his brother-in-law to the house. Jim was only in his third year of practice and hadn't been thrilled about getting involved in something that could mean his license. John had a feeling it was going to cost him big—as in Yankee play-off tickets big. But until he had time to arrange round-the-clock protection, they needed to stay under the radar.

"Yeah, I'm pretty sure her symptoms are more from exhaustion and dehydration, not to mention the blast, rather than from a concussion. No signs of trauma to the head. Now, do you want to tell me how you ended up caught in a warehouse explosion, and why this has to stay a secret?"

John shook his head. "Wish I could. But it's part of an undercover operation and Leah got caught up in it accidentally. She wasn't supposed to be there. I promise, once I can tell you, I will."

"Fine." Jim closed his black satchel. "Just do me a favor. Don't tell Carrie about this. She would absolutely freak."

"Promise." John held up his hand. The last thing he intended to do was tell his sister anything.

After walking Jim to his car, John returned to the house and stood at the end of the sofa, watching Leah sleep.

Two weeks. Less than two weeks since the day she cured me, and look at us now. Running like fugitives. A price on our heads from at least three different criminal gangs, and probably the police want us for questioning. We've saved each other's lives how many times over the past few days?

And none of it would have happened if she hadn't cured him that day in McDonald's. He wondered if their meeting was a blessing or a curse for her—after all, if she'd decided on pizza instead of a hamburger, he'd be dead but she'd be living a perfectly normal life, her secret still safe.

Would she be happy? That was hard to say. He was pretty sure she liked him, maybe was even falling in love with him. She'd talked about how lonely she'd been before meeting him.

Was that enough to counterbalance the sorrow and guilt she was feeling for everything that had happened? Or the terrors she'd gone through?

Could it ever be enough?

John hoped so. Because there were two things he was certain of.

He was definitely in love with Leah DeGarmo.

And he was never going to let anything get in the way of that love.

Part Two

Season of Change

The best thing you can do is the right thing; the next best thing you can do is the wrong thing; the worst thing you can do is nothing.

—Theodore Roosevelt

Chapter One

Leah had the cab drive around the block three times before she paid and got out. As far as she could tell, no one was watching her house. Not that she was an expert on surveillance, but she'd seen no trucks or vans parked anywhere, which was what they always used in movies. In fact, there'd been no vehicles of any kind parked on the street, typical for a weekday in her middle-class neighborhood.

She let herself in through the back door, using the key she kept in a fake rock near the door. Ten minutes, she reminded herself. That's how long she'd told the cabbie she would be. More than enough time to pack a bag and get out.

But that was before she'd walked in and realized this was the last time she'd ever see her house. The house she'd worked her ass off to buy, to decorate, to make her own. Everything in it reminded her of something in her life, something that had made her life *hers.*

The silver candleholders on the dining-room table. A housewarming gift from her parents, with the added comment that someday she might want to entertain a young man. The journals and medical books on the shelves, souvenirs of the many hours she'd spent perfecting her craft, even though she held the gift of magic in her hands. Photo albums from her younger days, back when she'd taken vacations and done things with friends.

Stop it. She wiped a hand roughly across her face, erasing the tears running down her cheeks. *It's for the best. Now get your ass in gear.*

It wouldn't take John long to discover she'd left the motel room where they'd been staying the past two days. He'd gone out for food. She'd told him she was going to take a long, hot shower. As soon as she was sure he was really walking to the corner market, she'd turned the shower on, shut the bathroom door and run out. Two blocks in the opposite direction from the minimart, she'd stopped at a gas station and had them call a cab for her.

She figured she had maybe an hour's head start. Ten minutes before he realized she wasn't in the bathroom. Ten for a cab to arrive. And then it was a fifty-fifty chance of whether he'd go to her house first or to the clinic. She had to assume the worst, that he was already on his way to the house.

So pack!

She did, thankful that when Nova dragged her out of the house he'd left her purse behind. Her license, which she'd need at the bank to close out her account. Cell phone, although she had to figure it was tapped. But she could use it in an emergency. Toothbrush. Makeup. Her iPod. A photo album she couldn't live without.

She felt tears threatening again and forced them down. Time for that later, when she was on a cross-country bus or train. A quick stop in the kitchen to grab some snacks and a few bottles of water, and she was back at the cab with two minutes to spare.

Tal Nova would be so proud. The sarcastic thought brought on another round of sobs, which the cabdriver judiciously ignored.

"Provident Bank," she told him, dabbing at her eyes with a tissue.

John watched Leah's house come into view and prayed he'd made the right choice. He'd had no idea Leah would take off; his first thought was she'd been kidnapped again, until the motel clerk mentioned he'd seen her walk past the office.

Damn her! What could possibly be the reason for ditching him? Did she still think he'd be safer if she was gone?

"Wait here," he told the driver. "I'll be right back."

He went around to the back door and cursed when he saw it hanging open. Leah, in and out in a hurry? Or one of the men looking for her? He cursed a second time and drew his gun, the short-barreled backup piece he'd picked up at his house before they checked into the motel. Only six shots, but if he needed more than that he was a dead man anyhow.

And this time Leah won't be there to save me.

He peeked around the corner of the door, presenting as small a target as possible. The kitchen looked the same as the last time he'd seen it. Past the small space, the dining room and living room seemed clear. Of course, there could be someone hiding behind a couch or chair, but he doubted it. The men they'd dealt with so far were more the stand-in-the-open-and-shoot-rather-than-hide type. Stepping into the kitchen, he crept forward to the base of the stairs, listening for any sounds from the second floor.

A floorboard squeaked behind him and he spun around, his heart thumping into overdrive, adrenaline surging through his body. Everything seemed to happen at hyperspeed—turning, bringing the gun up, tensing muscles—all faster than he'd ever moved before.

It wasn't fast enough.

Something hard and heavy struck him on the temple and lights exploded inside his head.

Then the fireworks disappeared, taking everything with them.

"There must be some kind of mistake." Leah leaned forward. "I had more than twenty thousand dollars in that account last week."

"I'm sorry, Ms. DeGarmo. But according to the computer, you transferred that money to another bank yesterday."

"Another bank? Why would I do that?" Even as she asked the question, a cold, nasty sensation filled Leah's chest. She had a feeling she knew what had happened to her money. Who would have access to her accounts besides her?

A man with the power of a multinational conglomerate behind him, that's who. Tal Nova.

"—want to speak with our manager? If this is a case of fraud, he has to call—"

"No." Leah shut her purse. "I mean, I'll be back. With my attorney," she added, knowing how lame it sounded but not having any other explanation for not wanting to find out where her money had gone.

Before the teller could say anything else, Leah turned and hurried away.

Damn him! He got to my money. And he's probably closed my credit cards as well; no sense even trying those.

She stormed out the bank doors and paused. Now what?

She had exactly sixty-three dollars to her name, no credit, and she probably couldn't even show her license anywhere. A bus ticket would most likely eat all her money and still not get her more than a couple of states away, leaving her alone, penniless and basically lost. Trains were more expensive than buses. She could steal a car, if she knew how. But she didn't.

Suddenly her plan of escaping and disappearing didn't seem as ingenious as it had when she'd thought she'd be leaving with twenty grand or so in her pocket.

The important thing is to get away. Worry about the rest later. She could always spend a few nights in a women's shelter if she had to; every city had at least one. They'd probably help her find a job that paid cash, too, if she lied and said she was hiding from an abusive husband. Any job would do, as long as it didn't involve the veterinary field. That would be too dangerous.

Her resolve strengthened again, she headed for the bus station.

Chapter Two

After three hours of watching an endless procession of malls, billboards and roadside diners go by—the monotony broken only by equally dull tracts of farmland—Leah was relieved when the bus pulled into the station at Elmira. The driver announced there'd be a thirty-minute layover before the next leg of the trip, which would take them to Jamestown. There she'd catch a different bus to Cleveland.

Faced with the option of sitting on the bus for the next half hour or spending the time in the station, Leah paused, unsure of what would be safer. Remaining on the bus meant fewer people would have the opportunity to see her. On the other hand, if someone wanted to kidnap her—or worse—then an empty bus was the perfect location.

In the end, it was her bladder that made the decision for her. Bus station restrooms were notoriously filthy, but even they were better than the cramped, foul-smelling toilet cubicle at the back of the bus.

Besides, her stomach was growling and there'd be snack machines in the lobby.

Keeping her eyes alert for any suspicious characters, she took care of business and then made her way to the vending machines, where she grudgingly parted with two dollars for a candy bar and a diet soda.

Leah frowned as she counted her remaining cash. Enough for three, maybe four meals at McDonald's if she stuck to the dollar menu. The ticket to Cleveland had eaten most of her money.

Taking a seat near the departure doors, Leah wondered again if she was being followed. She'd done her best to examine the faces of the people around her, but she had to admit her skills as a spy—or fugitive, depending on how you looked at it—weren't the best. Every gaze in her direction, every stranger who walked past, set her adrenaline pumping.

Finally, she forced herself to sit back and relax. After all, it wasn't as if Tal Nova or that other man, Del, could bring their thugs into a public place and just take her away against her will. No, if they were after her, they'd have made their move in Rocky Point, before she boarded the bus or when she'd been at her house.

Thinking of her house brought her mind back to John. He'd surely be frantic about finding her by now. She hoped that didn't put him in more danger. Would he be smart enough to go to the police once he was sure she was missing? Again, she hoped so. He could tell them whatever he wanted—even reveal her secret. She no longer cared.

Mostly because she no longer had a secret.

Leah looked down at her hands. The bruises and cuts on them were fading, but the very fact they were there at all was continued evidence her Power hadn't come back. She also still felt weak and run-down, another sign she'd changed. Although in the past she'd often ended up exhausted at the end of a hard workday, a good night's sleep always had her as good as new the next morning. Now, here she was, days after the explosion and the blow to her head, and she still felt like death warmed over.

Would it be so bad if my Power was gone? It was a question she'd been mulling over since she'd first realized she wasn't healing rapidly. Without it, no one would want to use her as a murder weapon. The people she loved—John, her family—would be safe. She might even be able to return to being a veterinarian, although it would probably break her heart each time she couldn't Cure a dying pet.

She'd actually considered calling Leonard Marsh, who she figured was behind everything bad that had happened, and telling him she was just an ordinary person again. Let them arrange a demonstration if they wanted. In return for them letting her go free, she'd promise not to say anything to the police.

Right, Leah. And they'll just let you go. After all, murdering criminals are famous for trusting people.

Not.

More likely they'd simply kill her.

Even with my Power gone, it continues to curse me.

Still, over the years she'd done a lot of good. John was right in that respect. She'd Cured hundreds of animals, made countless pet owners happy. Would she do it all over again, knowing what would eventually happen? Probably. If it weren't for Chastity's death, and John's life being in danger, it would be more than a fair trade.

A memory popped up from when she'd been shot trying to rescue John. She'd had a dream of being Jesus. Rather than blasphemous, the comparison seemed oddly appropriate. Two people with the Power to Cure the sick. One sacrificed himself so that his followers could be saved. And that was what she was doing now, in a way. Sacrificing her life to keep other people safe. Not that she felt saintly or Godlike, but the situation seemed to prove that "acts of kindness rarely go unpunished." Another of her mother's sayings.

My mother, who I Cured of cancer. And what did that act of kindness get me? Decades of tiptoeing around the truth, one of the few parts of our relationship that isn't perfect.

Secrets. Lies. Loneliness. Sadness. Violence. Death. What a list of consequences from having a so-called Power to do good.

I'm so much better off without it.

A middle-aged woman sat down in the seat across from her and cleared her throat. "Excuse me, miss. Do you have the time?"

Still deep in her own thoughts, Leah looked up at the clock. "Yes, its— Ow!"

A sharp pain in her shoulder made her turn around. Two well-dressed men stood behind her, one of them sliding a syringe back into his jacket pocket. Leah tried to scream but her mouth refused to open. At the same time, her body went limp and she was aware of the floor sliding up to meet her.

It's not the floor sliding, it's me. I've been drugged!

Her entire body felt wrapped in cotton, her senses of touch and hearing dulled and warped by the drugs. Only her vision remained clear, although she couldn't move her eyes to look in different directions. Her body rose again and she caught glimpses of the two men standing at her sides. Then her head drooped forward and all she saw were the tiles of the bus-station floor flowing past in a river of filthy gray.

Garbled voices reached her, some louder than others, the jumbled words disappearing and returning like a poorly tuned radio station.

"...what's wrong with...it's okay, we know...suffers from...escaped...call the...no, we have...be fine..."

Then she was outside, which she could tell because the gray tiles disappeared, replaced by cracked cement. The two men lifted her into a van and laid her on the floor. With her head facing up, she was finally able to see their faces. Neither of them looked familiar. Then the woman from the bus station stepped into view, and she did look familiar.

Even more so when she pulled her hair off.

You, Leah wanted to say, recognizing the man called Del.

He must have seen the comprehension in her eyes, because he nodded. "Nice to see you again, Doctor DeGarmo. Have a nice sleep."

This time the pinprick in her arm was barely noticeable.

The last thing she saw was Del's face growing fuzzy.

Leah woke up with the worst headache she'd ever felt, worse even than the time she'd done too many tequila shots at a college party. That one had lasted almost fifteen minutes, while her drinking partners had all ended up in the hospital with alcohol poisoning. At the time she'd thought she'd been lucky. It was only looking back, years later, that she understood it was more likely a side effect of her Power that kept her from getting her stomach pumped. And earned her a reputation for being immune to tequila.

This hangover showed no signs of letting up, and she wondered what kinds of drugs she'd been given.

That man. Del. It was him. Dressed like a woman.

Dammit. I should have stayed on the bus.

No, she consoled herself. It wouldn't have made a difference. If they had the audacity to drug her and carry her off in public, in broad daylight, then they'd have had no worries about boarding an empty bus to take her. Which brought up the next question.

Where had they taken her?

At the moment there was no way to tell. She was on a hard, cold floor of some kind, tile or maybe wood, her hands tied in front of her. The only light came from a nearby computer monitor, which showed the swirling, twisting rainbow colors of a screen saver. The monitor sat on a desk, but she couldn't see beyond that, couldn't tell how large the room was or what else it contained.

A scream threatened to break loose from her throat and she clenched her jaw, fighting the urge to give in to her panic. It terrified her that there could be a dozen men with guns not ten feet away and she'd never even be aware of their presence. Adding to her fear was the knowledge that something far worse awaited her, especially when Del found out she was no use to him anymore.

Leah forced herself to take deep breaths, which wasn't easy because the air stank of something foul, something that reminded her of the dissection labs in vet school. Was she in a morgue? God, she hoped not. Dead bodies all around...

Stop it!

She couldn't afford to freak out, not now. That could come later, if and when she got out of this latest mess. She laid her head against the floor, the chilly surface serving as a cold compress against her temple, bringing a bit of very welcome relief to her aching brain.

After a time, her rapid heartbeat slowed down, further easing her pain as the pounding in her skull diminished. With the headache retreating to a manageable level, she was able to think more clearly.

Somehow Del had followed her—had probably been watching her all along—and now that he had her again, odds were he was planning on completing whatever scheme he'd had in mind for her the first time he'd taken her.

"You're going to make me a lot of money," he'd said, or something to that effect. Was he planning on hiring her services to people like Nova and Marsh? Turn her into some kind of hit woman for hire? Or did he have something even more horrible in mind, like selling her to the mob?

Or a foreign government?

Images of being held captive by terrorists raced through her head, and her panic returned full force. Locked in a cell forever, starved, beaten, forced to constantly kill—

Wait. I can't Cure anymore. But Del doesn't know that. And if he wants me to kill people, that means I have to Cure someone first... Oh God.

John.

Del knew about John. He was the only leverage Del—or anyone else—had against Leah. Which meant they probably had him locked away somewhere as well, or were in the process of kidnapping him. And when they found out Leah couldn't Cure anymore, it wouldn't be just her life that was forfeit. It would be John's too because he was a witness.

No! It's not fair!

She'd run away to keep John safe, and she'd still basically condemned him to death.

They're going to come for me, and that will mean John's been shot or poisoned again. And what will I be able to do? Nothing. There's no way I can fake Curing someone. I'll have to stand there and watch him die. And I can't bear to see that happen.

Better they kill me first.

And how to accomplish that?

"I'll find a way," she whispered to the dark room.

Chapter Three

Del's men came for her sooner than Leah expected. Or maybe she'd been dozing longer than she thought. Between the drugs and being alone in the dark room, her sense of time was completely out of whack.

There was no warning to their entry; one minute everything was gray and silent, and the next a door opened, flooding the room with blinding light. She cried out and turned her head away, blinking back tears until she could open her eyes without pain.

"Let's go," the taller man said. She thought it might have been one of the two who'd pulled her out of the bus station, but she couldn't be sure.

"Where are you taking me?" Not that it mattered. Wherever it was, only death awaited. Still, as resigned to her fate as she felt, a spark of resistance remained inside her.

"The man wants to talk to you," her shorter captor said.

"You mean Del?" she asked as they lifted her to her feet. The two men glanced at each other, and one raised an eyebrow to his companion, but neither responded.

As they led her down a long hallway randomly lit by fluorescent bulbs, the rotten smell that had assaulted her earlier grew stronger, as if they were moving toward its source. It only took a few breaths for the odor to send her stomach into spasms, especially when she recognized some of the components of the stench.

Blood. Raw flesh.

Jesus, where the hell am I?

Her legs started to buckle, and the hands gripping her arms tightened their hold with bruising force.

"Relax, Doc. This ain't that kind of visit. You do what the man says and you'll be back in your little cave all safe and sound."

That's what you think. Leah held back a moan. The two men thought she was afraid of dying. If only they knew the truth—she'd welcome death if it meant John could go free. And they were also wrong about her safety. She'd never be returning to the dark room they'd had her in, not once she showed Del her Power was gone.

A door stood open at the end of the hall and the men steered her through it. When she saw Del sitting at a plain wooden desk, a cell phone to his ear, she knew her worse fears were about to come true. This time she didn't try to fight the whimper that escaped her. One of the men laughed softly as he pushed her into a vacant folding chair, and she felt a moment of indignation that dissipated as soon as it formed.

Let him laugh. What does it matter anymore?

Del smiled at her, held up a finger in an "I'll be with you in a moment" gesture and continued talking on the phone. Although she could only hear his end of the conversation, she got the idea he was setting up a meeting of some kind for the following day.

A meeting she was sure involved her in some way. A demonstration? Or maybe he'd already sold her? Looking at his boyish, nondescript features, she wondered how such an ordinary face could hide such a terrible person. At least Tal Nova had the decency to look like a murdering criminal. This Del person could sit next to you on a plane or bus, and you'd never know you were two feet from a cold-blooded killer.

Which was probably what made him so good at his job.

He thumbed the phone off and turned to her.

"Hi, Doc. Good to see you again. How are you feeling?"

If you didn't know better, you'd think he really meant it.

"I feel like shit, thanks to all those drugs." Except as she said it, she realized it wasn't true. Her headache was finally fading as the drugs left her system; all that remained was the nausea from the terrible stink filling the air.

"Sorry about that. But it's a pretty good bet you wouldn't have come with us willingly. What's in Cleveland?"

The question caught her by surprise, and for a moment she didn't understand what he was talking about. Then she remembered the bus ticket she'd bought.

"Nothing. A new life." *Dammit, why am I answering him?*

"A new life? Without your boyfriend?" Del raised his eyebrows in exaggerated surprise.

The mention of John sent a chill through Leah that had nothing to do with the cool air in the building. Did they have him here as well?

Del's next words confirmed her suspicions.

"I hate to see lovers separated. So you'll be glad to know Mr. Police Officer is resting safely not far from here."

"Please don't—" Leah stopped herself. What good was begging? It was obvious they intended to hurt him. Del already knew John was the key to getting her to use her Power.

"Don't what? Kill him? That's up to you. Play nice and he stays alive." Del's expression grew dark and menacing, as if the killer inside him had surfaced, and suddenly he was *very* scary indeed. "Try using your powers against me or my men, though, and I'll chop him into so many pieces even you couldn't ever put him back together again."

His words reminded her that she'd killed one of his men, passed on John's sickness and Del's own gunshot wound all at once. Did he feel hatred towards her for that?

Enough to kill her right here and now if she gave him the opportunity? She opened her mouth, fully intending to tell him that she'd lost the ability to Cure.

Nothing came out.

The words, so clear in her head, refused to leave her throat, leaving her gaping like a freshly caught fish.

"Don't look so surprised, Doc. You think I'm doing this for entertainment purposes? You're my retirement package, and I'll be damned if you ruin things for me by pulling some stunt like you did the other day. Now, you behave during tomorrow's little presentation, and I'll let you see your boyfriend afterward, maybe even have a little snuggle time. Consider it a reward for a job well done. If you don't, well, then your last memory of him won't be a pleasant one. Do we understand each other?"

Leah's inner turmoil turned into full-blown confusion. John was definitely in the building somewhere! And whatever they had planned for her, it didn't involve him. Which meant she could have a chance to say goodbye, to apologize for destroying his life.

If you do what Del asks.

And if she couldn't do it, he'd kill her.

"I'll take that as a yes," Del said, breaking in on her thoughts. "Have a nice night, Doc. Tomorrow's gonna be a great day." He motioned with his hand and his two men stepped forward and took her by the arms.

The walk back to her makeshift cell was a blur as Leah tried to make sense of the possibilities. Her thoughts were still in a whirl when the men locked the door. A tray sat on the desk, with a sandwich and a can of soda. The sight of them set her stomach rumbling and she grabbed the food as best she could with her hands still tied. The idea it might be drugged crossed her mind, but she didn't stop eating. A drug-induced sleep would actually be preferable to spending the night awake and worrying.

When she finished, Leah sat down on the floor and finally let loose the tears she'd been holding back. Sometime tomorrow she and John would both die. The only uncertainty would be who went first.

She prayed it was her.

She was still crying softly when the sedatives in her food took effect and put her to sleep.

Chapter Four

Leah woke to find a man bending over her, shaking her arm.

"Wake up. The man wants to see you in an hour. You need to use the bathroom?"

"What?" Leah tried to focus on his words. An hour? What time was it? Who was...?

Del.

Her thoughts grew clearer, cutting their way through the leftover haze of whatever they'd dosed her with. It was morning, and Del had some kind of demonstration planned, something that involved her.

Rough hands shook her.

"Hey! I said—"

"I heard you." Her words were as dry and cracked as her throat felt. "Bathroom. Yes."

She let the man haul her to her feet. The bathroom turned out to be one door down in the hallway. At one time it had been a public restroom with two urinals and two stalls. The guard started to close the door and Leah called out to him.

"Wait. My hands." She held up her hands, still bound at the wrists by a heavy plastic tie-wrap.

"No." He shut the door, leaving her alone in the musty room.

"Thanks a lot," she whispered, staring at her bound hands and trying to figure out how to get her pants down. In the end, it took a series of contortions before she could pee. Then it was a five-minute struggle trying to get her underwear and pants back on. As an act of defiance that meant little but made her feel better, she left the toilet unflushed. After splashing water on her face and struggling to get paper towels out of the dispenser, she tapped on the door to let the guard know she was ready.

A large cup of Dunkin' Donuts coffee was waiting in her cell, and she rushed across the room to it, the rich, dark aroma a siren call to her caffeine-starved body. Sipping the hot liquid, she found herself amazed at the human ability to find a bit of pleasure even in the most awful of situations. Here she was, most likely hours from her death, and still able to appreciate the simple joy of drinking coffee, experiencing an almost-sensual gratification from the complex flavors and scents.

If this has to be my last meal, I'm all right with that.

A morbid thought, but a real one. She'd been prepared for death since the renegade priest in the warehouse condemned her. She didn't want it—every fiber in her being craved life—but she was ready to accept it. Better death than a life of endless Curing and killing as someone's slave.

The door opened without warning, and she wondered if the room was soundproofed. And if so, why? What kind of place had this been before Del took it over for his own purposes?

Just like the last time, the long hallway stunk of stale blood and dead flesh, a metallic, bitter odor that coated her tongue and nostrils and kick-started her nausea again. It surprised her that she'd grown accustomed to the disagreeable smells, or at least to the less potent levels in her cell. In school she'd never gotten used to them, and had often felt like they lingered on long after she'd left the lab and showered, a phantom stench living inside her sinuses.

Either immune to the death smell or better at masking his displeasure, Del was at his desk when she arrived, still dressed in the same clothes as the previous day. She figured it was a good bet he'd stayed up all night, crafting whatever nasty surprise he had in store for her.

"Good morning, Doc. Sleep well?" he greeted, never looking away from the computer screen.

"What's going to happen to me?"

He shrugged. "Like I told you before, that depends on you. Are you ready to get started?"

"Please don't hurt John. He's been through too much already because of me." Leah's stomach churned as she spoke, her nausea mixing with guilt and anger at being in a situation that reduced her to begging.

"Well, you can relax. Your boyfriend's safe. At least for today," he added, and the guard behind her chuckled.

Del stood up and pointed at a second door across the office. "Right through there, Doc. Just do your magic and in an hour you can be holding hands or knocking boots or whatever you feel like with Mr. Police Officer."

Do your magic. Oh hell. Should I—

"I can't." Leah's feet, much like her mouth, suddenly decided to act on their own and she came to a stop by the door.

"What?" Del came around and stood in front of her, his face even with hers. The expression on it was not a pleasant one. Behind her, the guard gave her arm a little twist, making her wince. "What do you mean you can't?"

"I can't Cure anyone. Or anything. My Power. It's gone." Leah closed her eyes, anticipating a physical reaction. A punch, a slap. A broken arm.

"Bullshit."

The door opened on squeaky hinges and hands pushed her forward. She opened her eyes as she entered a much larger room. This one contained a video camera on a tripod, a computer and eight monitors lined up on a table. More cameras were mounted in the corners of the ceiling.

"Doc, this is no time to try and pull a fast one on me. I know all about you. I've got video of you killing one of my best associates, not to mention curing that cop. Bet you didn't know that, did you? I'm not an idiot. I plan things down to the last detail. You think I could set something like this up without proof? Now, you're gonna do as I ask or things are gonna get real painful for you."

Del took her arm and moved her to a position in front of the table.

Leah shook her head but didn't try to resist. "You don't understand. The explosion...in that warehouse. It...it did something to me. The doctor said it was exhaustion, and maybe a concussion. Ever since that day, I haven't been able to... I've been a normal person."

She looked at him, the man who'd caused her and John so much pain and suffering, and some of her old defiance rose up.

"So if you want to kill me, do it now."

She expected him to get angry, but instead Del just smiled, a grin that didn't reach his eyes at all.

"A concussion? Exhaustion? Sounds like a cop-out to me. Heard it all the time in the service. Psychosomatic bullshit. I think with the right, shall we say, incentive, you'll see how fast those powers of yours come back." He leaned forward, and his smile disappeared. "At least, you better hope so, for the cop's sake. Now, if you'll excuse me."

He moved to the table and flicked the computer screens on. As soon as they lit up, each one showed a different man's face. Leah recognized all of them as criminals; how she knew it, she couldn't say for sure, but there was something about their looks, something hard and cruel they all shared, despite looking nothing like each other.

"Good morning, gentlemen," Del said to them, and they returned his greeting with gruff hellos or brief nods. "You all know why you're here, so I won't waste your time with explanations. This morning you will see the demonstration I told you about."

"Is that her?" one of the faces, that of an older, swarthy man with gray hair, asked.

"Yes. And here is our test subject." Del motioned to his guards, and one of them opened the door, revealing two more men leading a large, very nervous animal on a leash.

A pig? They want me to Cure a pig? Leah eyed the beast as the two muscular men walked it in. It fought against the leash, and it took both men to keep it from breaking free.

I don't even want to go near that thing. She'd never handled a pig before. She estimated its weight to be at least two hundred pounds, recognized it as a half-grown Vietnamese pot-belly variety. A smart, intelligent animal. And dangerous. A pig that size could do real damage with its teeth, hooves and massive body.

One of the men drew a wicked-looking knife from his belt and held it against the top of the pig's fleshy neck.

"Gentlemen, what you are about to see will be—"

Before Del could finish, the pig emitted a loud squeal and leaped forward. It pulled the second guard to his knees and dragged him several feet before the leash yanked free.

"Shoot it!" Del shouted, dodging to one side. On the monitors, several of the video conference attendees called out, asking what was going on.

"A small delay," Del said, reaching for the keyboard. His hand never made it, as the pig changed directions, causing him to leap out of the way again. The man on the floor was crawling after his gun, which he'd dropped when he fell. The guard with the knife charged after the frantic pig, which was much more agile than its would-be captors.

Leah stood frozen, unsure of what to do. Thoughts of escape ran through her head, but brought with them an imagined bullet in the back from Del or one of his men.

Do something! she urged herself. Her body refused to obey, remaining locked in place. Then the pig was charging right at her, and it was too late to avoid it. At the last moment her paralysis broke but she only had time to get half her body out of the way.

The pig slammed into her at the waist with freight-train force, punching the breath from her lungs and knocking her onto her back. Hooves hammered her chest and face, shattering bones and sending thunderbolts of pain through her body. She tried to scream but a massive wall of flesh fell on top of her, covering her mouth and nose and pressing down on her injured ribs like a giant boot. Something exploded near her head and the muscular mountain sitting on her emitted a high-pitched shriek.

Then the weight and pressure disappeared, leaving her free to draw in a gasping breath. When it released, the scream that had been waiting in the wings came with it, a long, drawn-out cry of pain that triggered even more agony in her chest. Her vision dimmed, everything taking on shades of gray. A loud ringing in her ears made all other sounds seem fuzzy. Only the misery in her bones was sharp and focused, dominating her entire world. Words reached her, but carried no meaning.

"Look."

"Holy shit!"

"Get the camera!"

"I got it!"

"Put her in the chair."

"Ow! I got a shock!"

"Gentlemen, here is your demonstration."

Leah fought to breathe. Each movement triggered new agonies inside her until she grew numb to any further insults to her body. A wonderful feeling came to her, the pain washed away by a cool current, like sliding into a stream on a hot day or standing naked in a soft summer breeze. Her relief was a physical thing, similar to shedding a heavy weight from her shoulders. She felt free again and hoped she was returning to the dreamland she'd visited once before, the place she'd gone after the explosion in the warehouse.

The place she'd been longing for ever since she'd felt it. Heaven, or something so close it made no difference. A place of peace and rest and no worries.

Death.

"Thank you, God," she said to the encroaching darkness.

And then it claimed her.

Chapter Five

Del McCormick wanted to shout with joy. *From the ashes of destruction...*

Things couldn't have gone better if he'd planned them. First the vet saying she'd lost her supernatural mojo, then the pig getting loose during the web conference—the potential for disaster was so high he'd been lucky to keep his cool in front of the prospective buyers, each of whom would've been more than happy to have him killed for wasting their time.

And then the miracle.

Someone shouted "Look!" and he saw the lady vet on the floor, bruised, bloody and definitely hurt. Bad. He was no doctor, but her nose was obviously broken and she had to have some busted ribs from where the crazy pig had danced on her. She had cuts all over from its hooves.

And they were healing as they watched.

He wasted no time putting the camera on her so the deep pockets watching the fiasco could get a good look.

In the end, it was that same fiasco that convinced them—or at least most of them, two had dropped out—that DeGarmo's self-healing wasn't some kind of special-effects trick.

In less than a minute, every cut, every bruise, every broken bone had simply faded away, leaving behind an unmarked—and presumably healthy—woman.

After she was healed, he turned to face the six remaining prospects.

"Well, gentlemen, you've seen what she can do with her own injuries. She's just as adept at curing others, a talent I'm willing to demonstrate as well, but only in person. I take it all of you can be here tomorrow evening? Excellent. I'll text the time to each of you. Please come prepared with cash."

Del hit the End button, closing down the webcams and the connections.

"What are we gonna do with her?" a hulking man name Cyrus asked, pointing at DeGarmo.

"Tie her to the chair. Carefully. Wear gloves. I have a little surprise for her when she wakes up."

Del eyed the unconscious woman. *Lost your talents, huh? Either it was just a ruse, or that pig woke up whatever your concussion put to sleep.*

"Either way," he whispered, "you're gonna be a star tomorrow night."

Tal Nova stared at the telephone and silently cursed the day he'd heard about Leah DeGarmo and her powers. He'd just received word that Del McCormick was holding her captive, had her locked away in some podunk upstate town and was planning an auction of some sort for the top organized-crime families in the world. To sell her to the highest bidder.

The past few days had been the worst Tal could remember since that night in college when his freedom had hung by a thread. After losing DeGarmo, first to McCormick and then to Emilio Suarez and his religious fanatics, he'd been called on the carpet by Marsh, who'd gotten wind of the whole shitstorm through his own underground sources. Tal managed to give a slightly twisted version of what happened and succeeded in convincing the old man that he'd been double-crossed by McCormick (true enough), had tried to rescue the vet (not exactly accurate) and had failed (definitely true).

"Find her," Marsh had told him. "I don't care what it takes. She's too valuable to lose, dammit. This is on your head, Tal. Bring her back to me, alive, unharmed and grateful. And, Tal," he'd said, giving him one of those dead-serious looks of old, "I don't have to tell you what happens if you fail, do I?"

Tal hadn't heard that warning in many years, but he was well aware of the threat behind it. Exposure as a murderer, many times over. Sure, he had his own dirt on Marsh, dirt that would put the old bastard behind bars for the rest of his life. Maybe even enough dirt to get his own death sentence reduced to life without parole.

Maybe we'll get adjoining cells.

Of course, that would never happen. Marsh was a man with too many connections, too much money, to spend any time in the kind of prison where ordinary criminals ended up. No, he'd spend a few years free on bail while his lawyers fought the charges, and then if he did go to jail it would be a minimum-security facility where he'd get to watch TV, eat normal food and not have to worry about getting shanked in the yard.

And me? A black man convicted of multiple homicides? I'll be in general population, lucky if I last a month.

Which put him in a real dilemma, now that he'd located DeGarmo. If he brought the vet to Marsh, played the hero, she'd undoubtedly expose him to Marsh and the police for what he'd really done, and then Marsh would carry out his threat. And if he didn't bring DeGarmo back or she died in the process? Same result. So he was fucked either way.

So what do I do?

There had to be a third option. There always was. He'd built his career by finding creative solutions to impossible problems, had always considered himself pretty good at what the corporate world referred to as "strategic planning". Sure, Del had bested him this time, but only because Tal had never expected a professional like McCormick, whom he'd worked with so often in the past, to double-cross him.

And that's on me. I should have known better than to trust anyone, not when it came to something as unbelievably valuable as DeGarmo. Should've had Suarez and McCormick killed the minute I was done with them.

That was a mistake he'd learn from if he had the chance. Now, though, there were more pressing matters. Still tossing ideas around in his head, he opened a stick of gum and folded it into his mouth. The cinnamon burn triggered a release of saliva and woke his senses better than the strongest coffee.

Options...options. Anything to avoid prison or death.

Wait. That's it. Death. Learn from your mistakes.

What was the way to deal with loose ends? You get rid of them. Like he should have done with McCormick.

And what was Marsh but a loose end?

Like the fiery cinnamon cutting through the staleness in his mouth, a new idea exploded in his brain, cutting through the fog of stale ideas.

Tal smiled and reached for the phone. If all went well, in less than forty-eight hours he'd not only have his current problems solved, but he'd be looking at a very rich retirement.

Leah couldn't stop smiling.

She had a date! A first date. With a guy she actually was attracted to. The kind of date you should be on time for.

And not show up smelling of formaldehyde, either.

Which meant she had to hurry and finish her dissection of the cat she was working on for General Anatomy if she wanted to get back to the dorm, wash the stink off her hands and put on a clean top.

Turning back to the split, skinned and pinned corpse on the dissection board, she reached for her scalpel, her thoughts alternating between the lobes of the lungs and Hank Finn's totally kissable lips.

"Ow!" A sharp, stinging pain brought her attention back to the present. She looked down and saw she'd grabbed the wrong end of the scalpel. The surgical steel had sliced a two-inch gash along her thumb. As she watched, blood welled up and flowed out in a miniature waterfall.

"Oh damn." Instinctively she grabbed her injured thumb with her other hand and looked around for something to pack the wound. Paper towels, Kimwipes, anything. Naturally, there was nothing there.

"Shit. Shit shit shit!" Now she was really going to be late, doubly so if she had to go to the college infirmary for stitches.

Maybe just some Band-Aids... Praying for a shallow cut, she opened her hand and peeked at her thumb.

Under the red smears, a thin separation showed, with dried blood already crusting over the top.

"Wow." Leah breathed a sigh of relief. It was no worse than a paper cut. And yet it had bled so much...

I wonder if—

The buzz of her cell phone interrupted her thoughts. She pulled it from her purse and flipped it open with one hand.

"Leah, are you still in the Anatomy lab?" Kelli Chen's exasperation with Leah's perpetual lateness was evident even through the tiny speaker in the phone. "My God, girl, get your ass in gear or you're gonna stink like hell when he shows up!"

"On my way," she assured her roommate. *I can always come in early in the morning and finish.*

Lessons and cut both forgotten, Leah hurried for the door.

Leah's first thought when she woke up was that she'd fallen asleep on the couch again while reading, something she did more often than she liked to admit. A classic sign of a lonely life. Her dream echoed in her head, and she wondered why she'd thought back to that day her sophomore year in college. Back then, she hadn't been aware how her Power worked on her own cuts and bruises, kept her from catching the flu like other people. It was only years later, as she was finishing vet school, that all the little clues came together. After that, she never really thought about it. So why now? She had so much more—

Reality came barreling back, driving away memories and happy thoughts in an instant. She opened her eyes, afraid of what—or who—she might see.

Across from her was the table with the computer monitors. She tried to move and found she'd been tied—chest, arms and legs—to a wooden chair, probably the same one she'd sat in when Del had threatened her earlier.

Earlier when? she asked herself, which brought back other memories. The pig. Getting knocked down. Then...blacking out? From the numbness in her arms and legs, and the cold that had her shivering, she had to have been out for a while.

Someone cleared their throat off to her right and she turned her head.

Del sat in front of a computer, smiling at her in a way that immediately set her on edge. He looked as smug as a person possibly could, his grin a sure sign she was in worse trouble than she imagined.

"Hey, Doc. Welcome back. How do you feel?" His smile grew a little wider, like a little boy with a secret he couldn't wait to share.

"Cold. Not that you care." In no mood to play his game, she let her disgust for him show in her words. Once again her death had been postponed, and she was tired of waiting. Maybe if she antagonized him enough...

"Oh, but I do care. I care a lot. In fact, I'm happier than you can imagine to hear you don't have any aches or pains."

Aches or... Leah frowned. He was right. Other than being cold and stiff, she felt fine.

The pig.

She remembered it coming right at her. Its hooves. Snapping sounds... Bones breaking? So much pain...

No. It had to be part of her dream. A false memory from hitting her head again. That was it. The pig must've knocked her over, she'd hit her head and imagined the rest.

She looked around again. There was no sign of any destruction, although a faint but suspicious red swatch on the floor had her thinking about the explosion she'd heard just before blacking out. A gunshot? More than likely.

"Doc." Del snapped his fingers. "Pay attention here, okay? Remember what you were telling me earlier? How you're no use to me because you lost your powers? Well, I think you'll find this interesting."

He touched a button on the keyboard and the monitors came to life. A video started, showing a room Leah instantly recognized as the one she was in. Each monitor showed the same scene from a different angle, and as she watched the video play out, a sick feeling started in her stomach. At the point where the frantic pig charged her, Del paused the clip.

"Now watch this part carefully." He tapped one of the monitors. When the video started again, she found herself tensing as the animal trampled her. The sounds of screaming and bones breaking filled her ears.

It wasn't a dream. It was real. No, it couldn't—

"This is my favorite part," Del said, raising his voice over the sounds from the monitors. On one of the screens, the camera zoomed in and she saw two men lift her into the chair. One of them cried out as his hand touched her, but he didn't let go.

Leah's body started to tremble from something other than the cold.

No. Please, no...

The camera zoomed in farther, forcing her to watch as the massive damage to her body healed and disappeared. When her crooked nose slid back into its normal shape, Del touched another key and the screens went blank.

"Lost your powers, huh? I don't think so."

She understood his smile now. He looked like he'd won the lottery because he had. She'd proven what she could do to the people who'd been watching, and now she and John would be prisoners for life.

"What...what are you going to do?"

"That's a good question, and I think you deserve an honest answer. Tomorrow night some very bad men are going to come here, and I'm going to sell you to one of them. Of course, they'll want a live demonstration of your power, so your cop friend might have a few uncomfortable minutes. But if you're lucky, you'll be able to convince whoever buys you that you and your lover come as a pair."

He was basically admitting he'd be selling her into slavery, except she'd be raped in a different way. "Do you know what they'll do with me?"

"What the hell do I care? As long as I get my money, your next owner can spend the rest of his life having you keep his kids' pets alive. Of course, I'm guessing that what you'll end up doing will be a lot more dangerous, but then I figure you know that as well as I do."

"And that doesn't bother you?"

Del shrugged. "Honestly? No."

"You're a real piece of shit." Leah allowed all her contempt and anger to color her words.

Without warning, Del stood up and grabbed her by the hair, pulling her head against the back of the chair. He'd moved so fast she didn't even have time to cry out.

"Listen, lady. You don't know what makes me tick. There's a lot of fucking crap in this world that bothers me, but I know better than to try and get in its way. If these people want someone dead, that's what's gonna happen. All I'm doing is selling them a new weapon, no different than a gun or a knife. And trust me, I thought long and hard about this. I know what happens to people who know a secret. I'll be spending the rest of my life looking over my goddamned shoulder."

He let go and sat down again, his face returning to his normal calm expression.

"But at least I'll be looking over my shoulder in a beautiful beachside villa instead of a crummy New York apartment."

Leah stared at him. She wanted to scream out her frustrations, tell him what a horrible person he was, but she saw it would be no use.

Because he was crazy.

You wouldn't know it if you walked past him on the street, might not even notice it if you sat down and had a cup of coffee with him. But it was there, a deeply buried nugget of insanity, cloaked by ordinary looks and a friendly smile.

Not insane enough to shoot his golden goose, though, came the bitter thought. No, he was much too smart to do that.

And even if he did, what would it matter? He's not going to kill me, and apparently any other injury will just heal.

"Hey. Anybody home?"

With a start, she realized she'd become lost in her thoughts.

"What now?" she asked, expecting that she'd be locked up again until she was needed.

"I'm a man who keeps his promises," Del said, standing up. "You kept your part of our bargain, and now I'm keeping mine. Unless you don't want your conjugal visit?"

"My...?" Then it hit her. "John? I can see him?" As much as she'd told herself earlier that the best thing for both of them would be for her to be gone, the desire to be with him had never faded. In the battle between emotion and logic, logic might think itself the winner but emotion always ruled in the end.

"He's all yours from now until tomorrow morning. I'd make the best of it, if I were you," he added, opening the door and signaling to his men. Two of them came in and untied her.

The thought of seeing John again, hearing his voice, feeling his touch, had her so keyed up she hardly noticed Del's men gripping her arms with bruising force as they led her down the hall and into a different corridor, one that was even colder and fouler smelling than her own.

The moment they opened the door, she rushed inside, exclaiming John's name as he stood up.

"Leah?" The look on his face changed from shock to relief and joy, all in the few seconds it took her to cross the room.

The door slammed shut, locking them inside the murky room, but Leah didn't care. All that mattered was John's arms around her again, his chest pressed against hers, the wonderfully safe, sweaty smell of his body replacing the odor of death in her nose.

How long they stood there, embracing in silence, she didn't know, but eventually he stepped back.

"Are you all right? Did they hurt you? Did they make you...?"

She shook her head, wishing he didn't look so gaunt. She doubted he'd slept at all, unless he'd been drugged like her, and she wondered if he'd been fed or had anything to drink.

"I'm okay. They...they want to sell me to terrorists or the mob!" She hadn't planned on telling him right away, but everything just came pouring out in a flood of words and tears. Del's plans, the fact that she had her Power back and could apparently Cure herself.

"The worst part is he said whoever buys me might not want you, that I might have to convince them to take you too."

"Hey, it's okay." John wrapped her in his arms again, pulled her close. When he spoke, she felt his words against her cheek. "We'll figure something out. We've come this far, we're not going to give up now."

Leah sniffed back tears and mucous. "Del said...he said they were going to kill us both if I couldn't Cure anymore."

"If you couldn't... Wait." He pulled back from her. "Anymore? What do you mean? Is that...is that why you left?"

"No." She shook her head, feeling more tears ready to come on, this time the burning tears of shame. She'd never thought she'd have to explain why she'd run away. "I left because I thought maybe if I was gone you'd be safe.

After everything that happened to you, all because of me...I couldn't bear the thought of you getting hurt again."

"I can understand you feeling like that, but, Jesus Christ, couldn't you have talked to me first before taking off? I was worried sick. You should have known I'd go looking for you. If you'd stayed at the motel, we might not even be here now."

"I know!" Leah moved away, wishing there were something she could kick or punch, but the room was barren except for the single dusty light bulb overhead and a large blanket on the floor. "I was stupid and got us in more trouble."

"Hey, I'm sorry." John put his hand out but she stepped away. "I didn't mean it like that. I just... We work together better as a team than by ourselves. If we're gonna get out of this alive, we have to stick together, not be selfish."

"Selfish?" She turned to face him. "Is that what you think I was being? I was trying to save you."

"That's what you intended, but you were selfish because you weren't thinking about what I wanted, or how your actions would affect me. You came up with an idea and just did it. That's not how partners act."

"I'm not your partner." Leah knew she sounded like a petulant teenager, but his "selfish" comment had struck a nerve.

"That's right, you're not." For the first time, a note of anger crept into John's voice. "I thought you were more than that. Maybe I was wrong."

"You did? Think I was more than that?" Leah's heart did a happy dance. Did he mean what she thought he meant?

"Of course." John reached for her, and this time she didn't shy away. He took her hands in his, gripped them tight. "I know it's only been a couple of weeks, but I'm crazy about you. I was really hoping that we could...that this would...you know," he finished lamely.

Unable to resist a little teasing, Leah shook her head. "No, I don't," she said. "What do you mean?" She tried to hold back a smile but couldn't. Ever observant, John noticed it right away. He opened his mouth to respond, but she put her finger against his lips, stopping him.

"I know exactly what you mean," she whispered, pressing herself closer to him. "I feel the same way. And you were right; I was acting selfish and stupid. I'm sorry."

"Apology accepted," he said, his lips moving against hers as they both leaned toward each other. The kiss went quickly from a gentle pressure to full-on lip-smashing, tongue-wrestling passion. When they finally separated, they were both out of breath.

"Wow," John said. "That was—"

"Nothing compared to what's coming." Leah gave him a wink and started to unbutton her blouse.

"Wait." John looked around the room. "This isn't very private. I'm sure they have cameras hidden somewhere."

"So let them watch." She dropped her shirt and reached back to unsnap her bra, part of her amazed she was acting so boldly, part of her too fed up to give a damn. "This might be our last night together. I don't intend to waste it."

Her bra joined her shirt on the floor, and from the look in John's eyes, she knew he no longer cared about cameras either.

Then she let her thoughts go blank and lost herself in the magic of John's hands and mouth.

And she made sure he couldn't call her selfish.

Chapter Six

Tal Nova had just turned his computer off and grabbed his jacket when the intercom buzzed, eliciting a quick curse. He'd hoped to make a quick exit without talking to the old man.

He picked up the phone.

"Hello, Mr. Marsh."

"I just got information on where the DeGarmo woman is being held."

"If it's a meat-packing plant in Elmira, I got the same news a few minutes ago and I'm prepping a team to head up there." Another half-truth, but one the old man would be so happy to hear he wouldn't bother checking the details.

"Good. This is a top priority, Tal. I want her brought home unharmed and filled with gratitude for her rescue. Take the lead on this yourself. Don't let me down."

"I never have be—"

The line went dead, cutting Tal off. He stared at the phone for a moment before setting it softly into its cradle. This was one of those assignments where Marsh would brook no failure.

Tal smiled. He had no intention of failing.

Although in a day or so, Marsh would be wishing he had.

Leah nestled in the crook of John's arm, doubly comforted by his warm strength and the gentle feel of his chest rising and falling against her back. The afterglow of their lovemaking had quickly faded in the chilly air of their cell, so they'd dressed and lain down on the blanket, ostensibly to share warmth but, for Leah at least, it was also a desperate desire to hang on to their intimacy for as long as they could. She had no idea when Del's men would come for her, and if she'd ever see John again.

Well, that's not quite true, is it? she reminded herself. *You'll see him at least once more. When you have to Cure him.*

They'd talked for a while after snuggling up together, generalities and I-love-yous mostly, both of them avoiding any mention of impending death. She'd sensed John wanted to bring up the subject of escape, but each time he'd hinted in that direction—*"I wonder where they have the cameras hidden... How many men have you seen in this place?"*—she changed the topic, either by kissing him or mumbling sweet nothings against his neck, until he finally got the hint and stopped trying. Shortly after that, she'd rolled over and pulled his arms across her like a blanket, telling him she wanted to get some rest.

Even if the threat of death or slavery hadn't been hanging over her head, Leah doubted she'd have been able to fall asleep. The frigid cement was an inanimate vampire, sucking the warmth from her body, even with the rough blanket folded double beneath them. And despite her long exposure to it, the stench in the air still hit her at odd moments, proving you could never really get used to such an awful smell. Not to mention that lying on the floor with an arm as your only pillow was not exactly comfortable.

An involuntary shiver ran through her, and John's arms tightened in response.

"You awake?" he whispered, his breath rustling her hair so that it tickled her neck, sending another shiver down her back.

"Yes." She bit her lip, feeling a strong premonition of what was coming next. What was it about lying in a dark room that brought on serious conversations you hoped to avoid?

"Tomorrow, when it's time to cure me—"

"John, I don't want to think about—"

"Stop talking and listen. This is important."

She was about to interrupt again when she remembered their earlier conversation about selfishness and her promise not to be that way anymore. As much as it was going to hurt her to hear his words—and she *knew* what he was going to say—she owed it to him to listen. It was the courteous thing to do.

No, it was the *right* thing to do.

After a brief pause, he continued, "When it's time, don't cure me. Without me, they have no leverage against you. It's your only chance."

Conflicting emotions raced through Leah at John's words. On the one hand, she felt like laughing at a police officer who could be so naïve. On the other, she was shocked that he'd surprised her; she'd been sure he'd come up with some desperate escape plan, like for her to Cure him and then they'd attack the guards. Instead, all he had was a weak idea to sacrifice himself, leaving her alone to face the consequences. Talk about selfish...then it hit her that she'd planned on doing the same thing only a few hours ago.

I guess we're not so different.

She took a deep breath before responding, choosing her words carefully so as not to offend him.

"John, it wouldn't work. Even without you, they have plenty of leverage. They know where my parents live. Or they could just bring in strangers. Do you think I could stand there and let more people die because of me?"

She rolled over to face him in the dim light. His breathing sent sour odors her way, and she knew her breath had to be just as bad—two days of nothing but coffee and junk food, with no toothbrush—but she didn't care. The worst morning breath in the world would still smell better than the air in the building.

"No, I don't think that." His lips turned up slightly. "I guess it was a pretty stupid idea."

"Yeah." She smiled back. "We've had our share of those these past few days, huh?"

"Couple of real idiots, that's us."

"Well, you did have one good idea," Leah said.

"What was that?"

"You asked me out. I was so scared to say yes, but that was the best thing that's happened to me in years."

John's smile grew wider and took on a wicked glint. "Not as good as your idea."

185

"My idea?" Leah frowned. "For what?"

"This." He leaned forward and placed his lips against hers. At the same time, his hand slipped between them to cup one of her breasts. Despite her exhaustion and fear, she felt her body respond instantly to his touch.

And after he'd brought her to another screaming climax, she actually managed to fall asleep.

"Damn," Ken Pollack said to his watch partner, Eddie Spring, "I wouldn't mind getting me some of that."

"Take it easy." Eddie kept his eyes on the monitor, where grainy versions of the two captives had just gotten dressed and lain down again. "If Del even thinks you got ideas about touching her, he'll cut you from ear to ear, and he won't be letting the lady fix you."

"Yeah, I know. Still...hey, are they doin' it again?" Ken leaned closer to the screen.

"Naw. Looks like she's havin' a nightmare." Eddie laughed. "I'd be havin' bad dreams too if my ass was gettin' sold to some A-rabs."

"You think that's who's gonna buy her?" Ken opened a can of soda and took a long drink.

Eddie, a swarthy man with a fat ridge of scar tissue down the side of his neck, nodded. "That's my guess. Goddamn terrorists got more money than the Colombians or the mob."

"I'll take a piece of that action. Ten bucks says the Colombians. They're always trying to kill each other."

"You're on." Eddie wagged his chin in the direction of the monitor. "This time tomorrow, that cell's gonna seem like paradise."

"This time tomorrow, I'm gonna be whackin' off to a copy of that tape," Ken said, and they both burst into laughter.

On the screen, Leah continued thrashing back and forth on the blanket.

Chapter Seven

In Leah's dream, Death had her pinned face-first against a glass wall, his bony fingers gripping her neck and arm, his shoulder pressing against the back of her head, smashing her nose and lips against the glass. On the other side of the window, dwarfish imps, their bodies bathed in the green aura of sickness, danced around John's naked body, poking him with poisoned sticks. Although no sound reached Leah's ears, she knew he was screaming in pain, could tell by his wide-open mouth and taut neck muscles.

"Stop it!" she shouted, but Death just laughed and squeezed harder. Sharp nails dug into her flesh and she felt blood running down her back.

"They're killing him! I can save him!" She tried to break loose but the skeleton in the black robes was too strong.

"You can't save him this time, Leah," Death said, his ice-cold voice whistling through the bones of his chest and mouth like a winter wind. "Sometimes evil is stronger than good."

"I don't believe that," she whispered, but doubt colored her words, causing Death to laugh harder until he sounded like a freight train racing towards her.

"Do you really want to save him?" Death asked, his teeth clacking together right next to her ear.

"Yes." She tried to nod and her lips smeared the window.

"Would you do anything to keep him alive?" Now the voice was as soft as hers, each word an icy spider scurrying across the nape of her neck.

"Yes." She meant it too, but the admission brought with it a new fear, a fear that she'd just started a journey there was no coming back from.

"Good girl." The pressure against her disappeared. Leah turned around, expecting to see Death gone or retreated.

Instead, she found him less than a foot away, his fleshless mouth somehow grinning madly at her. Before she could do more than gasp, he thrust his hands forward, the bones of his fingers knifing into her chest as easily as sticks into mud. Leah shrieked in pain, each individual stab wound clear and agonizing. The assault grew worse, Death's wrists and arms following the fingers' lead. Talons pierced her lungs, robbing her of the ability to shout or breathe. Wide-eyed and helpless, she watched as Death pulled himself into her through the gaping hole between her breasts, his body deforming and twisting so that somehow the grinning skull remained staring at her while the rest of him raped her flesh. Then, with an impossible wink of one empty eye socket, skull and hood slipped inside her.

Only then did she have the breath to scream.

"No!"

Leah sat up, clutching at her chest. Next to her, John rolled over and got to his knees, hands up, ready to defend them. With his hair sticking up in all directions and his eyes wild with fear, he looked like a crazy homeless man.

It was that incongruous vision that calmed Leah more than anything.

"John! It's okay! It was just a bad dream." She placed a hand on his knee. He continued darting his gaze back and forth for another couple of seconds before his eyes narrowed and he looked at her.

"What? Are you... A dream?" His chest rose and fell in rapid motions, and she realized he must have been shocked out of a deep sleep by her shout.

"I'm sorry." Her other hand joined its partner on his leg. "I had a nightmare. I didn't mean to wake you."

"Wake me?" He took a deep breath and managed a tiny smile. "Jesus. You scared the freaking shit out of me!"

"Sorry," she repeated, feeling terrible for frightening him.

"It must have been a bad one." He took her hands in his, their warmth a reminder of just how cold she was. He must have noticed, too, because he switched from holding her hands to wrapping his arms around her.

"I've had better," she said, trying to make light of the nightmare. The attempt fell flat and she shook her head. "I dreamt about Death. A real shock, huh? No shrink needed to interpret that one."

John said nothing, just held her tighter, and she appreciated that. Sometimes a person didn't want words or advice or platitudes when they were upset, just a comforting touch. And one of the things she liked—no, *loved*—about John was his ability to know when to try and solve a problem, and when to just be there.

"John, I'm scared." She hadn't meant to say it; the words just popped out without warning. Once voiced, though, she felt better. As if admitting the fear was the first step in conquering it.

"I know," John whispered, stroking her hair. His touch was at once relaxing and sensual. "I know. Only a crazy person wouldn't be. But we'll figure something out. They need you alive, which means we'll have the opportunity to escape or call for help, or something. Even if you have to..." His voice trailed off, but Leah had a pretty good idea of what he meant.

Even if I have to use my Power to kill one of them.

The thought of it brought on a sudden anxiety. She didn't think John had any qualms about it; he was probably just being careful not to say too much, in case people were listening. Of course, he wasn't the one who had to consider murdering someone. She'd be the one who'd have to carry that guilt forever.

But why should you feel guilty? It's self-defense, not murder. You've done it before.

She thought about the man she'd killed in McDonald's. It seemed like a lifetime ago, although only a couple of weeks had passed. She felt no guilt about that, not anymore. And the man in the warehouse, the one who'd died because he touched her at the wrong time. That wasn't even her fault, she'd been unconscious. And she'd certainly been ready to kill Tal Nova on more than one occasion.

So why the desire to avoid killing now, even if it meant saving her and John's lives? Because it was premeditated?

It's not, though. It's just planning for a possible situation. A situation where if I don't do it we'll be prisoners forever.

The more she considered it, the more it seemed that guilt wasn't the problem. There was something else, something like fear, but colder, that gripped her whenever she thought about killing someone. The kind of fear better associated with opening the door to a dark cellar when you didn't know who or what was waiting for you at the bottom of the stairs.

A fear of the dark...

The pieces of the puzzle clicked. *The dream.* Death, wrapped in darkness, entering her, telling her good can't win.

I'm afraid there's an evil inside me, and killing someone will release it.

But that was stupid, wasn't it? She'd already killed—twice—and nothing happened. She was still the same person. Besides, if using her Power to kill was going to release some kind of supernatural evil, then what about all the animals she'd killed over the years? Why would that be any different? It boiled down to the same thing, after all: remove something bad here, insert something bad there. Take Death from point A and place it in point B.

It was all part of the same Power, the yin and the yang of it.

"God, I am such an idiot." She didn't realize she'd voiced the thought until John responded.

"What? Why?"

"That priest and those men with him, they convinced me I was evil, that my Power was something bad. That it came from the devil, not God."

"And I told you not to listen to them, remember?"

"I do. But you were wrong too. It's not a Power from the devil, or from God. It's not good or bad, it's just a thing. A thing I can do. The good or bad part comes from me. It's no different than any other kind of tool. Think about it. Guns, radiation, lasers, chemicals—they can all be used for good or bad purposes."

"I get it." One of John's eyebrows went up as he stared at her. "So what's this all mean for you?"

Leah shrugged. "That I feel better about myself. Even if someone forces me to do something I don't want to, I'll know I'm not a bad person, just a regular person in a bad situation."

She shook her head and let herself laugh a little. "Too bad my big epiphany doesn't involve any ideas for escape."

"Maybe it will. Maybe this will help you clear your head and—"

The sound of the door being unlocked cut short John's words. They both turned as the door opened, revealing four men holding pistols.

"On your feet," one of the men said. "Time to go."

Leah gripped John's hand.

"I love you," John whispered.

"I love you too."

Then two men pulled her away and led her down the hall. Her last glimpse of John was his back as he was dragged in a different direction.

And then he was gone.

Two miles away from the meat-packing plant where Del McCormick was preparing to start his auction, Tal Nova stood in front of his extraction team, anticipating the brutal destruction they were about to unleash. He'd handpicked the entire group, ten of the nastiest guns for hire he knew. He'd used them all before, mostly for wet work in Third World countries where fear and bloodshed got things accomplished much more quickly and effectively than diplomacy or even cash. At least three of them were wanted for questioning by Interpol and the FBI—three that he knew of. It wouldn't be a stretch to figure there were others. It had cost Tal serious cash and favors to get them all into the country unnoticed. The cost would be well worth it, though, if he ended up with DeGarmo in his possession.

Watching McCormick endure a slow, painful death would be the icing on the proverbial cake.

"All right, it's just about go time." Tal looked at the men, all of them armed to the teeth. "You all know the drill, right?"

"Capture the girl alive, kill everyone else," one of the mercenaries, a hulking man almost equal in size to Tal, said.

"Emphasis on 'capture the girl alive'. I need her unhurt, understand? We are expendable, she isn't."

The men nodded.

"Okay. Let's move out."

Tal checked his own weapon and then followed them to the waiting vehicles.

Chapter Eight

With every new person the guards escorted into the room, Leah felt her spirits sink even further. Each one seemed more dangerous than the last, despite their expensive suits and polite mannerisms. Six men in all, of varying ethnicities. They said very little, so she couldn't ascertain their accents, but at least two seemed Middle Eastern, with thick, unkempt beards, and one Italian, with swarthy good looks. Another, pale-complexioned and broad-shouldered, appeared to be Russian or of some similarly Slavic origin.

Criminals. Terrorists and mobsters, most likely. They stared at her from across the wide room with varying expressions of hunger, eagerness and suspicion that made her feel degraded, as if she was nothing more to them than a piece of meat.

And in a way, that's true. This is the modern version of a slave auction, with me as the slave girl.

There was no compassion in these men, no hope for respect. Their gaze promised brutal treatment and suffering, worse than anything Del or Tal Nova had done to her.

The door opened a final time and Del walked in, his smiling countenance the total opposite of the hard looks his guests wore.

"Good evening, gentlemen," he said while his guards took up strategic places around the room. "Thank you for coming. I know several of you have traveled a good distance to be here, so I won't waste your time."

"This better not be bullshit." The man who'd spoken, a skeletally thin black man with more gold on his fingers than Leah had in her entire jewelry box, cast a scowl in her direction.

"I assure you, this is not bullshit." Del went to a small desk, which held a laptop. It showed a revolving screen saver, the same image displayed on the large flat-screen TV positioned at one end of the table where the six criminals sat. Leah had been placed in a chair off to one side, but she could still see the TV.

Del touched a button on the keyboard and the picture on both screens switched to a view so grotesque Leah felt herself go numb. John, seated in a chair, surrounded by deadly-looking hooks that dangled from the ceiling. Two armed guards stood a few feet away.

An involuntary gasp made it past Leah's lips before she clamped her mouth tightly closed. It was too late, though; several of the men at the table glanced her way. One of them raised an eyebrow and turned toward Del.

"You're wondering about her reaction?" Her captor nodded to the group. "Consider him the carrot on the stick. Please watch carefully. Go ahead."

Del's voice had risen, and one of the guards with John looked up and flashed an okay sign. Then he turned and pulled out a pistol.

John's eyes went wide.

"No!" Leah jumped up as she screamed, knowing what was about to happen.

Rough hands forced her back into her chair.

On the screen, the guard pulled the trigger. There was a sound like a child's cap gun going off and John tumbled off the chair. A black hole in his shirt disappeared as a red stain quickly formed in the center of his stomach.

"Let me go!" Leah struggled against her guard's iron-strong grip. "He's going to die if I don't get there."

"Not just you, Doc." Del nodded to the guards and they opened the door. "We're all going, so these gentlemen can see firsthand what you can do."

Leah fought harder to break free, but her struggles were in vain until all prospective buyers had left the room. Only then did the guards let her up. She ran for the door, where another guard took her arm and guided her down a side corridor.

"Hurry!" She tried to pull free but the man held her arm too tightly. "Please!"

They rounded a corner and she saw the others entering a room a few doors down. The guard let her go and she raced down the hall.

She was only a few feet away when the world exploded around her.

John stared at the sky and wondered why it was so dark. Was it going to rain? He was cold, but it was a good cold. It numbed him, took the pain away. He'd been shot. In a room. So why was he in the water now, sinking down. So hard to breathe. Drowning? That didn't make sense. He was waiting for Leah. Where was she?

How would she find him in the water?

The sky grew darker and he closed his eyes.

I'll just rest until she finds me.

Tal Nova ran down the corridor in a crouch, a pistol in one hand and his other pressed against the earpiece he wore so he could hear the updates from his team over the noise of shouting and gunshots. The concussion grenades had done their job, putting at least half of McCormick's men out of commission. Those deeper in the building were fighting back to some degree; the rapid *bang-bang-bang* of automatic weapons echoed through the hallways, but it was a losing battle against superior firepower. Already he was hearing reports of clear corridors and rooms.

He'd split away from the team as soon as the shooting started, knowing Del's instinct for self-preservation would have him heading in a direction away from the conflict. And wherever Del McCormick was, DeGarmo would be with him.

Turning a corner, Tal nearly stumbled over the very person he was looking for: Leah DeGarmo. She lay on the floor, moaning, her hands over her ears. He assumed she'd been at the periphery of one of the blasts; had it caught her full-on, she'd have been out cold. After checking to make sure no one else was around, he leaned down and poked her with his gun.

"Hey! Can you hear me?"

She let out a scream when she saw him.

Her expression quickly changed from fear to something worse, a combination of terror and hatred that made Tal's heart sing. Not only did she recognize him, but she was aware enough to remember how dangerous he was.

"Get up," he said, motioning with the gun.

She reached out to him and he backed up a step, shaking his head.

"Don't even try to touch me. Now get your ass up." He motioned again, in case she couldn't hear him.

Without warning, she lunged at him.

He reacted without thinking, his finger instinctively squeezing the trigger, a reflex ingrained in him by hundreds of hours spent training for, and experiencing, life-or-death situations.

The hollow-point bullet caught her in the right shoulder, tearing a fist-sized hole through her and sending her back-first against the wall.

"Goddammit!" Nova stared at her body. Blood poured from her wound and her eyes had already closed. How could he have been so stupid? He'd always prided himself on thinking before acting, and now he'd gone and fucked up everything for himself.

Then again, maybe not, he thought, noticing a slight movement. Her chest was rising and falling, which meant she was still alive. If he could get her back to the van, they had emergency medical equipment there, and at least two of his mercenaries had battlefield first aid training.

He holstered his weapon and knelt down. Before he could slid his arms under her and lift her, her eyes opened and her lips twitched. He bent closer to hear what she was trying to say. Her hand closed over his wrist.

Tal Nova screamed as fire filled his veins.

Leah knew only darkness and pain. They surrounded her, encased her in walls of black fire. There was no conscious thought, no sense of body or mind. Just endless torture.

Just when she thought she might explode from the pain, a glowing sun appeared in the distance, its light enticing her with salvation from the eternal hell of her existence. Without being aware of moving, she reached for the golden promise of deliverance.

The moment she touched it, the brilliance poured through her, melting through the burning dark in waves of cool, soothing pleasure that was like nothing she'd ever felt before. Better than an ice-cold drink quenching a parched throat, better than stepping into a frigid mountain stream on a hot day. She let the waves wash over her, wanting to bathe in them forever. As the yellow light grew stronger, she felt its energy recharging her, revitalizing every cell in her body. In her mind she shouted with laughter as conscious thought returned.

This was it! She'd finally reached heaven!

Leah opened her eyes, wanting to see the beauty of the afterlife.

And found herself face-to-face with a monster.

All of Leah's good feelings shattered at the sight of the shriveled, twisted mummy standing less than a foot away from her. She cried out and jerked away, but it followed.

It's got me! It's got—

Realizing she was holding on to the creature and not the other way around, she let go, her hand unclenching like she'd grabbed a red-hot pan. The thing slowly toppled backwards and hit the floor next to her, its limbs as shrunken and deformed as its face.

Leah gasped as she recognized the monster for what it really was.

The corpse of Tal Nova.

Her first thought was *What the hell happened to him?* But even as the words took shape in her mind, a cold suspicion followed in its wake, an impossible idea that nevertheless wouldn't go away once it had formed.

The beautiful light in the dark.

A fear like nothing she'd ever felt before took root in her guts.

She remembered Tal pointing the gun at her. Deafened by the explosion, disoriented, she'd reached out to him, desperate for help.

Had he shot her?

She couldn't recall. But it seemed likely, based on what she did remember—the terrible pain, the darkness. It made sense. He'd always been afraid of touching her, ever since the night in her clinic. So in his fear, he'd shot her, at close range.

She'd been dying.

And the light in the darkness? Tal? His essence, his life force? Had she somehow sensed it? Touched him?

The light growing stronger. That was me drawing the life from his body. My Power working...in reverse? Instead of passing on my injury, I used him to Cure myself.

The epiphany struck her with the force of a fist to her stomach.

She'd known for a long time she could heal her own body. Had understood in her subconsious even before she admitted it to herself. Cuts and bruises that faded faster than they should. Never getting sick. But until the concussion... the pig... she'd never realized she could Cure serious injuries just as easily. And she'd never considered how. After all, she'd never passed those injuries on to anyone or anything.

She looked again at Tal's dessicated form. Remembered seeing Del's guard jump and cry out when he handled her battered, broken body.

All these years I've been taking something from the people around me, their energy. Storing it inside me.

"Jesus," Leah whispered to herself, "I'm like a vampire."

It all made sense. All the physical contact of daily life—shaking hands, holding animals, brushing up against people, maybe even just being near people—each time, she took a tiny bit of their healthy energy and stored it like a battery.

To be used when she needed it.

Like with Tal Nova. She'd drained him, pulled every last bit of life out of him. More than enough to Cure her wounds; that was why she'd felt so wonderful, so full of...

Life.

Life. Oh my God.

"John."

The rest of her memory returned. That was where she'd been going. He'd been shot too. Then the explosion. Tal—he must have attacked Del's hideout to get her. His men might be searching for her right now. To take her away.

Away from John.

She stood up. How long had she been unconscious? They'd shot John in the stomach. Was he still alive? She had to find him.

She took off in the direction they'd been taking her.

Chapter Nine

Leah found John less than a minute after leaving the corpse of Tal Nova behind, but the delay had been costly.

He was dead.

She wanted to shout her anger at God and the heavens, beg them to bring him back. She'd arrived only a few minutes too late, after fighting through the smoke and dust that filled the hallways.

A few minutes too late. His body was still warm, despite the icy air of the meat locker they'd left him in. However, the puddle of blood growing cold and tacky beneath him was no longer spreading. Frustration, anguish and hatred raged inside her. Damn Tal Nova! Even in his final act of life, he'd still managed to ruin hers.

A few minutes. That's all she would have needed. Del would have let her Cure John—*wanted* her to Cure him—and then they could have done whatever they liked with her. Sold her to the mob. Let Nova bring the whole damn building down on top of her. As long as John was alive.

But no.

Instead, she'd been knocked senseless, unconscious just long enough to make her too late to save him.

She knelt on the frigid cement, staring at his face. He looked too serene. Death shouldn't look that calm. He'd died waiting for her to save him, waiting for the miracle inside her, the miracle that never came.

Were his last thoughts that I let him down?

Guilt gnawed at her insides, a vicious, starving animal that wanted to swallow her whole. He'd trusted her, counted on her, depended on her.

She'd betrayed that trust. Not on purpose, but purpose didn't matter. Only results mattered.

And the result was she'd failed when it mattered most.

"Oh, John, I'm so sorry."

Leah reached down and paused.

He's only been dead a few minutes.

The room couldn't be much more than forty degrees.

The brain stays viable longer in the cold...

Leah slammed her hands down on John's chest before the logical part of her brain could force her to consider the possible consequences.

The agony that raced into her was so much worse than anything she'd ever felt before. It was beyond pain, a misery so profound that just being aware was pure torment. It was Death, a wave of darkness both fiery hot and icy cold at the same time, a river of dry ice pouring through her veins and stopping her heart. Writhing fingers of sorrow and despair tore into her brains with claws made of acid, until she couldn't take it any longer.

She closed her eyes and let it consume her.

Life! It filled every vessel in John's body, stuffed his cells to overflowing. There were no words to describe the feeling, but he knew it for what it was.

Life.

A butter-yellow sun rose in his brain, casting warmth and goodness over everything. He recognized Leah's Power immediately, similar to the other times he'd felt it, but so much stronger. He imagined it was how plants felt each morning when the first rays of sun touched them, triggering the creation of energy, turning on the machine of growth.

The pure ecstasy of it coursed through him, wakening his arms, his legs, his fingers, his individual hairs. His heart started up, strong and proud. No faltering, no hesitations. He wondered if it had stopped, and if that meant he'd died. And if he'd died, where had he been?

He didn't care.

His lungs woke and he drew in a deep breath. Breathing meant life, not afterlife, which was fine by him. He inhaled again, savoring each distinct aroma. Smoke. Dust. Rotten meat.

Leah.

It was her. A scent that was part apple shampoo, part body wash and part sweat. The same odors that had filled his nose the previous night, as they'd lain together after making love.

She was there, and it had to be her power he felt bringing him back to life. John opened his eyes.

And wondered if he was in hell.

A walking corpse from a horror movie leaned over him, wearing Leah's face and clothes. Her skin was bluish gray, her eyes a deathly milky white. Her hair fell in limp strands around her shoulders. Her mouth gaped wide, frozen in a soundless scream. Waves of terrible cold radiated from her, cold and something else, something that physically repelled him. It was nothing he could see or touch, but it was there.

As a cop he'd trained himself to trust his instincts. And those instincts were telling him to run the fuck away.

Leah stared at him with her dead eyes and he shrank back, trying to put space between them. His repulsion grew worse. He felt defiled by her gaze, as if just being near her was contaminating his soul.

She reached out with one hand and his bladder released.

This is it. I'm going to die.

There would be no coming back if she touched him. No miracle to save him.

Her hand grew closer and he felt the corruption and freezing cold rippling down from it. Burning him from the inside out.

Two men in combat gear appeared in the doorway. One of them shouted and raised his gun. Fired at Leah.

The bullets punched holes in her side, holes that sealed themselves an instant later. Leah turned and looked at the men.

The one who'd pulled the trigger cried out as blood sprayed out from two gaping wounds under his ribs. The other soldier turned and ran.

Leah stood up and headed for the door.

John watched her leave, torn between thinking he should follow her and wanting to get as far away from her as possible. Out in the hallway someone screamed and then went silent, his cry cut off in the middle.

Someone else is dead.

At some basic level John understood that anyone near Leah was in danger of dying a horrible death. Just like he understood she was no longer completely human, that she'd changed, succumbed to—or been taken over by—the dark part of her power.

She'd become Death incarnate.

Except she's also Leah. Not on the surface, maybe not even consciously, but Leah is still in there. She cured me. That means...

A sickening thought surfaced. Leah had cured him. Which meant she'd taken his wound into herself, just like the other times. But she'd never changed before. So why now?

What was different?

He'd been shot. That much he remembered. Close range. Right in the stomach. But he'd been shot before and she'd cured it. More than once. So it wasn't being shot that was different.

Did I die?

He'd wondered that same thing while experiencing the euphoria of her cure. If that was true, and she'd tried to cure him anyhow...

It meant she'd taken all his death into herself.

And what Leah took in, she had to release.

"Jesus Christ." Once the idea of it appeared in his mind, it seemed so right he couldn't consider any other possibility. It would be so like Leah to try something like that, even knowing what it could do to her.

Except she probably only expected to die. Maybe even hoped for it, considering her frame of mind the last few days.

She'd have never expected to turn into a monster.

Another scream somewhere in the building, farther away.

She's going to kill them all. And then what? What happens if she still has death to release afterwards? Or worse, if she releases it all and there are still some of Del's men left?

They would kill her.

I can't let that happen.

As much as his mind rebelled against doing it, John got up and made his way to the door.

He had to be there for her when she needed him.

Just like she'd been there for him.

Chapter Ten

The moment the attack started, Del McCormick knew he was in trouble. Based on the reactions of his invited guests—anger, fear—none of them was responsible. Which left only one person.

Tal Nova.

And from the detonations rocking the building, he'd come with a goddamn army. Del's men were well trained and well armed, but they wouldn't stand a chance against what sounded like concussion grenades and explosives.

Time to cut my losses.

A firm believer in being prepared, Del had an emergency escape plan. "Just in case," as he liked to say. He veered down a side hall, no longer concerned about making enemies of the powerful men he'd convinced to attend the demonstration, no longer caring about Dr. Leah DeGarmo and her powers.

Only one thing mattered, and that was staying alive and safe. He could always figure out another way to get the good doctor away from Tal Nova and set up his auction somewhere else.

Things he couldn't do if he was dead.

Two of his guards followed him, which he assumed was out of self-preservation rather than a desire to protect him. Whatever. If they were still with him by the time he left the building, fine. If not, too bad for them. At the end of the hall, he veered right then ducked into the first door he came to. He'd spent some time checking out the old meat-processing plant before bringing DeGarmo in and setting up the different rooms. Each wing of the facility now had one room set aside for emergencies.

Like the other three serving the same purpose, the room contained nothing but a wooden crate with a dirty tarp thrown over it. Del tore the tarp away and opened the lid, revealing an assortment of handguns, a briefcase that contained several IDs and some cash, and three hand grenades.

After grabbing the briefcase, two guns and a grenade, Del told the guards to take what they wanted.

"You're gonna need them before we get out of here," he said, heading for the hall again. By the time they caught up with him, he was several doors down.

His strategy was to make his way through several side hallways to one of the stairwells leading down to the basement. In the basement was an access tunnel that led to another abandoned warehouse next door, which had also been owned by the same company. They shared maintenance functions, such as the boiler room and electrical plant.

The perfect escape route since Nova wouldn't know about the tunnel.

Something exploded a few halls away and Del increased his pace. There was still a good ways to go before he reached the basement, and Nova's men were moving fast.

Maybe they'll find DeGarmo and just leave.

He mentally crossed his fingers as he ran.

Following Leah's path was too easy. Even if you couldn't hear the gunshots and screams, the dead bodies she left in her wake littered the hallways like morbid breadcrumbs left by a deadly Gretel.

John cringed as he came across two more mummies. Like the others he'd seen, it looked like they'd had all the liquid sucked out of them, leaving behind dry husks, skin stretched tightly over bone and mouths open in silent screams. While trying to catch up with Leah, he'd come across several of them. Plus the others—the ones that had died more conventional, although equally gruesome deaths. Limbs missing. Bodies riddled with holes.

He assumed the ones with the bullet holes in them had tried to shoot her. He had no idea how she mummified the others—he had his suspicions, but they were too terrible to contemplate for very long—and he hoped he never had the chance to find out.

Although he feared he would.

He turned a corner at a full run and ended up falling as tried to stop himself. A small group of men stood fifteen feet away, guns pointed at the demonic entity occupying Leah DeGarmo. She looked worse than before, terrifying and yet somehow beautiful, in the way that a tornado or hurricane is frighteningly beautiful even as it destroys a neighborhood. Her hair and clothes whipped back and forth as if she stood in the center of a vortex. Or was transforming into a fury of nature.

John shouted for the men not to shoot, but they paid no attention to his warnings. Three of the six opened fire, their guns filling the hallway with explosive reports. Leah's body jerked back and forth, slugs tearing through her.

Pressed to the floor to avoid the gunfire, John cringed, knowing what was coming next.

The three men who'd fired screamed in unison as bullet holes appeared in their chests and limbs. Blood flew in all directions, splattering their two companions and the walls around them. The three mortally wounded men fell to the floor.

Leaving the other two standing there while Leah walked toward them.

"Run!" John shouted at them. They remained statue-still, frozen in place while the supernatural wind emanating from Leah ruffled their hair and clothing.

Leah ignored them as she passed, but her dark powers didn't. Their eyes went wide and their mouths fell open, whether from pain or terror, John couldn't tell. Then the most awful thing he'd ever seen took place. Their bodies began to shrink inside their clothes, fat and muscle disappearing magically from beneath their skin, which tightened and hardened at the same time. Their eyes first bulged out and then shriveled in their sockets.

By the time Leah was past them, the two men were nothing but stick figures wrapped in flesh-colored jerky.

They tumbled over in her wake.

John's stomach clenched. Now he knew where the mummies came from.

He got to his feet and continued after Leah, this time careful to keep half a hallway between them. A shifting, smoky-black aura appeared around her, pulsating in a weird rhythm that made John think of an octopus's color changes as it glided along the ocean floor.

She moved down the hallways, walking in a slow but steady fashion. There seemed to be no rhyme or reason to her path. She never paused when she reached intersecting halls. Sometimes she continued straight. Other times she would turn left or right. Rarely would she go more than a few hundred feet before encountering more armed men.

None of them survived her passing.

On one occasion, she stopped after crossing a junction and turned around. John froze, certain she'd decided to suck the life out of him as she'd done to so many of the others. But she merely turned down one of the side corridors. After pausing to calm himself and say a quick prayer for being spared, John went after her.

The hall turned out to be a dead end. A half-dozen men were crowded against a set of double doors that refused to open. Two of the men pounded at the lock bars while the others jostled with each other, trying to use their companions as human shields against the advancing Angel of Death that was Leah.

John was about to shout a warning when he noticed something about the men was off. They had the hard-looking faces of career criminals, but they wore expensive designer clothes and carried no weapons. Then he understood.

Those are the men who came to bid on Leah. And possibly me.

Rather than continuing forward, John stepped back and watched from around the corner as Leah drew closer to the group.

Heavy winds buffeted the men. The two at the doors increased their efforts, kicking the unyielding metal and slamming their bodies against the lock bars. The other four cowered together, hands raised and faces turned away from Leah. Although he couldn't hear them, John saw their mouths moving as they cried for mercy.

This time Leah came to a halt a dozen or so feet away. She raised her arms, palms forward. The crazed winds increased to a point where John felt them at the other end of the hall.

One of the men screamed so loud it was audible above the noise of his companions' desperate attempts to break through solid steel.

Then they were all screaming, a horrible chorus of shrieks and wails that made the hair on John's arms stand at attention.

The pulsing aura around Leah grew darker as she drained the life out of the would-be slave owners. Tiny, angry bolts of red lightning flashed silently inside the unearthly glow encompassing her body.

Her victims fell to their knees and tumbled onto their sides, their bodies shriveling into brittle husks. One of them remained standing, withered fingers wrapped in a permanent death grip on the metal push bar of the doors. Open mouths revealed tongues that resembled sunbaked slugs. Wrinkled, shrunken eyes stared out of cavernous sockets like albino prunes.

The gale surrounding Leah dissipated to a heavy breeze. She stood still for a moment, her back to John, framed in the throbbing circle of energy. Then she turned around so quickly it caught John by surprise.

He froze like a rabbit on the highway, pinned in place by Leah's dead eyes. A second later his senses returned and he ducked back around the corner, praying she hadn't had time to see him.

Heavy winds roared down the hall.

Jesus. This is it. I'm dead.

John debated running versus trying to reason with Leah. Could she even be reasoned with? Was she even human still? It was entirely possible she'd died while curing him and was now some kind of otherworldly force or creature.

No. I can't believe that. Leah is still in there somewhere. She has to be. I can't give up on her. She wouldn't give up on me. In fact, if it wasn't for me, she wouldn't be like this at all.

John stepped around the corner to face Death.

And then dove to the ground as gunfire sounded behind him.

Del McCormick cursed his own stupidity for trying to shoot while running at full speed. He'd missed the cop by a mile and now the son of a bitch had gone around the corner and could be in any of a dozen rooms.

Seeing the cop alive had surprised Del only for a moment. Obviously DeGarmo had managed to find him after Tal Nova's men attacked. She'd done her magic on her boyfriend once again. The real question was, where had DeGarmo disappeared to? She couldn't be too far away. Not with the cop right there. Which meant there might still be a chance to grab her and get the hell out of the building.

His two remaining guards close behind him, Del sprinted toward the intersection where the cop had disappeared.

"I want DeGarmo alive!" he shouted to his men. Implicit in his command was the understanding that anyone else was fair game.

Del slowed and threw himself into a forward shoulder roll as he came to the corner. He let his momentum take him to the opposite side of the hallway and rose to one knee, gun aimed ahead of him and ready to fire, his body shielded by the wall.

It was the only thing that saved him.

A blast of air hit him like a hurricane and spun him back and around. His head struck the wall and the hallway disappeared behind a dazzling shower of multicolored stars.

What the—?

The lights faded. He tried to focus on the floor tiles but they kept moving and turning into doubles of themselves.

Seeing double. Explosion. Nova's men. Gotta hide.

Del climbed to his feet, using the wall for support. Somewhere in the other corridor a gun fired and a man screamed. Not trusting his eyesight, Del hugged the wall and felt with his hands until he located a doorknob. Opening it, he entered a room and staggered across it to a stack of broken, moldy wooden crates. With his last few ounces of strength he pushed his way between the shattered frames and the wall.

And then let the darkness claim him.

In the corridor, Del's bodyguards picked themselves up off the floor. One of them rubbed at his eyes, trying to clear the grit and dust from them, while the other shouted for Del.

They were still trying to get their bearings when the impossible became a reality.

Tendrils of black lightning emerged from the side hallway and wrapped themselves around the men before they knew what was happening. The slithering lightning split into twisting vines that snaked across the guards' bodies and burrowed into their ears, mouths and noses. Miniature supernovas of red exploded within the lines of energy. The two men collapsed to the ground in unison, their legs and arms contorting in ways human limbs were never meant to move.

The sound of snapping bones filled the air and the grotesque St. Vitus dance came to an end as the men went still. A moment later, both bodies collapsed into themselves, deflating like empty balloons.

The storm winds picked up again and filled the halls with a roaring sound. Dark-gray fog rolled into the corridor, a ground-level thundercloud inside of which black and red lightning flashed in all directions.

Death marched down the hall in search of its next victim.

Chapter Eleven

John didn't understand what was happening at first. He'd seen Del and two other men coming at him and he'd automatically ducked back around the corner.

Straight into Leah's oncoming path.

There'd been no time to think. He'd sprinted for the closest door and dashed inside. Slammed the door closed and then backed across the empty room. The opaque window in the door obscured his view, but not so much that he couldn't see the hall grow dark. Flashes of weird lightning had splashed the glass with red and howling winds rattled the door in its frame.

At one point, something that looked like a snake made of negative energy slipped under the door and rose up, waving back and forth like an ebon cobra from another world. It had paused for a moment—a moment in which John was sure he was about to die—and then retreated back under the door.

Agonized screams reached John's ears over the shrieking winds. Del? His men? John found he had no regret for their dying. They deserved it for what they'd done, what they'd planned on doing.

His lack of remorse surprised him. He'd always believed that vigilantism was a poor substitute for the law. Criminals taking out other criminals didn't help the system in the long run; it just made it harder to maintain order.

But the retribution Leah was raining down…there was something primal about it. As if Nature herself was pissed off and had decided to do a little cleansing.

And what if that cleansing includes you?

The question came up out of nowhere. John didn't want to believe Leah could ever hurt him. She'd had multiple opportunities and so far he was still alive. Which made him think maybe there was still enough of the real Leah inside the she-demon roaming the halls.

Except, on all those occasions, she'd been distracted by other targets. Maybe she was just going after the worst offenders first.

It did seem like the presence of something—of what? evil? past sins?—attracted her like a magnet. And where did that leave a person who'd basically led a good life but wasn't by any stretch perfect? Last on the list? Or would she leave him and go out into the world, a hurricane of destruction, killing anyone with some type of darkness in their soul?

Was she simply a greater evil than all others, or was she the hand of God, come down to purify the world?

In the end, what she was wouldn't matter. Not to the people outside the building. They'd see her as a threat and deal with her. Do whatever it took to stop her.

Or destroy her.

"Can't let that happen."

John got to his feet. Leah deserved a chance to be normal again. If that was even possible. Which meant he had to be there in case she needed his help. He owed her his life several times over. He wasn't going to let her die because of saving him.

"Okay, God. Let's see if I'm right, that she's not going to suck the life out of me."

His hand shook as he grabbed the doorknob.

If he was wrong, he was going to wish she'd never cured him.

A heavy wind pulled the door from John's hand the moment he cracked it open. Glass shattered as it slammed against the wall. Although whatever was happening was out of sight around the corner, the effects of Leah's supernatural form were evident in the gale-force gusts that swirled through the halls and the flashes of red light in the other corridor.

Someone cried out for help. It didn't sound like Leah, but John broke into a run anyhow, the instinct to provide assistance a part of him after so many years as a cop. He rounded the corner and found the hallway blocked by a roiling cloud of black mist. Reddish lightning flashed inside it, illuminating a vaguely human form that he knew had to be Leah. Dark tendrils of energy—like the ones he'd seen before, but larger now—whipped back and forth and all around, making him think of a wounded octopus. As the hellish nimbus churned the air, John caught a glimpse of two men on the other side.

Men who were writhing on the floor like they'd been plugged into the world's largest electrical socket. The absolute terror on their faces made John glad he couldn't see what new changes had happened to Leah.

He didn't want to know what she looked like, what she'd turned into. He just wanted to make sure she stayed safe. And if there was no chance of her becoming human again, he wanted to make sure he escaped to let someone know about the imminent danger she represented.

One of the night-black tendrils separated from the others and slowly extended in John's direction. He remembered how fast they'd moved before. In contrast to those lightning-fast strikes, this one seemed to be toying with him. Or trying to make up its mind about what to do. Then it rose up a few feet and John knew it was about to attack.

Except before it could, the hallway filled with the metallic chatter of heavy automatic gunfire, large machine pistols, or possibly MACs or HKs. The living storm cloud blocked most of his view, but he saw shadowy figures moving toward where the two men now lay motionless on the floor.

Something zipped past him like a wasp on steroids. Belatedly, John realized he should've hit the ground when the shooting started. Machine pistols packed more than enough punch to tear through a person and kill anyone unlucky enough to be behind the intended target.

So why hadn't he been hit?

Sparkles of light caught his attention. Tiny fireworks were exploding around the edges of the churning cloud that surrounded Leah. He remembered the way the other men had shot at her with no effect.

The safest place to be is right behind her.

John darted forward, positioning himself directly behind the center of the dark mass. He kept one eye on the weaving tentacles as he stayed in step with Leah's protective shield, which was slowly advancing on the men attacking her.

More of the tentacles formed and shot forward.

A second later the gunfire took on a disjointed rhythm and then stopped. Somebody screamed a long, drawn-out wail that was joined by others. Just as quickly, they all ended.

In the resulting silence the sound of John's breathing and the blood pounding in his ears seemed like cannon fire. The cloud ceased its forward movement and dissipated slightly, allowing him a view of a pale, human-shaped object in the center.

An object that was rotating around to face him.

Later, John would thank all the gods in the universe that he never got a clear look at Leah in that moment. He believed with all his soul that seeing her face would have assuredly stopped his heart, like a modern Medusa. Even obscured by layers of gray and black, it was too much to bear, so inhuman that her previous dead-looking countenance was pleasant by comparison.

John fell to his knees as sharp pains coursed through his guts. His bowels threatened to release and he squeezed his eyes closed, petrified the cloud would part and her lethal gaze would melt him on the spot.

A terrible sound filled his head, a cross between insane laughter and the growl of a prehistoric beast. Teeth clenched and body shaking, he waited for the cold touch of a tendril on his neck, a teasing stroke before it wrapped around him and drank the life from his body.

When several heartbeats passed, and then several more, with nothing happening, he carefully opened his eyes.

And found Leah lying unconscious on the floor.

Chapter Twelve

Leah opened her eyes to ghostly faces hovering over her. Three of them, their features blurred to the point where they almost disappeared into the background of gray and white. Smaller shapes moved within the orbs and sounds reached her, timed with the movements.

The faces are speaking, her brain told her. She tried to understand the words, but her hearing was working as poorly as her vision.

One of the faces moved closer.

"Aya. Aya. AYA. C...n...you...ear me?"

Leah wanted to shout at the face to speak more clearly, but when she tried, her lips refused to move. The rest of her seemed paralyzed as well. That worried her. Had she been in an accident? Broken her back or neck? She closed her eyes and tried to focus on her body. See if she could sense what was wrong.

Something sharp jabbed her in the arm and her eyes popped open of their own accord. The face staring at her was a bit clearer now. Familiar.

John?

She still couldn't speak his name, but he seemed to sense she was aware of his presence.

"Leah. You're okay now. Everything will be fine."

Feeling began to return, a pins-and-needles tingling like her foot had fallen asleep, only instead of her foot it was her entire body. She tried again to move, and this time her arm rose up. She reached for John, desperate to feel his touch, to have him comfort her and take the fear away.

He glanced at her hand and backed away.

Why? she wanted to ask him. *What's wrong?* She felt hurt, betrayed, sad and other things that she couldn't express, even to herself. Because it was too hard to think about them.

And she was getting sleepy.

She closed her eyes, unaware of the tears sliding down her cheeks.

Images filled the darkness, a hundred different movies playing on a hundred different screens that surrounded her. No matter which direction Leah looked, dozens of movies played in endless loops.

A man on his knees begging for his life.

A wild-haired demoness floating in a black cloud.

Desiccated mummies crawling across the ground.

John bleeding to death on the floor.

Cement and plaster exploding in a strange hallway.

The face of a dead woman who looked like—

No! That's impossible. I'm not dead. Just dreaming. My eyes were open. I saw…

John.

Had she seen him? Was he still next to her? She pushed at the darkness, trying to force it back. Trying to sense the outside world.

Sounds.

Beeping. Voices.

I'm here! she screamed, but the voice was only in her head. Was she awake or still dreaming? Or in a coma? Did people in comas imagine they were conscious?

Maybe I'm blind. Sudden fear motivated her. She concentrated on her eyes. Feeling them. Moving them.

Opening them.

Straining like she was lifting a heavy weight, she forced her eyelids to rise. Nothing happened at first, and then a pale strip of gray appeared. The strip turned into a small window, and then a larger one. The gray evolved into something brighter, almost white. Shapes appeared. At the same time, the voices and beeps grew clearer.

"—hear me? Leah? Can you hear me?"

"John?" Attempting to speak was an automatic reaction to hearing him. The word came out as more of a whispered croak.

"Hold on," a second voice said. A woman. A hand appeared with a Styrofoam cup. A straw poked out of a plastic lid. It drew closer and Leah eagerly moved to meet it.

Cool liquid touched her tongue and throat, a magic elixir that washed away the dry, scaly feeling from her mouth, moistened the arid tunnel that was her throat, and poured energy into her body with each sip.

The cup pulled away, leaving Leah feeling unsatisfied but a thousand times better.

"That's enough for now. You can have more in a few minutes." The woman stepped away and adjusted a machine next to the bed. "I'll give you two a few minutes."

Woman. Machine. Bed. She's a nurse. I'm in the hospital.

"John?" She turned to the side, afraid she'd hallucinated seeing him before. Memories—real or imagined, she couldn't be sure—jostled each other in her head. *John on the floor, dying. John turning away from her when she needed him.*

John cowering on the ground?

"I'm here." His hand patted hers, and she clutched at it. Real. Solid. Warm. "How are you feeling?"

Leah thought for a moment before answering. How was she feeling? Weak, but her strength was returning. Confused. Tired, the kind of tired that comes from mental exhaustion rather than physical exertion or lack of sleep. But, otherwise, she felt...okay.

"All right, I guess. I... How did I get here? What happened? I remember...I saw you...they..."

John glanced at the door before speaking. "Shot me. But you cured me. Again. I think I'm losing count of how many times that is now."

He gave her a ghost of his usual sunny smile that triggered a twinge of guilt in her chest. He had to be as exhausted as she was. Whatever had happened, he'd undoubtedly been right there with her, just like he'd been there for her all along. He was the one who'd been shot, poisoned and who knew what else. And yet she was the one in the hospital bed, while he watched over her.

"It's me who owes you. I was the one who got you in all this mess, and you're the one who pulled me out of it. Or tried to. I guess I should have listened more."

Continuing as if he hadn't heard her, John asked, "So seeing me get shot. That's the last thing you remember?"

Leah bit her lip as she tried to make sense of the image and memory snippets that were flashing in random fashion through her thoughts. "Del...he ordered them to do it. We watched on the computer... I begged him to let me help you—"

"We?" John interrupted. "We who?"

"The other men," she said, as the scene cleared up in her head. "The ones who came to see what I could do. To buy me."

"Dressed real nice, but tough looking? Some of them were foreigners?"

Leah nodded. From the way he'd said it, she had the feeling he'd seen them. But when?

"Yes. And then Del had his men lead everyone down to the room where you were. And..." She stopped as a new memory popped to the surface.

A mummy lying across her, a dead thing that somehow looked familiar...

"Leah?"

"There was an explosion. In the hall. Someone was pointing a gun at me... Tal Nova! That's who it was. But he didn't shoot me. He...I...I think I did something to him."

She looked at John and saw something in his eyes, something she'd never seen there before. Not fear. Not sympathy, either. Something she couldn't identify, but she knew it wasn't good.

"John. You know something. Tell me."

He stared at her for a minute, his lack of expression betraying the fact that he had bad news for her. Then he sighed, and she recognized the emotion filling his brown eyes.

Pity.

With another sigh, he started speaking.

Leah waited until she was positive John wasn't returning before letting her tears spill out. She wasn't sure what had her crying worse—losing John, knowing she was the cause of his leaving, or finding out she was a monster, something no longer human.

She lay on her side, clutching one of the thin, almost-useless hospital pillows to her chest. It was almost too much to comprehend. She wanted to just close her eyes and sink into dark oblivion. Return to her coma-like state and never wake up. Except now she knew even that would offer no respite from the hell her life had become. John's words—awful enough on their own—had acted like magnets on her broken memories, rounding them up and piecing them together until the whole picture became clear inside her head.

Drawing the death out of John and replacing it with her own life force.

Sucking Tal Nova's essence from him until only a husk remained.

Becoming something other than herself, the opposite of herself, a thing that delivered death instead of life.

Killing the men who'd held her hostage, who'd attacked her.

And worst of all, *enjoying it.*

Most of the previous day was still fuzzy, but parts she remembered were more than enough to let her know she'd turned into a freak. A monster. She'd sensed John hadn't told her everything, either. He'd been vague about describing what she looked like when he encountered her in the hall. But she'd seen how his face turned pale, how his hands trembled in his lap.

Whatever he'd seen—whatever she'd *been*—it hadn't just frightened him.

It had *terrified* him.

Which was why she shouldn't have been surprised at his response when she said that the one silver lining was they didn't have to worry about Tal Nova or Del anymore, and after she was released from the hospital they could go back to the way things were.

"I don't know, Leah... I...I need to think about things. After what's happened, what I've seen...I need to process it. I think I'm going to take some vacation time. Get away. Clear my head."

He'd left right after that. No goodbye. No "I love you, we'll work this out". Just there one minute and gone the next.

Leaving her alone.

Alone.

The *beep-beep* of her monitor and the hushed *swoosh* of the IV drip—glucose and saline to rehydrate her—emphasized the quiet of the room, which in turn underscored the fact that she had no one. No one to hold her hand. No one to take her home and have a glass of wine with. No one to help her celebrate surviving a horrible ordeal...

Of course not. Who could be with you? You're the embodiment of Death. You suck the life out of people. You hold the Power to Cure or Kill. And who knows if you have any ability to control it. Why should John want to be with you when you might drain him dry, turn him into a mummy creature, because you let yourself get tired or you Cured the wrong animal?

You're alone, and you should be. It's not safe for you to get close to anyone. Even if you don't kill them yourself, there's always the chance somebody else will find out about you and, and then what? The lives of everyone you know will always be in danger.

So that was it. Leah rolled over, wiped her eyes and stared at the water-stained tiles overhead. She was doomed to be alone. Which, when you really thought about it, wasn't much different than how her life had been before she met John. Go to work. Cure some animals. Go home. Wake up and start over.

She'd been doing fine for years—maybe not totally happy, maybe not living the life she'd dreamed about as a girl, but not bad, either. She could do it again. Start over. A different state. And this time she'd be more careful. A clinic with no windows, for one thing.

And no Curing people.

I can do this. It's for the best.

She fell asleep still trying to convince herself it was true.

The long, black limousine glided to a stop just as the sun disappeared behind the buildings on the Jersey side of the Hudson River. Del McCormick waited for Leonard Marsh to get out before he exited his own vehicle, an SUV he'd stolen specifically for this meeting. He'd leave it in the parking garage when he was through.

"Thank you for meeting me," Del said. At the same time, he looked past the billionaire and caught a glimpse of at least two bodyguards in the limo.

"You said you had a proposition for me." Marsh's words were measured, his tone cautious.

Del was pretty sure he knew why. Tal Nova had fucked up the whole DeGarmo thing on so many levels, turned it into a nightmare that showed no sign of ending anytime soon. At any moment a piece of evidence could turn up linking them all to Nova's idiotic actions.

"Your associate had certain plans for our mutual friend." Del kept his words purposely neutral, just in case Marsh was wired.

"My associate was a fool. As was I for trusting him. You can see what it got him in the end." One of Marsh's bushy, gray eyebrows rose up. "Speaking of which, I was rather surprised at your...continued involvement."

Del allowed himself a small laugh at Marsh's euphemism for his being alive. "You and me both."

How he'd survived the attack on the slaughterhouse he had no idea. Just like he had no idea what happened while he was unconscious. As best he could figure, his own men and Nova's had pretty much killed each other off. In the confusion, DeGarmo and her boyfriend had either hidden or been rescued by the cops. By the time Del regained consciousness and emerged from his own hiding place, the forensic teams were already hard at work. It had taken some effort, but he'd managed to sneak out without being seen.

The end result was there'd been no one left alive who could rat on Del, and DeGarmo was very much alive and kicking.

"So what is it you wanted to speak to me about?"

"Well, I have to admit that I had some ideas which sort of ran in the same vein as our friend's. But upon further reflection, I think I've found something, er, safer, which could still make us both a lot of money."

Marsh nodded. "I'm listening. Although I'm no longer sure that dealing with that woman is in my best interests."

"This might change your mind." Del was hoping it would. "Tell me, Mr. Marsh. How much do you think certain politicians, and men of business such as yourself, would pay for the chance to dramatically extend their life spans?"

Chapter Thirteen

Leah opened the door to the clinic and nearly passed out from the smell. The police had warned her but she hadn't expected something so rank. She should have. After all, it'd been close to three weeks since she'd been there. Her absence, and the subsequent discovery of Chastity's murder, had created quite a stir in town.

The police had investigated the clinic as a potential crime scene and arranged for the transfer of any animals who'd been recuperating or boarded at the clinic. However, no one had thought to do anything with the fish tank in the waiting area. Or Chastity's two hamsters that she kept in the file room. Or the various plants. And no one had cleaned any of the cages or emptied the food dishes.

The stench of rotten food, old feces, scummy fish water and dead rodents not only turned her stomach it brought back unwanted memories of the slaughterhouse where she'd been held captive. Dozens of flies buzzed through the room. She imagined each one carrying little packages of rot and disease on its feet.

On top of everything, someone had turned the air conditioner off and the office had the hot, stuffy feel of a desert tomb that had just been unsealed after a thousand years.

One hand over her nose and mouth, Leah ran from window to window, opening them all despite the ninety-degree temperatures outside. Then she set the A/C to sixty degrees and turned on the two portable fans she kept in the supply closet in case the A/C ever broke down. Finally, she doused every room with Lysol until the antiseptic fog made it almost impossible to breathe.

After that began step two: packing. She'd made her decision the night before while sitting alone in her living room with all the lights on. She couldn't stay in Rocky Point. Not only was it a place of bad memories now, but she didn't feel safe. She'd been attacked in her home. Attacked in her place of work. Being in the dark was impossible; she kept having waking nightmares of Tal Nova entering her bedroom and completing his threat to kill her. Since her release from the hospital, she'd been sleeping on the couch. Even then, it usually took several glasses of wine and an Ambien before she could drift off without jumping back awake several times.

So she'd come to the clinic to clean it and pack up her files, get everything ready so she could sell the practice. After that, she'd put the house on the market but she didn't intend to stick around until it sold. She'd find herself a new town, set up shop and rent until someone bought the house. They could send her the money; she didn't even plan on returning for the closing. Why bother? Rocky Point held nothing for her anymore.

Since her release from the hospital two days earlier, the only phone calls she'd had, other than her parents, were from the police—"We'd like to go over your statement once more"—and the press—"Why did those men kidnap you?"

Nothing from John.

She'd stuck to the story she and John had worked out back when they'd been holed up in the motel. The same one he'd apparently given, based on what she'd read in the newspapers.

Unknown people had kidnapped her because they wanted drugs. John had been there at the time and had been taken as well. In the process, they'd killed Chastity and then used Leah and John as hostages. There'd been a gunfight with a rival gang. John and Leah had escaped, but then were captured again before they could get to the police. In a second gun battle, John had gotten Leah to safety.

She'd seen in the paper, and on TV, that John was getting a medal for heroism. He'd also announced he was retiring from the force.

Leah had turned down all requests for interviews.

Her goal was to disappear as fast as possible from the spotlight, and it was working. This morning there'd been no reporters out in front of the house, so she'd gotten dressed and dashed out as fast as possible. A quick trip to an office supply store for file boxes and here she was.

Getting ready to throw away everything she'd worked so hard to attain.

Stop feeling sorry for yourself. What's done is done. Get your ass in gear.

For the next six hours she did just that—cleaning, tossing bags of garbage into the dumpster out back, filling red medical-waste bags for disposal and applying liberal amounts of bleach to every countertop and floor. After a quick break for a late pizza dinner (delivered, there was no way she was taking a chance and going to a fast-food place again), she got to work on packing her files.

As she put together several of the packing cartons she'd purchased, she realized that for the first time in days she hadn't thought about the downward spiral her life had taken.

"Maybe it's true what they say," she said to the empty room. "Hard work really does clear your head."

She'd just started stacking files in the first box when the door buzzer rang.

"Damn." She paused, debating whether to answer it or not. Most likely it was a reporter who'd noticed the lights on in the clinic.

Or it could be John.

Unlikely. But could she take the chance that it wasn't? A delightful shiver ran through her and she cursed herself for anticipating something that surely wasn't reality. Odds were, she'd open the door and get barraged with unwanted questions.

Still...

The door buzzed again.

Oh hell. Just open it.

A peek through the blinds covering the glass revealed the face of a man she didn't recognize. He wore a dark suit and sunglasses, and she immediately crossed reporter off her list. A cop? Possibly. If so, a detective. Or was he FBI? Had something else been uncovered during the investigation? Had they found out about *her*?

For one brief instant Leah considered turning and running. Then common sense took over. The man knew she was here, had seen her looking at him. And if the government was really there to take her away, they'd have come in force.

She opened the door, just enough to lean out.

"Can I help you?"

The man nodded and flashed a badge, the black leather case flipping open and closed again so quickly she only had time to catch a glimpse of gold.

"Dr. DeGarmo? There's an urgent matter I need to speak to you about."

She wished the man would take his glasses off. What was it about detectives and government types that they always wore dark glasses? It made reading their expressions so hard. Maybe that was the reason they did it, even at night.

At night...?

The man was already stepping forward. Leah put more weight against the door, blocking him. Something wasn't kosher...

"Can I have your name, please? And see your ID again?"

He nodded again, but this time when his hand came out from inside his suit it held a small but deadly-looking pistol.

"Inside, lady. Now." Like a chameleon, his voice and manner changed, becoming rougher. The formal tone of his words disappeared as well.

Leah stepped back, her heart slamming against her ribs.

Not again!

She turned to run away. There was no thought, no plan of action. Just an instinctive reaction to the sight of the gun.

Six men stood in the hallway leading to the examination rooms. All of them held guns.

Their unexpected presence was enough to freeze Leah in her tracks. Worse was recognizing one of them.

"Hello, Ms. DeGarmo," said the man she knew as Del.

"We have some unfinished business."

Chapter Fourteen

Leah tried to make sense of what was happening. *Men. Guns. Del. Here.* But her brain refused to work correctly. It stuttered and stopped and went nowhere, like a car stuck in the mud. A car with a record player that had a wicked scratch.

You're not making sense!

Reboot. Reboot. She had no idea where the computer reference came from, but it seemed to help. The flurry of words and ideas settled into a semblance of logical order.

Del didn't die. Jesus Christ. I killed practically everyone in that building, but Del didn't die.

And now he's going to kill me.

That had to be the reason he'd shown up. He'd escaped the slaughterhouse, evaded the police and waited until she was alone. Considering he'd already shown that he had no problem kidnapping her in public, the only reason for secrecy now had to be because he wanted revenge.

She wondered how he'd gotten away. It couldn't have been easy, judging by the bruises and cuts on his face. He looked like he'd gone through the windshield of a car. His injuries weren't the only difference about him, either. Before, she'd only ever seen him either with a calm, serious expression or a sardonic smile. Now, however, his face was a mask of barely controlled fury.

Together with his wounds, it made him finally look as dangerous as he actually was.

"How did you get in here?" The moment the words came out, Leah cursed them. It wasn't what she wanted to say; it wasn't even what she'd been thinking. What the hell was her brain doing?

"I think that's the last thing you should be worrying about," Del said. "Grab her."

At his words, two of his men holstered their guns and stepped forward. Their eagerness, combined with their air of menace, promised pain.

"No!" Leah stepped back, only to have her arms grabbed by the man who'd posed as a cop.

Del shook his head. "Sorry, Ms. DeGarmo. We've been watching you for hours. You haven't worked your magic on any animals, which means you can't make anyone sick by touching them. And that means..." he stepped forward, his expression growing even uglier, "...I can do *this*."

She never saw the fist that struck her in the stomach. All she knew was one instant she was standing there, and the next her whole world exploded in a supernova of pain. Colored lights flashed in her eyes, her lungs refused to work, and her legs buckled. Only the strong hands gripping her arms kept her from falling.

Her first thought was that he'd shot her. Then her lungs turned back on and she recognized the bruising trauma in her midsection.

Del let her take two huge, gasping breaths before he punched her again in the same spot.

Leah saw it coming this time. Not that it mattered. His fist hit her like a battering ram. Her feet slid out from beneath her and her stomach, unable to take the abuse, let loose its contents in a volcanic eruption of half-digested cheese, dough and pepperoni. Some of the puke splattered on Del's shoes.

He cursed and pulled her out of the other man's grasp. Shook her so hard her teeth clacked together and pinched her tongue. The metallic taste of blood added to the burning acids of the pizza sauce and stomach juices, and she gagged again.

"Don't you dare puke on me."

The hands holding her let go and then she was falling. She tried to cover her face but ended up landing chest and elbows first on the hard tile. The pain stabbed at her like steak knives dipped in vinegar.

As she lay moaning in the warm puddle of her own vomit, she heard one of the men laugh.

"She don't seem so tough to me, boss."

A new sensation bloomed in Leah's stomach, a burning that had nothing to do with the punches she'd taken. The fire spread quickly through her, setting her face to tingling. She recognized the feeling. Shame.

On the heels of the shame came something stronger than anger. A ferocious rage that swept through her thoughts in a red wave, leaving behind only black hatred for the people who had reduced her to this, degraded her.

And with the black came the cold. And the wind.

Leah smiled as her body rose into the air.

This time there would be no forgetting.

Del's first thought was that a freak storm must have rolled in. Papers rolled and twisted in the air as gusts of wind blew through the reception area with enough force to ruffle shirt collars and send hats flying.

"Find that window and shut it!" he yelled, glancing around to see where the wind was coming from. An open window was an invitation for nosy neighbors to look in, something he definitely didn't need.

Then he heard someone gasp.

"Jesus fucking Christ!"

Del turned back just in time to witness DeGarmo not just rising to her feet, but floating. Fucking levitating like a goddamn magic trick. Her hair blew in all directions as if the unexpected storm was centered right over her.

Or came from *her,* he thought, as an impossible mass of dark clouds formed around her. Jagged bolts of red lightning, each no larger than one of his fingers, flared in random patterns within the miniature storm.

He was so distracted by the lightning that he never looked at her face until she spoke.

"Del."

The word sounded in his ears and inside his head at the same time. It was DeGarmo's voice, yet it wasn't. It was darker, colder.

Evil.

His eyes moved to her face, which was now directly across from him.

He screamed.

Several of his men cried out as well, but he barely noticed. All he could do was look at the thing hovering in front of him.

Whatever DeGarmo had become, he knew instantly it was something deadly. Her eyes were like the eyes of corpses he'd seen pulled from the river, fish-belly white all the way across. Black tears ran down her cheeks. Blue veins stood out on her face and arms from beneath translucent flesh that was mottled with gray and green blotches.

The storm grew stronger, the winds reaching gale force in the confined space. Office supplies joined the debris sailing through the room. The blinds on the windows and doors snapped up and slammed down so hard they sounded like cymbals crashing at the end of an opera.

"Del." This time it was only in his head. Her blue, cracked lips never moved. *"Del, we have some unfinished business."*

Her arms started to rise and in a flash Del understood the cause of those two mummified corpses he'd stumbled across during his escape from the slaughterhouse. At the time he'd thought Nova's team had used some kind of chemical weapon.

Now he knew the truth.

Well, she wasn't going to turn him into a fucking mummy.

"Fuck you, bitch." He drew his gun and fired. His men, all combat trained, did the same. The roar of the guns in the small room was deafening, louder than the wind or the smashing of objects against the walls. Louder even than the freezing-cold words that continued to speak in his brain, telling him his time was up.

The barrage of bullets punched dozens of holes in DeGarmo's body. They tore her shirt and pants to ribbons. The few that missed created kaleidoscopic patterns within the black clouds around her.

None of the men stopped shooting until their guns were emptied.

What was left of Leah DeGarmo's face and body looked like a road sign in the rural South, so filled with bullet holes it was unrecognizable.

"You had your fun, Del. Now it's my turn."

For the first time in his life Del McCormick knew total, utter terror. Nothing in all his years as a military operative, mercenary, or private gun for hire had ever come close to what he felt when DeGarmo's words pierced his brain, letting him know she wasn't dead. His gun fell from his hand as the body in front of him healed its wounds. There was no scarring, no blood. Just the holes disappearing like a movie run in reverse.

Someone yelled "Run!" and Del's body reacted in Pavlovian fashion, his muscles tensing in preparation of movement.

That was as far as he got.

Ink-black pseudopods of pure energy appeared inside the storm cloud. In less time than the blink of an eye they extended out in all directions, dozens of them, elongating like the arms of an octopus. The tentacles whipped and curled among the men, coiling around arms, legs, necks—whatever they could reach.

Screams quickly turned into choking gasps. Del watched in horror as the captured men went into convulsions. Arms and legs kicked and flailed.

Two of the tentacles encircled Del without touching him. He tried to duck underneath one and it dipped in time to his movements. As he straightened up, his arm brushed against the rippling, amorphous surface and a brief but powerful electrical shock burned his skin and sent him to his knees in pain.

By then all of his men lay dead on the floor, their bodies reduced to desiccated, crusty shells, skin stretched tight and thin as plastic wrap over tendons and bones.

All of the tentacles withdrew into the supernatural tempest surrounding the apparition hovering in front of him.

"You should have left me alone. That's all I wanted."

Del shook his head, unable to answer the telepathic accusation. The smells of roasted meat and ozone assaulted his nose, mixed with the sickly-sweet odor of a taxidermy shop.

"Look at me, Del."

It took him a second to realize she—it—had spoken the words aloud. He lifted his head.

And stared into the eyes of Death.

There was no other way to describe what DeGarmo had become. She was a living corpse, a dead thing come to life. She looked dead. She smelled dead.

When she smiled, her blue-gray lips cracked in several places, releasing droplets of black, rancid fluids.

"You hurt me, Del. Now I'm going to hurt you."

Her hands reached out towards him, the same hands that had once saved his life when he'd been shot.

Now they would end it.

Del closed his eyes.

Cold, damp flesh touched the sides of his face.

This time the shock was so much worse. It was napalm igniting in his veins, hammers pounding his bones, giant hands twisting each of his organs. The agony grew and grew, expanding until every cell of his body screamed for an end to the torture. It grew until his mind snapped and conscious thought disappeared.

And still he felt it when his chest and head exploded.

Chapter Fifteen

Leah stared at the dead bodies littering her waiting area and wasn't sure how she should feel. Emotions warred with each other inside her—fear, rage, disgust, gratification. She remembered everything that happened. Changing into something else, a process that had been surprisingly easy and painless. The intoxicating sensation of sucking the life force out of the men who'd hurt her. Tried to kill her.

The satisfaction of finally putting an end to the man named Del McCormick. Her contact with his mind had been brief; just long enough for her to see his name and understand that while he held some compassion for her plight and some hatred for her continued thwarting of his plans, mostly what he felt was simple greed. He saw her as a retirement plan, a commodity to be sold or traded, and there'd be no guilt afterwards.

She'd also seen herself as he had in the moment before his death, a monster from hell, a living embodiment of the Grim Reaper.

What she hadn't seen was the name of the person who Del was working with.

The telepathic connection had been completely unexpected, and it had broken the moment Del's head burst like a dead animal left in the sun for too long.

With the immediate danger gone, Leah had returned to normal, the process now as effortless and natural as waking from a nap.

Unfortunately, the Death-her had left the human-her with a gigantic disaster. Mummified bodies littered the floor, and her memories told her there were a couple more in the back, individuals who'd tried to run rather than stay and fight. Add to that the scattered gobs of flesh, blood and body parts that had once been Del McCormick, and the police were going to have a field day with her.

Police that will be here any minute, thanks to all the gunfire, she added to herself. *Instead of being able to Cure and Kill, why can't I just turn invisible when I need to?*

"Quite a mess you've got here."

Leah couldn't help a frightened gasp at the sound of a man's voice. She turned and froze, stunned by the person who stood in the hall leading into the examination areas.

Leonard Marsh.

He held up his hands in mock surrender. "Please don't be alarmed. I'm not here to hurt you or kidnap you. In fact, I'm here to assist you with your..." he gestured at the grotesque mess on the floor, "...problem. But we need to move quickly, before the police arrive."

Leah let some of her dark Powers rise up, Powers she still didn't understand completely, just enough to create a breeze in the room. From the look on Marsh's face, her own features must have changed as well. Dead eyes? Mottled skin? She knew from Del's mind what she looked like in Death mode.

"You have no reason to trust me," Marsh said, his hands still held out, palms up. "But consider this. I came here because I learned what Mr. McCormick had planned for you. Unfortunately, I arrived too late to help. Not that you needed it, apparently."

"You saw what I did?"

Marsh nodded. "Very impressive. Almost as impressive as your ability to grant life to a very grateful man with enough money to make this..." another gesture at the room, "...go away. If you'll let me."

"And in return?" Leah knew a person like Marsh would never offer to help for free. There had to be a catch.

There was *always* a catch.

"Nothing." Marsh shook his head. "I'm the one who will forever be in your debt. There are some things I'd like to talk to you about—things involving me helping you, not the other way around—but only if you choose to speak with me."

Leah chewed her lip. A siren sounded in the distance, quickly joined by others. There was little doubt they were on their way to the clinic.

What choice did she have?

"Okay."

Marsh smiled. "Excellent. Please come with me and let my people take care of everything."

A group of men in dark-blue coveralls entered from behind Marsh, and Leah wondered where they'd been waiting. She also promised herself to install better locks on her next office. Marsh offered her his arm and led her through the halls to the back door, which stood open, presumably from Del and his men's entry. A long, stylish limousine idled at the curb.

Leah hesitated when Marsh opened the door.

"I promise this is just to get you away from anything that might link you to more bad press. We can go to your house, or anywhere you feel safe."

A gentle summer breeze drifted past, bringing the scents of mown grass, barbeque and roses. Leah shivered, not from a chill but from the incongruous transition from violence to serenity.

"You said you wanted to talk to me about something."

He nodded. "Several somethings."

"All right. For now, let's just drive around town." She got into the car, hoping that if Marsh did have something nasty planned, she'd be able to handle it.

Or at least her Death persona would handle it.

"How are they going to explain all that to the police?" she asked as the limo pulled silently away from the curb. The crushed-leather seats hugged her, and she realized that, compared to Marsh's personal car, the limos she'd ridden in with Tal Nova were at the bottom of the luxury list.

Marsh, sitting across from her at a distance longer than her legs could stretch, pressed a button and a center console slid open, revealing a selection of sodas and waters.

"Please help yourself. There is no alcohol in the car, I'm afraid. Since you, er, alleviated my illness, I've been on something of a health kick." He took a bottle of sparkling water and she did the same, listening carefully for the *pop-hiss* that let her know the bottle hadn't been unsealed.

"First, I want to sincerely apologize for the actions of Mr. Nova. His only orders from me were to invite you to the office so that I could make amends for my treatment of you. What he did—the kidnapping, the brutal treatment of your boyfriend—I knew nothing about that."

She didn't want to believe him—how could someone so rich and powerful not know what their right-hand man was doing?—but his face and voice both sounded totally sincere, nothing at all like the self-absorbed, high-and-mighty asshole he'd been the last time she'd seen him. When she'd Cured him.

"I also want to thank you for not mentioning me in the story you gave to the police," he added.

"I didn't do that for your benefit." A bit of anger rose up and Leah welcomed it. It felt good. "I just figured no one would believe me, and I certainly wasn't going to tell anyone about my ability to Cure."

"Still, you could have tried to throw me under the bus, so to speak, especially when it came out that Tal was one of the dead discovered in that slaughterhouse."

Marsh dipped his hand into the cooler compartment and took out a candy bar. The label was in French, but Leah read the words *chocolat fondant* and figured it was some type of fancy chocolate. When he offered her a piece, she took it gladly.

"How did that all work out?" She wanted to say more, but the heavenly taste of the chocolate robbed her of the ability to speak. Light, velvety, with hints of raspberry peeking out from below the bittersweet tones of the dark cocoa, it put any other chocolate she'd ever had to shame. By itself, it was worth the chance she'd taken by getting into the car.

"In my business, you have to plan for any eventuality. Between the evidence at the slaughterhouse and what they found in his home, the authorities came to the appropriate conclusion that he'd secretly been smuggling drugs for years and had gotten into a turf war with another gang. Of course, I made sure to remove any mention of your abilities from his work and home computers."

"Then I guess it's me who should be thanking you." Leah ran her tongue across the roof of her mouth, savoring the remaining splashes of flavor.

"No. You saved my life. And there are only two things I can offer you in return. Safety and financial freedom."

"What?" Chocolate heaven forgotten, Leah sat up straighter.

"You turned down my money the last time," Marsh said. "One of the reasons I asked Tal to bring you back to my office was so that I could try to convince you to accept my payment. Now I'm offering you something further. One hundred thousand dollars for your clinic. Another hundred thousand to set up a foundation for veterinary education in the name of your assistant, the one Tal murdered. And on top of that, my security team will completely outfit your home and your clinic with state-of-the-art security systems and provide personal protection for a period of one year."

"I...I don't know what to say..." Leah's voice trailed off. She had no idea what to do. She didn't even know if she could believe him.

"It's hard to trust me." Marsh gave her a smile, as if he could read her thoughts. Or maybe he was just used to not being trusted. "I was a selfish man for a long time, Ms. DeGarmo. But after you...did what you did...I realized that using your power as a personal tool, like you were some kind of supernatural masseuse or private physician, just wasn't right. You did more than heal me. You changed me."

She was tempted to say no again, despite the enormity of the offer. Maybe Marsh hadn't been involved in her kidnappings and John's torture. It was still because of him that it all happened in the first place.

It was still dirty money.

The word *dirty* reminded her of something John had said to her the night they'd found Marsh's check on the door.

"The minute you cash that check it goes from dirty to clean just because of the good it will do."

Think about it, Leah. The animals. The Chastity Summers foundation providing grants for veterinary students.

Safety.

Her answer came easily after that. "I accept your offer."

She felt no guilt, no sense of making a deal with the devil.

"On one condition," she added.

"Of course, if I can." Marsh's eyebrows rose, expressing his curiosity.

"I'd like one of those chocolate bars." She pointed to the wrapper.

For a moment Marsh just stared at her; then he burst into laughter. "Dr. DeGarmo, I'll see to it that you get a lifetime supply!"

Twenty minutes later, Leonard Marsh watched Leah DeGarmo unlock the door to her house and go inside.

"Back to the city," he said to his driver, and the limo eased away from the curb. During the short trip through town to the highway entrance, Marsh considered what he'd achieved that night.

He'd turned a potentially deadly enemy into an ally.

He'd quietly removed the last chances of anyone connecting him to the mess Tal Nova had created.

He'd set himself up to broker possibly the largest business deal of his life.

Tal and Del had been small thinkers; that was their problem. One considered DeGarmo a weapon. The other had been ready to sell her like she was some kind of street drug. They'd both been right—she was a weapon and a longevity medicine, to be sure. But that was only the tip of the iceberg.

Who knew what other abilities she possessed?

He took another sip of water. Sure, he'd just spent close to half a million dollars between the cleanup and his payments to her. But it was a small price to pay for gaining her trust.

And the potential returns…

It was time to see what they would be.

He took out a cell phone from the console, a so-called burner phone he'd had his engineers work on so that no GPS signal emanated from it. There was one preprogrammed number in it, which he activated.

"Hello, General. Remember the individual we discussed. She's everything I said and much, much more. It's time for us to meet."

Chapter Sixteen

Leah walked away from Marsh's limo feeling better than she had since...well, since the day she'd come home from the hospital. In her pocket were two checks.

While they'd driven, Marsh had arranged to have one of his security specialists—the same one currently posing as an FBI agent at her clinic and keeping the police out of the building—stop by in the morning and begin work on the new security system. He'd also had his driver stop at a 24-hour pharmacy and purchase a plain pink T-shirt to replace her tattered one.

She was grateful there were no reporters hovering around the yard, which meant he'd been successful at keeping the events at the clinic from reaching the press. That was key. She needed time to decompress, to come to terms with the thing she'd...

What? Mutated into? Maybe you haven't become anything, Leah. Maybe this is who you've always been, and it just needed to be woken up.

Therein lay the problem. Were these all just new manifestations of her Power, or had something happened when she took John's death into herself?

Most importantly, would she be able to control it in the future? What would happen the first time she Cured an animal and then had to pass its illness on? Would it be the same as before, or was she going to turn into some kind of modern-day Kali, raining hell down on anyone in her path?

She opened the door and was halfway across the darkened living room before someone spoke her name.

"Leah."

The light beside the couch came on at the same time she recognized the voice.

"John? What...what are you doing here?"

He looked haggard and old, and not just from the sharply angled shadows thrown by the small lamp. Although still as handsome as ever, he had the appearance of a man who'd gone too many nights with too little sleep.

"I came here to talk to you. I...needed to talk to you. There was no one here, so I used the spare key to come in and wait."

Damn. She'd meant to get rid of the key she kept in a fake rock in the outside planter. God, she really did need security help!

"You're leaving." He said it not as a question but as a statement.

She glanced into the dining room, where she'd left the suitcase she'd packed the day before. He was right, although she hadn't planned on leaving that night.

"I...I don't know." It was the truth. After accepting Marsh's offer, it seemed like a cop-out to leave town. Chastity's foundation deserved to be in Rocky Point. And all her patients were here.

Why should she be the one who had to leave? It wasn't as if the bad memories wouldn't follow. They were a part of her now, just like her Powers.

"I was planning to," she said, "because I had no reason to stay. My practice was destroyed. You...you were gone..." Her throat tightened and tears welled in her eyes. She turned away, ashamed at showing how much he'd hurt her.

"Hey." John stood up and approached her. He stopped a few feet away, close enough that she could smell him, feel his warmth against her back, but distant enough that he wasn't invading her space.

"I never said I was going anywhere. I said I needed time to think about things. To clear my head. A lot of shit went down in that place, Leah, shit you don't know about. I saw things..."

"I think I have a pretty good idea of what you saw." She turned back to face him. "Me. Dead and floating in the air. Killing people, right?"

John's eyes went wide, then narrowed. "Wait. You said you didn't remember anything that happened after you cured me."

"I didn't. I still don't."

"Then how... Jesus Christ, did it happen again? Are you all right?"

Leah shrugged. As much as she trusted John—even now, even after he'd let her down, just walked right the hell out on her, she still trusted him—she didn't feel comfortable telling him about the events at the clinic.

"Let's just say a man named Del won't be a problem anymore."

A strange look came over John's face, a look that made her regret saying anything at all. Sadness? Fear?

Disappointment.

He doesn't know I was attacked. He thinks I killed a man for revenge.

Not that she could be faulted, even if that's what she had done. But she was still human enough not to go all vigilante on people. John should have known that.

Why? The last time he saw you, you were a one-woman death squad. It's amazing he's even here talking to you.

That made her stop and think. Why had he come over, instead of just calling? And if their positions were reversed, would she have been able to go anywhere near him? A supernatural monster that could suck the life out of people?

The truth was, his being there with her, after everything he'd seen, showed that he wasn't afraid, that he still trusted her with his life.

"I'm not a killer," she said. It sounded lame, even to her own ears.

"I didn't say you were." His dark eyes bore into her, silently telling her he wanted to believe her but she wasn't giving him any reason to.

"He showed up at the clinic. I...I'd been cleaning all day, getting it ready to...you know, because I planned on..." Leah paused, feeling guilty and trapped by the lie she was spinning and afraid her dishonesty was already obvious.

"Running away," John supplied, but there was no malice or accusation in his voice.

"Yes. Running away. I admit it. He and his men...they surprised me there. He grabbed me and..." She took a deep breath before continuing. The words might not be truthful, but the emotions behind them were, and she hoped that sold the story to him. "And it just happened. The Power rose up, only this time I was aware of everything. All the different ways I could kill him. What I looked like. But it was under my control. My thoughts were my own. I was planning on just scaring him but then he shot me and the Power responded. It was automatic, just like when I Cure someone."

John stared at her for a moment, and she shriveled inside.

He knows I'm lying! He's a cop for God's sake.

What would she do if he demanded the truth?

But he didn't. Instead, his expression slowly softened.

"Automatic or not, it was self-defense. That's different than murder. You shouldn't feel like you did anything wrong. Except...what did you do with the body?"

This time the lie came easier.

"I drove it twenty miles out of town and tossed it in the river. It was all dried up, like a mummy—"

"I remember what they look like."

"So no one will be able to connect it to me."

There was another moment of silence, a space of heartbeats in which Leah felt sure John was analyzing her. Listening to the lie detector in his head.

"That must have been awful. Why didn't you call me?"

"Call you?" All her worries vanished, driven away by a sudden rush of righteous anger. "Call you? You walked out on me! Said you weren't sure if we could ever be together. Said you needed 'time to think'." She added finger quotes to emphasize the words. "Left me high and dry in the hospital after telling me I'd used some kind of mental superpower to kill a couple dozen people. Is any of this ringing a bell?"

She would have gone on, but he stood up and shouted over her words.

"Hey! Who's the one who isn't remembering everything? You're the one who planned on killing herself before I talked you out of it. You're the one who ran away from me at the hotel. You're the one who's still planning on running away to God knows where. All of which I'm supposed to not get pissed about. In the meantime, in the past couple of weeks I've been shot and poisoned more times than I can count, kidnapped three different times, and I had to lie to the police—my own friends, some of them—about everything that happened. I had to quit my job because everyone there thinks I'm some kind of hero and I couldn't go to work every day living that kind of lie. And on top of all that, the woman I fell in love with suddenly develops the power to turn people into corn husks without even touching them. But if I say I need a few days to think about things, I'm the jerk who abandoned you?"

He stopped, his face red, his hair out of place on his forehead.

Leah took a step back. Not out of fear—never once during his tirade had she felt threatened, worried about physical violence—but out of amazement. She'd never seen him lose control of his emotions like that, not even when people were threatening to kill him.

All those things he mentioned, they were because of me. Yes, I Cured him. Even brought him back from the dead. But if he'd never met me, none of this would've happened.

If he'd never met me he'd have died in that McDonald's.

It was all too confusing! The what-ifs, the maybes. One thing was clear, though.

She'd acted like a selfish bitch. Again. After promising not to do it. All he'd asked for was a few days, and she'd been unable to wait because his need for time away had come when she felt he should be standing by her. Supporting her.

And yet, despite how she had acted, was *still* acting, he'd said he...

Loved her.

"You still love me?"

John rolled his eyes, eyes that mirrored the warmth of the gentle smile he gave her.

"I've always loved you. I just had to make sure the other stuff—your powers, my getting killed—wouldn't get in the way of that love. I needed to think hard about committing to you so that down the road I didn't end up hurting you."

Staring into his dark-chocolate gaze, all the things she wanted to say fell apart, got jammed in her throat like logs in a river.

Instead of speaking, she burst into tears and threw herself into his arms.

He held her tight, and nothing in the world ever felt so good.

Part Three

Into the Future

All great changes are preceded by chaos.

—Deepak Chopra

Chapter One

To Leah, opening her eyes the next morning wasn't just waking up, it was being born all over again. A new beginning. A second chance at life.

An emotional and psychological resurrection.

The sun angled in through the window over the bed, draping the sheets and floor with a warm, yellow blanket. The pastoral sounds of birdsong, buzzing insects and lawnmowers created the suburban version of white noise. John continued to sleep peacefully next to her and she considered just rolling over and snuggling next to him. However, her bladder was telling her that wasn't going to be a comfortable option and the rest of her body was craving a cup of coffee. Preferably in the kitchen, with the windows open and the paper on the table.

She glanced at John once more, reluctant to do anything that might disturb the perfect serenity of the morning, and then gave in to the inevitable. Besides, Marsh's men would be there soon to begin work on the alarm system, which meant she had to be up and dressed.

And tell John at least part of the truth.

She'd already decided what to say. Thinking about it had kept her awake long after they'd finished their lovemaking and John had drifted off, one arm around her and his breathing a comforting lullaby behind her head.

"He came by the house. Apologized. Offered me money and safety. This time I took him up on his offers because of what you told me last time."

Putting it that way would not only keep John in the dark about what happened at the clinic, but also give him no leg to stand on if he tried to argue her out of accepting the money and help.

Most important was keeping her meltdown—or blow up?—at the clinic a secret. The cover-up was bad enough. But her gut feelings told her that now was not the right time to tell him not only how many people she'd killed, but that there was a part of her—the dark part, she now recognized—that'd enjoyed it.

That last fact was something she was still trying to wrap her head around. She had enjoyed killing Del and others, in a masochistic, vindictive sort of way. The way you might feel as you stomped a bunch of ants in your kitchen or punched the kid who'd just knocked down your little brother. There'd been no remorse afterward—although that fact, in itself, had made her feel a little guilty. As of yet there was also no desire to repeat the act, no yearning to suck the life from someone. So she was hoping it wasn't a Power that would become addictive.

Curing people never was, either. It was just something that I could do, and I was happy to do it because it made the animals, and their owners, feel better.

She was hoping the Kill Power was the same as her Cure Power: just a tool to be used when necessary. One she prayed wouldn't be necessary any longer.

As Leah poured water into the brew pot, a nasty thought still haunted her, the same one that had haunted her at night while she'd tried to sleep.

All your life you've been subtly stealing the life-force energy from the people around you to fuel your ability to Cure yourself and others. Where are you getting the Power to Kill?

And what will it mean in the long term for John?

An hour later, after sharing the paper and the single bagel Leah had in the house, John finished his second cup of coffee and leaned back in his chair.

"So what's on the agenda for today? Finish cleaning the clinic and get ready to reopen? Or is today a rest-and-relax day?"

They'd spoken the previous night about Leah coming to the decision that despite everything that had happened, she wasn't going to leave Rocky Point. Getting John back in her life just made that choice more definite. Since he wasn't working, he'd offered to help her with any cleaning or repairs that needed to be done before reopening.

Leah hesitated before answering. What if Marsh's men hadn't finished their own cleanup yet? And even if they had, would John's police-trained eyes pick up any subtle clues left behind? A poorly patched bullet hole in a wall? A droplet of blood under a chair?

A chiming of bells sounded before she could answer. *Damn! The security specialists are here.* A welcome distraction from John's offer to help, but it also meant it was time to tell him about her and Leonard Marsh.

"I'll get it," she said, rising from the table. She'd let the men get started and explain everything to John upstairs while they got dressed for the day. Or maybe on the way to the bank to deposit Marsh's checks.

When she opened the door, a muscular man with piercing blue eyes and a crew cut stood there smiling at her. Leah paused with the door half-open. It wasn't the same person Marsh had said would be handling her home security.

"Hello. Can I—?"

His hand rose up and she had just enough time to notice he held a small, dark object. She felt something like a bee sting on her arm.

Then everything disappeared.

Leah's return to consciousness was not a pleasant one. Her head throbbed, her thoughts were fuzzy and disjointed, and each movement created waves of nausea that sent the ceiling tiles spinning. She tried closing her eyes and counting to fifty, but when she opened them nothing had changed. She felt off-kilter, like she'd had too much to drink and was trying to balance in an elevator.

Drugged. I've been drugged. I don't take drugs. Why would someone drug me?

"Leah? Can you hear me?"

A familiar voice. Someone she knew.

Of course it's someone you know. That's what familiar means!

Leah glanced to her left. A man stood several feet away. She recognized him.

John. His name is…John. He's my boyfriend, I think. Why is he just standing there?

She stood up, only just then noticing that she'd been reclining on a metal cot. The room wobbled and the floor tilted downwards. Leah stumbled but didn't fall as she took two steps forward. After a break to catch her breath, she took two more. Then two more. Slowly, concentrating hard on putting each foot down, she made her way to where John still stood looking at her.

"Leah, be careful. Don't—"

Something hard struck her in the face and arm just as she reached John. She grabbed at him for support but her hand smashed into the same invisible barrier.

"What…?" She placed her hands against it. Cool. Smooth. Solid.

"Leah?"

It came to her. Glass. The room had glass walls around it.

That's silly. Why make walls out of glass?

"Leah? Are you all right?"

John again. Still talking. Repeating himself over and over. Like a rabbit.

No. Not a rabbit. That doesn't make sense!

She looked at him. He was frowning.

"John. You're not a rabbit."

His frown deepened. Why? Had she said something to make him angry? She tried to think. He'd said something. *How are you all Leah, right?*

That didn't make sense. There was only one of her.

Oh! He must be drugged too.

"John. Did they drug you too?" She spoke slowly so he'd understand.

It worked. His frown disappeared. He shook his head.

"No, I guess they only drugged you. But that explains a lot. You should go sit down and rest."

"Okay." Rest sounded good. She *was* sleepy. She lowered herself to the floor. Placed her head on her arms.

Maybe I'll feel better when I wake up.

Four men watched Leah DeGarmo fall asleep. Three of them wore green uniforms, the other a tailored black suit. The youngest of the soldiers, a red-haired man in his twenties with the triple stripes of a sergeant on his shoulders, sat in front of a series of computer consoles. The other two, one bearing the twin bars of a captain and the other with the single star of a brigadier general, stood behind the sergeant with the man in the suit, their eyes on the largest of the three computer screens.

"The dose is too high," the man in the suit said.

"I'm not sure we should go lower," replied the captain. "According to Marsh's report, she has the ability to heal herself rapidly. If we reduce the concentration of the sedative she's breathing, we risk her being able to activate her powers."

The general's eyes never left the screen as he considered the words of the two other men. Finally, he spoke.

"Sergeant, how quickly can you raise the sedative concentration to where she's incapacitated?"

The sergeant tapped a red button. "If I hit the emergency switch, I can flood the room with enough gas to knock her out in fifteen seconds."

The general nodded once.

"Good enough. Lower her dosage fifteen percent. I want her aware enough so she can converse coherently, but woozy enough that you wouldn't want her handing you a hot cup of coffee."

"Yes, sir." The sergeant entered a change on the keyboard.

"Sir...?" The captain let his question hang in the air.

"Fifteen seconds," the general said. "Even if she manages to overcome the sedatives, there's no way she can do any damage before she's out cold. You've read the reports. Seen the pictures. The moment you sense anything going wrong, see her eyes start to change or whatever, just give us the signal and we'll take care of the rest."

The man in the black suit cleared his throat. "I'll leave you to it. General, I want a report on my desk first thing in the morning."

"Yes, sir." The general snapped off a salute as the man turned and exited the room. Then he turned to the captain.

"Let's grab a coffee. I want to go over the script once more before she wakes up."

Chapter Two

Leah said nothing as the man in the military uniform entered her room. He wore a clear plastic mask over his nose and mouth, with circular filters on either side.

She'd woken up on the floor about a half hour earlier—it was hard to tell without any clocks and with her thoughts still fuzzy—and for a moment thought she'd dreamed of talking with John through a glass wall. Then she'd realized she really was in the room from her dreams, but someone had lowered a metal panel on the other side of the glass—which turned out to be some kind of clear plastic, actually.

Feeling much less nauseated than before, she'd gotten up and inspected her cell. Approximately fifteen by fifteen, with a cot bolted to the wall. Other than that, there was a toilet in the back (which she used as soon as she saw it) and two folding chairs.

All the walls and ceiling were made of the same clear plastic, and the choice of material didn't make sense until she noticed a black box on the outside of the ceiling with several tubes running from it.

It's an airtight chamber, like the ones where people work with viruses. Not the kind with the double air-lock doors, but it's pressurized, for sure.

Her suspicions were confirmed when the uniformed man opened the door and a breeze rushed past her, accompanied by a *whooshing* sound.

That doesn't make sense, though. She struggled to focus on the thought. It was hard; she kept getting distracted by the man's clear-plastic air mask.

The breeze blew toward the door. Out of the room. But these rooms are supposed to keep things from escaping. I'm not contaminated, though. Which means they want to keep something outside from coming in. What? The only thing outside is air...

Her eyes went to the man's mask again. He must have seen something on her face because he gave her a quick smile and a nod.

The mask. Air. Something in the air...

They're still drugging me! The machine on the ceiling. It's pumping something into the air, something to keep me sleepy.

"You bastards." The words came out slightly slurred, as if she'd had a few too many drinks.

"It's for your own protection, Ms. DeGarmo," he said, his words slightly muffled by the mask. "Well, yours and ours. We—I—want to talk with you, and it's hard to do that if we're afraid you might decide to kill everyone."

The man stepped farther into the room and took a seat in one of the folding chairs. Leah kept her eyes on him, trying to size him up despite her muddled brain. About fifty, with brown hair in a short military cut that made his ears look extra large. His eyes were a murky greenish brown, as if his head were filled with swamp water. That almost made her laugh out loud and she had to bite her lip to control it.

The man motioned to the other chair. "Please sit down. I'll answer any questions you might have."

Leah didn't want to go anywhere near the man, but moving around the room had made her tired. It would feel good to sit down. And she did have questions...

She slid the chair a few feet farther away from him and sat down. He continued to stare at her and she wondered why he didn't say anything. Then she remembered she was supposed to ask questions.

"Why...why am I here?" Even in her drug-induced haze she knew it had something to do with her Powers. But which one? And what was their plan for using it?

The man smiled. "First, let me introduce myself. My name is Captain Leo Green, US Army. And the reason you're here, Ms. DeGarmo, is because of the amazing things you can do."

"So you want me to, what, kill people for you?"

"No." Green shook his head. "We want to figure out how it is you do what you do. Powers like yours would be very helpful to soldiers."

Leah knew she should be scared. He was talking about studying her like some kind of lab animal. Maybe even cutting out her brain. But all she felt was numb. And tired.

"You want to study me. And what if the answer isn't in my blood? Or my cells? Then what? You kill me? Dissect my brain?"

"Honestly, I don't make those decisions, Ms. DeGarmo. My job is just to make sure you cooperate. If you do, I can make life better for you. Visits with your boyfriend. Television and movie privileges. Special meals. Maybe even some privacy." He gestured at the toilet in the back of the room.

"And if I don't cooperate? You make my life hell, right?" Leah tried to put some anger in her voice but her words came out flat and weak, victims of the drugs in the air.

"It's better if we think positive," Green said. "Will it help if I tell you we're not planning anything more painful than a visit to the doctor? We'll draw some blood, do a few x-rays and MRIs and such. Ask you to demonstrate what you can do on a few lab animals."

"But you never let me go, do you? I'll never be free."

Green shrugged. "Freedom isn't always what it seems. Were you free before we found you? You were kidnapped by criminals who wanted to sell you into slavery. Sure, you escaped. But you were going to have to spend the rest of your life looking over your shoulder, wondering if you were safe. Is that freedom? At least here your life isn't in danger. And neither is Mr. Carrera's." Green motioned with one hand at the far wall, where the metal panels blocked her view of John's cell.

"You don't need him." Leah felt sick knowing John was again caught up in the mess that was her life. "Let him go."

"We can't do that." Green shook his head. "Too much of a security risk. But, again, if you cooperate, then I don't see why the two of you can't share a nice apartment. Just think of it as working for us. We run the tests, and you get a life paid for by the US military."

"I don't think so." It took all her strength, but Leah forced herself to stand up and take a step toward Green. She tried to ignite the Power inside her, kick-start it to life. For a moment something flickered in her chest, the beginning of a vibration, the hint of the Death force she remembered from the events in the clinic.

She had a quick glimpse of Green's eyes going wide. His hand dipped into his pocket and she wondered if he had a weapon hidden there.

Then her feeling of triumph disappeared and the room turned black.

Captain Leo Green's finger was still inches away from the emergency trigger in his pocket when the prisoner fell onto her side. His hand shook as he turned and motioned for the door to be unlocked, the memory of DeGarmo's face still vivid in his mind.

Her eyes as she stood up. The color disappearing from them, replaced by a sickly bluish gray. A faint smell of rotten flesh, despite the mask he wore.

What would have happened if she hadn't passed out?

Green cursed his own hesitation as he walked down the hall to meet with General Moore. He'd frozen. It was hard to accept, but it was true. The sight of DeGarmo turning into—what? A corpse? A demon?—right in front of him had done something no battlefield disaster ever had.

Can't tell anyone about this. Leaders—at least those working for General Butch Moore—don't freeze. Don't show weakness.

What would have happened if she hadn't passed out?

I would have died.

Despite his orders to report immediately to Moore's office after the interview with DeGarmo, Green stopped at a bathroom to splash water on his face and take several deep breaths.

I would have died.

It took almost three minutes before his hands stopped shaking.

"What's your assessment, Green?"

Leo Green pointed to the video screen mounted at the far end of the room. On it, Leah DeGarmo had just woken up and was making her way to her cot on unsteady legs.

"The level of sedative is perfect. She's coherent but unable to muster any real strength. As you saw, she tried to threaten me with her powers and it was too much for her. My only concern is that in her present state, she won't be able to demonstrate those powers when we need her to."

Green sat down, leaving unvoiced his additional thought that they were all better off with DeGarmo unable to cure or kill.

"That defeats the purpose of having her here," General Butch Moore said from the head of the conference table. Beneath his gray, thinning crew cut his skin was a mottled red, lingering mementos of chemical burns he'd received while leading a top-secret mission in Iraq two decades earlier. "Can't we lower the concentration? You've got the damned button."

"The button's worthless if he can't use it," said the third man at the table, the one in the dark suit. Green had yet to learn his name, but based on his conservative haircut, tailored clothes and quiet arrogance, he figured the man must be a high-ranking member of one of the intel agencies. DARPA, most likely. Or perhaps CIA. They had had their dirty fingers in every black op.

"Why wouldn't he—"

"Not wouldn't, couldn't," the unnamed spook interrupted. "As in, if the woman's powers come on faster, Captain Green is going to be one very dead soldier, and the rest of your men will soon follow. Or am I the only one here who noticed how badly she got the jump on him last time?"

Green's heart thumped and he tried to cover his surprise by forcing a deep scowl. "Got the jump on me?"

"Oh please. I was watching your hand, Captain. It was barely into your pocket when the lady keeled over. That means another two or three seconds to press the button, followed by fifteen seconds before the soporific gas floods the chamber. That's close to twenty seconds. Judging by how fast she started to change, I imagine that would be more than enough time to mummify your ass."

"Green? Is that right?" Moore's eyes narrowed as he waited for a response.

"Um, possibly, sir," Green conceded. Still hoping to hide his own poor response in DeGarmo's presence, he added, "But I wasn't moving at full speed. I'd already noticed how sluggish she was, and I felt confident she wouldn't have enough energy to actually pose a threat."

"You hesitated," the agent said.

"No, I reacted properly to the situation. Since you were watching, you probably also noticed that I never left my seat. Had I felt in danger, I would have not only pressed the button but headed right for the door."

"Hmmm." The agent raised one eyebrow and then returned his attention to the papers in front of him.

"Well, from now on, no heroics, understand?" General Moore tapped a finger on the table. "The second she starts to change, you hit the button and get the hell out of there. Full speed."

"Yes, sir," Green said, aware he'd dodged a bullet when the agent didn't press the issue of performance.

Or cowardice. Something tells me that man is fully aware of why I didn't sound the alarm. And that means I need to watch him as closely as he's been watching me.

The nameless agent looked back up, a smile on his face that made Green feel a lot like a mouse who'd just emerged from his hole to find King Tabby staring right at him, paw raised and ready to strike.

"Well, since Captain Green is certain he can react with more alacrity than he showed today, I see no reason not to lower DeGarmo's sedative levels. Captain, first thing tomorrow we'll see if you can convince our guest to play nice."

The agent stood, nodded to them and strode out of the room, house-cat grin still plastered on his face.

It took all of Green's willpower to not groan out loud.

Chapter Three

Leah wasn't sure what was worse, sitting alone in her cell and wondering what the army had planned for her, or knowing John was only a few feet away yet totally unavailable to her.

Either way, depression and loneliness had her on the verge of tears. They were also making it impossible to sleep, despite the fact that someone had turned the lights off hours ago.

Of course, I slept half the day away, if not more than that, came the bitter thought, *thanks to their drugging me.*

Wait...

The drugs in the air had made her tired and sleepy, so sleepy she couldn't even muster the energy to use her Powers.

So why wasn't she sleepy now?

They've lowered the dose. The only question is, do they just do it at night, or did they decide they need me more awake?

The latter made more sense. If they wanted her to Cure something—or Kill something—she'd have to be alert. They already knew that if she was half-asleep she didn't pose a threat.

I still don't feel right, though. Her legs and arms seemed to weigh twice as much as they should. And while normally she'd have been full of pent-up energy and pacing her cell, the thought of making the effort to get off the cot seemed too much of a strain.

So they're still drugging me with something, just not as much. But my brain's working a thousand times better. That means my Powers should be too.

And *that* meant someone was in for a surprise tomorrow.

Captain Green showed up with coffee, donuts and a hard look behind his mask. The moment he entered the cell, he spoke to her in a loud voice.

And it turned out Leah was the one to get surprised.

"Ms. DeGarmo. Please don't try anything like you did yesterday. There are people watching us right now, and if you make any attempt to harm me, your friend John will suffer the consequences."

He stood by the door, waiting on her response.

As tempted as she was to still go into full Death mode, Leah knew she'd been outmaneuvered.

"I won't do anything."

It didn't help that the smell of the coffee and sight of the food had her stomach rumbling and her mouth salivating.

Food and love. That's all it takes to break someone, or at least me. Deprive them of food and love.

Feeling like a traitor to John and herself, she lowered herself into the same chair as the previous day and remained silent and motionless while Green approached her and set the tray down on the floor before taking the seat opposite her.

"Go ahead." He motioned at the food. "We've got a long day ahead of us, but if you cooperate, tonight you'll not only be eating dinner with your boyfriend, but sharing the same room."

Leah frowned but refrained from speaking any of the comments that came to mind. She was well aware he was testing her, prodding her with veiled insults and threats disguised as friendly advice. "If you cooperate" was another way of saying "do as you're told or else". And the offer to eat dinner and share a room with John was dangling bait, the same way a zookeeper would use a piece of meat to get an animal to follow instructions.

They consider me a guinea pig, a lab rat. They think they can tame me, train me to follow orders so I can get my reward at the end of the day. Well, I can play along for now. But sooner or later someone will slip up. And when they do, there will be hell to pay.

Leah looked at Green and smiled as she took a bite of donut.

And that hell will be me.

After she finished her coffee and donuts, Green called someone on his cell phone, and not two minutes later a woman in a white coat and a face mask like Green's had wheeled in a cart with two cages on it. One held a small mixed- breed dog with an unhealthy green glow surrounding it. Even without her Power, though, she'd have known it was sick. Its eyes were glassy, its tongue lolling and dry, and its fur lusterless. The other cage held a healthy, happy terrier pup.

"I think you know what to do," Green said, as the tech left the cell. He pointed at the sick dog. "It has late stage distemper."

"I won't kill an innocent animal." Leah crossed her arms and gave Green what she hoped was a defiant glare. Inside, she was worried. She'd promised to do what they asked in order to keep John safe, and now here she was refusing to cooperate before the first experiment even started.

But they wanted her to kill a puppy, and that went against everything she believed in.

"Ms. DeGarmo, you agreed—"

"I agreed to demonstrate what I can do, not kill healthy dogs for you. That's not how it works."

"Don't bullshit me. I've read the reports. You take the sickness out of one animal and place it in another."

"Your report isn't complete, then. After I Cure something or someone, I pass it on to an animal that I can't Cure because too many people know it's dying. I'm a doctor. You think I go around making healthy animals sick?"

Green's eyes narrowed. "So what you're telling me is...?"

Leah let out a breath. "What I'm telling you is that both animals have to be sick. One of them should be old and about to die anyhow, the kind of animal that if it suddenly appeared to get well people would be very suspicious. Understand?"

Green stared at her and she had a heart-stopping moment where she thought maybe she'd gone too far, been too sarcastic. Then he spoke into his phone again and asked for another animal to be brought to them.

That reminded Leah of one other thing.

"Wait! We'll also need something to put the dog down. Sodium pentobarbital, preferably."

Green raised one eyebrow behind his mask.

"You want me to hand you a needle filled with poison?"

"You don't have to hand it to me. You can inject the dog yourself. But when I pass the disease to that other animal, it's going to feel a lot of pain, possibly for hours. I try to time it so that I pass it along right before the animal dies."

"Fine." He made another call and then hung up. "Anything else?"

"No," she said, ignoring his sarcasm.

During the five-minute wait, neither of them said anything.

The next animal to arrive was exactly what she'd asked for, and she remembered the old adage about being "careful what you wished for, you might just get it". Because it wasn't a dog.

The rhesus monkey was ancient, its gray fur balding in patches and its joints swollen to grotesque size by arthritis. Cataracts gave its eyes a bluish tint, reminding her uncomfortably of the way her own eyes looked when she transformed into her Death persona. It lay on its side, refusing to move even when she tapped on the cage door.

"Can we get on with it now?" Green asked, impatience giving his words an acid tone.

"Yes." In fact, Leah was more than ready to do what needed to be done. The poor monkey was in obvious pain and deserved to be released from it.

She opened the cage containing the dying mixed breed and carefully reached her hands toward it, wary of being bitten. As she touched it and felt the sudden, familiar shock that signaled the Cure, she realized how long it had been since she'd simply used her Power to help an animal. Since the day Tal Nova kidnapped her, she'd only Cured—and Killed—humans.

Healing the dog was like getting back to her roots, her true self, and she understood that at some deep level she'd been missing it.

The dog gave a yelp and backed away from her, its eyes already alert and bright, its fur filled with color and life. The green glow was gone.

At the same time, a vague feeling of nausea settled in Leah's stomach. Nothing major, not yet; she knew from past experience she had an hour or more before her symptoms became life threatening. But unlike when she was at work, here there was no reason to wait and pretend nothing was wrong.

Speaking like a teacher demonstrating a procedure to a class, she explained the next steps in the process to Green as she carried them out.

"The dog is Cured," she said. "Right now I'm carrying the disease inside me. If I were to wait too long, it would kill me the same as it would have killed the dog. Which is why I pass it on to another animal as soon as I can."

She motioned at the cage containing the monkey.

"You should inject him now and then step away. I wouldn't want you to be touching it at the same time I do."

The implication of her words caused Green's face to go a little pale. Beads of sweat formed on his forehead, although Leah wasn't sure if he was afraid of her or the monkey. As he reached between the bars, she wondered if he had any experience with injections. She'd never thought to ask. However, he expertly pinched a section of skin between his fingers and injected the contents of the syringe.

The rhesus, already on its deathbed, barely flinched.

"You've got about sixty seconds," Green said, backing up.

Leah didn't respond. She grasped the monkey's paw and felt the muted shock of transference. The monkey jerked once and then turned its rheumy gaze towards her, as if to ask why she was inflicting further torture on it.

"I'm sorry," she whispered, stroking its palm.

The monkey closed its eyes and let out a final breath.

Leah wiped tears from her eyes, wishing she didn't always cry when she had to sacrifice an animal. The soldiers watching her would no doubt take it as a sign of weakness, something to exploit. She walked away from the cart and sat down, pausing to rub the dog's ears as she went by.

"That's it?" Green asked from his position by the door.

"What did you expect?" Leah felt bitter inside and it flavored her words. "Lightning? Storm clouds? The trumpeting of angels? I thought you did your homework. That stuff only happens when I feel threatened, not when I'm Curing something."

Green wisely didn't answer. Instead, he made another call, requesting someone to take the two animals to the lab immediately.

Alarmed, Leah stood up. "You're not going to sacrifice that dog I Cured, are you? Because if you do, my cooperation is over."

"No, we're not." Something in Green's voice told her he was telling the truth, at least for now. "Blood tests, that's all."

A masked tech arrived and the door whooshed open, reminding Leah there must still be at least some soporific in the air.

Have I grown used to it? Am I tired and I don't even realize it?

Lost in her thoughts, she didn't notice Green exiting the cell with the technician until the door was almost closed.

"Wait!" She motioned with her hands. "When do I get to see John?"

Holding the door open with his foot, Green shrugged. "That depends on you. We have to run this same experiment again, except this time with some diagnostics hooked up to you. Can you, you know, do it again today or do we have to wait until tomorrow?"

Curing more than one animal in a day wasn't any hardship; she'd done as many as four in one day. But she wasn't about to let them know that.

"I can do one more," Leah told him, putting a note of exhaustion in her voice. "But that's all."

Green nodded.

"I'll see you in an hour."

Chapter Four

That evening, after a quick cheeseburger and fries in the officers' mess, Green joined General Moore and the intelligence agent he mentally referred to as Spooky—as an homage to Agent Mulder in the X-Files—in the General's conference room. Moore and Spooky were already poring over the diagnostic reports from the two experiments.

"I thought the meeting started at six," Green said, opening his own file.

Moore glanced up at him, his expression hard.

"Gotta be ahead of the pack if you want to win the race, Captain."

"Have you reviewed the reports, Captain?" Spooky asked, never taking his eyes off the data tables he was reading.

"Yes, earlier. Nothing really exceptional, from what I could see. Blood pressure, pulse, oxygen levels, all almost identical before and after she cured the rabbit. Same with her blood panels and EEG."

"And you don't find that exceptional?" Spooky's dark eyes narrowed and he looked back and forth between Green and Moore. "The woman somehow transferred a carcinoma from the test animal into herself and then passed it on to another animal, all without her brain waves, blood chemistry or even heart rate changing, and you don't consider that exceptional?"

"Not really. To her, it's no different than picking up a book and putting it down somewhere else." Before anyone could comment, he pointed to a blip on the EKG. "There is one change, right here. Right at the point where the cancer was in her. A slight increase in heart rate and blood pressure. But it goes back to normal before she passes the cancer on."

Spooky nodded. "The time corresponds to when she told us she gets that nauseated feeling, after she's taken in the disease. Fluctuations that small could result from feeling ill, stress, worry, any sort of emotional change. Then her body adjusts. No different than if you or I stubbed a toe or got a piece of disturbing email. Statistically insignificant."

Moore frowned. "So on the one hand you say we should consider her results exceptional, but on the other you say the deviations are insignificant. You're not making any sense."

Spooky turned to Green, obviously ignoring Moore's comment.

"Captain Green. Your background includes several years in bioterrorism, does it not?"

Green said nothing. The question wasn't one that needed answering because Spooky had undoubtedly read his file, knew of his research experience with various biological and chemical agents of destruction. It was one of the reasons he'd been chosen as DeGarmo's prime handler.

"Tell me," Spooky continued, "in your professional opinion, what do these results mean?"

Green glanced down at the reports again, aware of the two men waiting for his answer. What had he missed that Spooky had obviously seen? He read through the data again. And again.

Totally normal.

No physical deviations of any kind.

No physical...

No, it couldn't be.

A chill ran down Green's back, amplified by the cool breeze from the air conditioner on his suddenly damp neck.

"No physical reaction means that most likely there's no physical cause." Even saying it in general terms sounded like madness.

Spooky, however, seemed positively thrilled with his answer.

"Exactly! Cause and effect, except in this case we're seeing the effect and trying to determine the cause, instead of the other way around."

"Will someone please explain what the hell the point of this is?"

Green clenched his jaw so he wouldn't smile at General Moore's obvious frustration. The man's face was taking on a reddish hue that made his scars stand out more than usual. Spooky—apparently secure in his higher status on the ladder of rank—actually let out a chuckle. Green hurried to answer before the General's head exploded.

"What it means, sir, is that whatever energy DeGarmo is using to do what she does, it doesn't come from within her. Rather than being natural, it's...supernatural."

"Bullshit!" Moore slammed his hand on the table. "Just because you haven't found an explanation doesn't mean there isn't one. You just need to look harder. Cut her brain open if you have to."

"I'd rather it not come to such a...permanent choice," Spooky said. "At least not until we've exhausted all other options. But I have to agree with the Captain. In the absence of a natural cause, we must consider the supernatural."

The agent held up his hand before Moore could object again.

"I'm not talking about ghosts or demons, General. Although the physical changes she displays could support such a hypothesis, for sure. I'm speaking of the paranormal. Abilities beyond the norm. You're familiar with the experiments the military—both ours and other governments'—have done in the areas of far seeing, mind reading and telekinesis?"

"More bullshit," Moore said. "Waste of time and money."

Spooky's left eyebrow rose and his smile grew cooler, as if he was remembering something unpleasant.

"You might not say that if you'd read some of the same reports I have. But that's neither here nor there. The fact is, there have been people who've shown limited psychic abilities and, like Ms. DeGarmo, nothing unusual registered in their clinical data while they were doing so."

Watching the man's face, Green wondered what he'd read. And hoped he never had to find out for himself.

"Sir, excuse me, but if I'm interpreting you correctly, what you're saying is that it's possible she's harnessing some sort of internal or external energy, and we just can't measure it yet?"

"Yes. For now, it falls in the realm of supernatural because we can't quantify or qualify it. That may change with our next experiment."

Green glanced down at the reports.

"I don't see anything here—"

"It isn't in there," Moore said, his gruff, assured tone back as he stepped into the familiar role of leadership. "We decided on it just before you arrived. Tomorrow you're going to have DeGarmo demonstrate her other talent."

Green's heart sped up so fast it almost hurt.

"You want me to have her kill someone?"

"Not yet," Spooky said, his meaning obvious. Sooner or later they were going to have her kill someone. "This time it will just be a something."

The very thought of being near her when she changed into her alternate self made Green want to run for the nearest exit and never return. She'd nearly killed him once already, and she'd been wasted to near unconsciousness at the time.

What would she do—what *could* she do—if clearheaded?

Hoping to get them to reconsider, without appearing like a coward for suggesting it, Green shook his head.

"You heard what she said today. She only goes into that mode when she feels threatened."

Moore shrugged.

"So threaten her. But get her to change."

"I feel like a lab rat."

Leah and John were lying together on her cot, his one arm draped over her. Shortly before the evening meal was served, two guards had escorted John to her cell and locked him in with her. After a frantic greeting of hugs and kisses, they'd sat down and she'd told him everything that had happened since the previous night.

"At least you don't look like one anymore." John brushed his fingers across one arm, sending delightful shivers across her flesh, despite the fact she knew he was only indicating the places where an array of needle marks and bruises had discolored her skin just a few hours earlier.

"Self-healing, it's a wonderful thing."

Leah felt guilty about not having yet told John the whole truth about where the energy for her healing—and presumably killing—Powers came from, but under the present circumstances it was impossible. Odds were, someone was watching and listening at all times, so sharing secrets would have to wait.

In the meantime, lying in John's embrace not only felt good, it was probably also recharging her. That brought on more than a few twinges of shame as well; she was using him, in a way. But tempering the guilt was the knowledge that her body obviously never took anywhere near enough energy to actually harm someone. She was more like a sock or balloon getting dragged across a carpet, gathering tiny bits of electricity as she went. A little here, a little there. A hug here, a handshake there, a pet to a dog's head.

Over time, though, the bits added up.

After a few more minutes of silence, Leah spoke again.

"I'm scared of what they'll ask me to do next."

She'd already told him about Curing the dog, and then a rabbit. Passing the diseases to the two monkeys had been hard, but John had agreed she'd been doing them a favor just by ending their wretched lives as test subjects. She'd also told him about the blood tests, EKGs, brainwave monitoring and even a urine test, which had been especially humiliating.

"What? Like a CT scan? Or a human subject?" John's voice grew agitated. "I hope they don't think they can make you handle criminals."

"I'm thinking worse." It had been on her mind all day, and now, lying in the darkened room with nothing but John's body to distract her thoughts, it was on her mind again. "They've seen me Cure animals twice. But I don't think that's what they're really interested in. That was just to see if I'll do what they say. I think they want me to...you know..."

John's arm tensed and then relaxed.

"Become the other you and kill something."

"Yes."

"And you're afraid you won't be able to do it."

"No." She turned around so she was facing him, their noses only inches apart, close enough that she could smell the coffee and mustard on his breath from dinner. "I'm afraid that if I do it, the power will go to my head, make me overconfident, and I'll try something I shouldn't. And then they'll either kill you or me or both of us."

Staring into his eyes, Leah wondered how a conglomeration of colored cells could express so much emotion, even when you couldn't see the rest of the face. John's eyes, so dark they almost disappeared in the dim light, seemed to soften and grow warmer, like two pieces of chocolate sitting in the sun. She could feel his compassion radiating from them.

"Sometimes you just have to trust yourself. I don't know much about these powers you have, but I get the feeling they're a lot like you: stronger than you think."

Leah wasn't sure what to make of John's statement. It sounded like a compliment, but a cryptic one. Was he telling her to go for it, let her Power loose? Or that he trusted her to keep it under control?

She kissed him, long and hard, and then rolled back over so they could spoon again. She needed to think, and she couldn't do that while looking at him.

Long after John drifted into sleep, she was still awake.

Chapter Five

Leah wiped sweaty palms on her pants. She'd lost count of how many times she'd repeated the gesture since Green and two soldiers had come to take John back to his cell and remove their breakfast trays. After they left, a technician had arrived and stuck an assortment of wires to her forehead, chest and arms. The leads all disappeared into a black box that hung from a canvas belt at her waist. Two other technicians set up digital recorders on tripods outside the clear walls of the cell.

Since then, she'd been waiting almost fifteen minutes for Green or someone to return, and her anxiety was getting so bad she'd started pacing just to burn off some of her nervous energy.

Something was going to happen. She could feel it like a change in the air before a thunderstorm. Even though she couldn't see any people, a sense of expectancy charged the atmosphere.

Something is going to happen.

She just hoped it didn't involve her or John dying.

Almost a half hour after Green left, he finally returned, this time with four guards who held large, odd-looking pistols. Behind his mask, Green's forehead was beaded with sweat and his pupils dilated.

He looks more nervous than I feel.

It's going to be something big, that's for sure.

"Please take a seat on your bed." Green's words came out faster than normal, another sign of his agitation.

He waited until she sat down before continuing, "We're going to bring in another test animal. We need you to—"

"I know what you want. You want me to kill it, like I did those men at the slaughterhouse. I told you, though, it's not something I can just turn on like when I Cure an animal."

Green smiled, but it was an unappealing smile, knowing and gloomy, all at the same time.

"I don't think that will be a problem." He turned and left, two of the guards accompanying him. The other two took up positions outside the door, their backs to her.

Leah leaned back against the wall, hoping she didn't have long to wait this time. It turned out she didn't; only a couple of minutes passed before two masked technicians appeared, rolling yet another metal cage on a cart.

This one contained a medium-sized Labrador retriever.

Leah felt the anger rising inside her. They wanted her to kill a dog? Just thinking about it made her furious. And when the cage was wheeled into her cell and she saw the poor Chocolate lab trembling, her jaw tightened and her fists clenched in her lap.

No way. I am not doing this!

The technicians quickly exited the cell and shut the door. Only after they left did a maskless Green come down the hall.

This time he didn't enter the cell.

"Anytime you're ready," he said. He hadn't pressed any kind of button outside the door, so she figured there was some kind of speaker system that he'd activated before showing up.

"No. I won't kill a helpless animal for you. Not like that."

"I told them you'd say that." Green tapped a Bluetooth earpiece and spoke, "Bring him."

A cold mass formed in Leah's belly. There was only one thing he could mean.

Two guards came down the hall guiding a handcuffed John between them. They stopped a few paces away from Green and one of the guards jammed a gun into John's ribs.

"Ms. DeGarmo. I don't like being a hard-ass. But you're not leaving me a choice. In two minutes I'm going to give the order for Max there to pull the trigger. You can either kill the dog and prevent that from happening, or you can watch your boyfriend get shot and then kill the dog so you can save him. But that door doesn't open until the dog is dead."

"You bastards!" Leah took one of the chairs and threw it against the plexiglass wall. The dog yelped and cringed, but no one on the other side even twitched. "You goddamn bastards! You're worse than Tal Nova or any of the others!"

"Ninety seconds," Green said, ignoring her outburst.

Leah glanced at John. She expected him to say something, tell her to forget about him, or at least shake his head in nonverbal communication.

Instead, he winked at her.

That caught her completely off guard. *A wink? What the hell did that mean?*

"Sixty seconds." Green's tone let her know he was serious.

John must know that too. Which means...

Leah found herself smiling as she remembered his words from last night.

"Sometimes you just have to trust yourself. I don't know much about these powers you have, but I get the feeling they're a lot like you: stronger than you think."

Okay then.

They were about to find out just how strong she was.

Closing her eyes, she opened herself to the darkness.

In the control room, General Moore motioned at the monitor he and the agent he only knew as Smith were watching.

"This is it! She's starting to change. Holy shit, look at her eyes."

Moore never noticed Smith get up and leave the room.

Leo Green found himself backing away from DeGarmo's cell. It was like a miniature hurricane had formed inside the room, with the young woman as its eye. A heavy wind circled around, sending chairs and bedsheets tumbling across the floor. The Labrador huddled in a corner of its cage, clearly terrified.

This time DeGarmo's transformation didn't stop with her eyes. Her skin turned a sallow grayish-yellow and her hair stuck out in all directions like she'd stuck her finger in an electrical socket. She looked taller too, until Green noticed she was floating several inches off the ground. Black lines appeared on her arms and it took him a moment to realize they were the outlines of veins. Her lips split open in places, dark fluids dripping down and then getting whipped away by the wind.

Still, it was her eyes that were the worst. Glazed in bluish white until the pupils disappeared.

The eyes of a corpse.

Next to him, John Carrera gasped. So did one of the guards, despite being briefed on what might happen.

"Hold your ground, men. She's not a danger to us." Green hoped he was right. Who the hell knew what she might do?

"General, are you getting all this?" he said into the Bluetooth phone he wore.

"It's goddamn spectacular!" came the reply.

"Enjoy while you can," someone said, and Green turned to see Carrera staring right at him, wearing a very smug expression.

Something about the man's smile made Green look back at DeGarmo's cell.

She was floating within a raging storm cloud, red and yellow flashes of lightning exploding all around her.

And she had moved past the dog.

"Shit. Shit shit shit!"

"Green? What's the matter?"

"I think we have a code red, sir!" DeGarmo glided closer to the door, her black, oozing lips almost a perfect duplicate of Carrera's knowing smile.

General Moore shouted something in his ear, but Green didn't hear the words over his own bellowed orders.

"Shoot him!" He pointed at Carrera. "Shoot that motherfucker right now!"

The guard hesitated for a split second before pulling the trigger, an almost imperceptible delay, but one that allowed Carrera to jerk his body back and out of the grasp of the two men. The gun went off and two screams sounded simultaneously. Carrera fell to his knees, clutching his midsection. Next to him the second guard, a man named Kellogg, collapsed to the floor as well, blood already staining his uniform and pooling on the cold tiles thanks to the the bullet that had passed right through Carrera

Green's hand was still moving toward his own weapon when a new sound drowned out Moore's frantic shouts and the echo of the gunshot. It was a sound he'd never heard before, a deep, booming *crack!* reminiscent of river ice shattering on a warm day, only amplified a hundred times.

He knew what it was even before he looked.

The two-inch bulletproof Plastiglas—guaranteed to withstand a direct hit with a mortar—was spiderwebbed with cracks that radiated outward from a center point.

Right where the undead thing that was Leah DeGarmo had her hand.

"Oh shit." Forgetting about Carrera, General Moore and protocol, Green turned to run away. One of the remaining guards called out a warning but it was lost in a thunderous explosion. An invisible hand slapped Green in the back and then picked him up and tossed him down the hallway. Ragged pieces of Plastiglas ricocheted off the walls and floor around him.

He landed hard on his right shoulder. There was a moment of blinding agony and the branch-snapping sound of bones breaking, and then he was tumbling over, unable to see or hear, his entire world nothing but bright light and hammer blows of pain. He finally came to a stop fifteen feet from the cell, sprawled on his left side. Despite the multicolored spots obscuring his vision, he made out a dark shape taking up most of the hallway. He tried to focus but the effort just made things more blurry.

Through the ringing in his ears, he heard someone scream.

Chapter Six

The moment Leah opened herself to her Power, she knew she was going to break out of her cell.

What she hadn't expected was that it would be so easy.

She'd simply placed her hands on the wall and concentrated on the lightning surrounding her, guiding it, channeling it, focusing it all on one point.

The resulting explosion had startled her so badly she'd actually faltered for a moment, felt her feet brush the ground. Then she was floating again, moving out of the cell. John lay on the ground, his stomach stained with blood, but something in her sensed he was still alive so she shifted her attention to the other men. The ones with the guns.

The ones who wanted to hurt her and John.

There was no need to aim, no need to chase them. Thinking it brought her Power into action. First the two guards next to John, the one who'd fired the pistol and the one who lay dying on the floor. She imagined her energy grasping them and siphoning off their life force, replenishing the energy she'd spent breaking out of her cell.

As fast as her thoughts appeared, so they became real. Dark tendrils with openings at the end like elephant trunks snaked out and wrapped themselves around the two men. The open ends closed over their faces and Leah felt the energy rushing into her, reveled in the ecstasy of it the same way she would delight in gulping down a cold drink on a sweltering day. She wrung them out, squeezing every last drop of life from them until they were as dry and dead as cactus husks in a desert. Then she let them go and turned her attention to the other two guards who were halfway down the hall and running at full speed.

It made no difference.

She laughed as they froze in midstep and collapsed, their bodies shriveling into human raisins, their skin shrinking, becoming so tight their bones shattered and their organs appeared as visible bulges beneath their clothes.

That left only Captain Green.

His body lay awkwardly atop shattered chunks from the wall of her cell. Blood dripped from his arm where a jagged piece of bone protruded halfway between his elbow and wrist.

Compound fracture of the ulna, the veterinarian part of her mind diagnosed. *He's in shock from the pain and losing blood too fast. Definitely severed at least one artery.*

He tried to raise his head but the effort was too much and it thumped back onto the floor.

His life is draining away.

In that instant, a memory came to her: the battered and broken dog Del McCormick had brought into her clinic. Like Green, it had a compound fracture. And also like Green, it had been dying.

Like a fire doused with water, the fury inside her sputtered out.

I'm not a killer. Just because I have the ability doesn't mean I should use it. I never did before.

The Power to Kill had always been there, an aspect of the Cure. There'd never been a desire in her to pass pain or illness on to people, even people who some might think deserved it. She'd never once thought about becoming a vigilante, doling out secret death. In fact, she'd hated that part of her Power, the part which required her to pass on what she took in.

Leah sensed as much as saw the storm clouds around her fade away, taking with them the gale-force winds. Her feet touched the floor, letting her know she was no longer levitating. She imagined that if she looked in a mirror just then, her skin and eyes would no longer resemble a corpse's.

She knelt down next to Green and placed her hand on his arm. There was the familiar electric shock as she Cured him. Then his arm was whole again and his breathing settling into a normal rhythm. He opened his eyes and looked at her.

"What...what did you do?"

"Cured you," she said, standing up again. She moved over to where John lay on the floor and touched his stomach, aware that she could now control whether she Cured someone or passed on an injury. This time the shock was greater, whether because she'd already Cured someone or because John's wound was more serious, she couldn't tell. Already her arm was beginning to ache and now her stomach joined in.

"Hey, there," John whispered, grasping her hand. "I told you."

"You were right," she said, her voice equally soft. She knew he was referring to their conversation the previous night. "But I don't want to be that person. I just want to be the old me again, not a monster."

"Too late."

Leah turned at the sound of Green's voice. He was standing again, his pistol aimed at her. She opened her mouth to say something but never had the chance.

He fired.

In the moments between his pulling the trigger and his death, Leo Green had time for several thoughts:

This is my chance, before she changes again.

Her eyes! Jesus God, it's happening too fast!

Wait—she's not even—

Why didn't the bullet—?

And the final thought, as a hole opened in his belly, its twin ruptured the flesh of his chest. the bones in his arm snapped and tore through his skin, and he screamed so loud the lining of his throat ripped:

The two have become one.

Leah felt the bullet strike, a split second of pain like a hammer blow between her breasts, and then there was a more familiar sensation, the electric shock of Curing something.

Ten feet away, Green let out the most awful shriek she'd ever heard a man make. Blood exploded from his mouth, chest, belly and arm.

He fell to the floor and his death registered to her as a second jolt, only this time it was more like the energy kick of that first strong cup of coffee in the morning.

She looked down at herself. No storm clouds. No supernatural displays. No levitation.

Just her.

And yet she'd not only evoked the other side of her Curing Power, she'd also Killed. All at a distance.

What was happening to her?

Alarmed, she turned to John, who'd pushed himself to a sitting position against the wall.

His eyes went wide.

"Leah? Can you... Are you there?"

She nodded.

"It's me. I think. Why...?"

"Your eyes. The rest of you is...normal. But your eyes. It's like when you...change."

"No!" She had to see. She ran down the hall, ignoring John's shouts for her to wait. Past unmarked door after unmarked door until she came to one that stood partly open. Entering it, she saw a console with several computers and video screens, along with a lot of controls.

The screens all showed her cell and the hallway outside from various angles.

Putting her face close to one, she focused on her eyes.

And gasped.

They were the eyes of a corpse. Milky gray in the partially transparent reflection, but she knew they'd have a bluish tint when seen straight on. The cloudy haze extended over the pupils and iris, and then gave way to yellowing, bloodshot sclera.

She squeezed them shut and rubbed them, concentrating on their turning normal again. Maybe this was just her reaction to the danger Green had posed. Her adrenaline was too high. She took a deep breath and counted to twenty, trying to calm herself.

Opening her eyes again, Leah looked at herself once more.

"Oh God."

No change.

This can't be happening! Why won't they change back? I'm not that monster anymore!

A noise behind her, footsteps on tile. *John.* He must have followed her. She turned, wanting nothing more than for him to hold her, to tell her she hadn't mutated into some kind of freak.

A stranger in an army uniform stood there, an odd-looking gun in his hand. Before she could even think about reacting, he fired.

A bright halo of light exploded around her and the world suddenly spun in circles while thunder filled her head. The next thing she knew, she was on the floor, her ears ringing and her skin crawling with a tingling, burning sensation like she was covered in angry fire ants. She tried to move but her limbs wouldn't respond.

"They told me you were the perfect weapon, but I never realized how perfect," the man said, gesturing at her with the weird gun.

"Who…?" she tried to say, but all that came out was a slow exhale. *Who did he mean? Who had told him? I have to find out.*

Ignoring her attempts at forming words, he continued talking.

"We will find a way to turn you, even if it means torturing or killing everyone you hold dear and locking you in a goddamn impenetrable cave until your mind snaps."

As he spoke, his voice escalated in volume and his face grew red from the vehemence of his words. His terrible burn scars stood out in sharp contrast.

He has crazy eyes, Leah thought.

And then, without warning, he had a third eye, this one black and directly over his left one.

A trickle of blood leaked out of the black circle, and the man slowly collapsed and fell over.

Leah watched as a larger pool of blood formed beneath the other side of his head. A shadow appeared; she tried to turn her head but couldn't. She closed her eyes and waited for the unseen man to shoot her. Time passed.

Someone was calling her name, over and over. The voice grew closer, and despite the buzzing in her ears, she recognized it as John's.

He appeared in the doorway just as she was able to get her mouth to move.

"John...help me." This time her words were audible.

"Leah! Are you hurt?" He hurried over to her.

"No." She shook her head. It was an effort to move, but each breath seemed to bring a little more strength. "Did you shoot him?"

"What? No, I thought you—"

"No. I have to Cure him. He knows things...help me over there."

A frown crossed John's face but he didn't hesitate or question her. He half lifted, half slid her to the dead soldier and then stood back as she placed a shaking hand on his cheek.

She wasn't prepared for the tremendous shock when her flesh touched his. The prone body spasmed and her hand flew back. A searing pain erupted in her face and scalp, worse even than the sharp bite of the bullet wound he'd suffered.

"Turn him on his back," she gasped, fighting not to cry from the scalding fire digging into her skin. She prayed she never experienced burns like his, not if this was even half of what it felt like.

John shifted the soldier whose head wound was healed and his face unmarked.

The man's eyes opened.

"Who do you work for?" she asked him. "Who told you about me?"

The man stared blankly at her. His mouth opened. A trickle of drool ran over his lip and down his neck.

"Uh-uh-uh..." He stopped and then smiled. At the same time, he let go a loud fart. His smile grew wider, but there was no humor in it. Only satisfied pleasure.

"Dammit!" Leah backed away. She wanted to slap the man, kick him, punch him until he spoke.

Except she knew he never would.

Chapter Seven

Leah stared at the man she'd Cured and silently cursed the gods who'd given her an imperfect Power.

"What the hell's wrong with him?" John asked.

It took her a moment to regain her composure before she could answer.

"His brain. I Cured the bullet wound, and everything else that was wrong with him. Brought him back from the goddamned dead. But his brain...even though the cells were healed, they don't contain his memories, his personality. He's alive, but he's..."

"A vegetable," John finished.

"Yeah. I guess repairing a brain isn't like repairing other organs, even for me."

She started to get to her knees, almost losing her balance in the process. John held out his hand to her but she pulled away.

"Don't touch me. I've still got his injuries inside me, and I don't know how long I can hold them in check."

"So give them back." John poked the man with his foot and the soldier stared at the spot for a second before returning his gaze to the ceiling. More drool had puddled on his neck and the floor beneath him.

"No." Lea pushed herself to her feet, using one of the consoles for support. "I won't kill an innocent man. And he's about as innocent as they come."

Keeping one hand on the countertop to steady herself, she placed her other hand against the center of the equipment, felt the muted hum of the electronics through her palm.

"Energy comes in many forms, but in the end it's all just energy." A professor had said that many years ago, during one of her college physics classes.

Oh my God. Could it be that simple?

She let the death and pain flow out, the same as if she were passing on a terminal illness to an already doomed animal.

Sparks exploded from the console and the video screens shattered. There was a series of muffled *pops!* from the computer drives. At the same time, all the lights in the room and the hallway went dark.

Somewhere deeper in the building, alarms began to sound.

"Damn!" came John's voice in the darkness. "Did you do that?"

"I think so."

Leah felt inside herself. No trace of pain in her head, no acid fire on her skin. She'd done it! More than anything she'd learned about herself, more than any of the new Powers she had gained, this one ability was the greatest thing that could have ever happened to her.

"John, do you know what this means?" She reached for him in the dark, felt his doing the same. They clasped hands. "I passed those wounds into the computer system. From now on, when I Cure an animal, I don't have to kill something else!"

"That's great," he said, and she could tell he meant it. But there was something else in his voice, an urgency. "Right now we have to get the hell out of here."

She nodded and let him lead her out of the room, but her mind was still on the major transformation in her life. She'd always felt so guilty every time she killed something, even though the sacrifices were animals that were too old, too sick for her to Cure without raising suspicion. But she'd had to; there'd been no other options, not if she wanted to Cure at all.

For all those years she'd consoled herself by rationalizing it as the circle of life: animals lived and died, it was the natural order of things. She wasn't playing God by Curing her patients, she was merely making that circle of life last longer. The same thing doctors and people had been trying to do since the dawn of civilization.

And now? It was a question with as many possibilities as the branching corridors John was guiding them through, and filled with just as many dangers.

Her first thought was that she'd be able to Cure every animal that came to her, regardless of its diagnosis. Except that would quickly lead to complications. People wondering how their dying pets suddenly had completely recovered. Dogs and cats that were healthy and young well beyond the time they should have died from old age. Complications like that would bring more unwanted attention, which, in turn, would lead to situations just like the one she was in.

And you're not unstoppable, she reminded herself. *Look at what that soldier did, paralyzed you with a single shot.*

Of course, he hadn't used an ordinary weapon, The flash of light and strange sound told her the gun had to use some kind of laser or sonic disruption—or maybe a combination of both—to temporarily jumble a person's synapses. And who knew what other weapons the military might have developed? After all, it *was* what they did for a living.

John broke her train of thought by roughly pulling her into a doorway.

"Ssshhh." It came out as a whispered hiss.

Leah pressed her back against the door and listened for whatever he'd heard. Scattered red emergency lights set in the ceiling turned the hallway into a corridor to hell, their dim glow ensuring a potential enemy could be dangerously close before you could see them.

Then, over the thump of her own pulse in her ears, she heard the sound of footsteps.

Someone was coming!

Leah let go of John's hand, prepared to defend herself—defend both of them—if she had to.

And then froze.

Because she had no idea what she would do or how she would do it. Would her Power still work at a distance? Did she have to Cure before she could Kill? Would her previous supernatural form manifest itself if needed?

In that moment, she realized her biggest weakness was her own mind. A simple hesitation was all an enemy would need to put her down the way that soldier had.

The footsteps slowly drew closer, each one adding to her inner quandary, until the men were so near she could hear their breathing.

Just then, the crackle of a handheld radio echoed in the dark.

"We've found the general! Medical assistance needed in video room A!"

"Let's go!" a voice said, so near and loud that Leah actually jumped and had to bite down a surprised cry. A second later, two men ran past the doorway in the direction John and Leah had just come from.

"This is our chance," John said, pulling her into the hall.

They followed the main corridor, ignoring side hallways, for what seemed a million miles to Leah. Each branch heightened her anxiety at getting caught again. The silence—except for their footsteps—made things worse. Why weren't there any alarms going off? She'd expected blaring sirens and packs of soldiers in the wake of her escape. Instead, she felt like they were being stalked by ninjas.

She was about to ask John if he had any idea of how they would get out when a dancing light appeared up ahead. John stopped and Leah's heart jitterbugged in her chest as she recognized it: the bouncing beam of a flashlight hitting the corridor walls.

"They're coming right at us," John whispered. "Quick, back this way." He turned and led her to a side hallway they'd just passed. They moved deeper into the hall, past several doors, and waited for the soldiers to go by.

Leah tried not to breathe while they stood there, backs pressed against the wall. Seconds ticked by, turning into minutes. Afraid someone might sneak up behind them, she kept glancing back into the darkness. On the fourth or fifth time—she'd lost count, her brain ready to explode from tension—she noticed something was different.

There were lights. Still far away, but definitely there.

Oh shit.

She tugged on John's sleeve, not wanting to speak for fear of the other men who had to be close to them by then and must have turned their lights off because the corridor was dark. She felt him turn in her direction and she pointed down the hall at the lights.

And realized how stupid *that* was, since he couldn't see her.

"Down there," she said in a whisper so soft she could barely hear it herself. "Lights."

John's body tensed under her hand and he leaned past her. Suddenly he grabbed her arm and started pulling her down the hall. Toward the lights.

Has he gone crazy? Leah tried to pull away but he just held her tighter and ran faster, practically dragging her as his fingers bruised her arm.

Then she saw it.

A door! An unlit red-and-white *EMERGENCY EXIT* sign sat high up near the ceiling. And the lights...they were shining through around the edges of the door.

John hit the door at full speed, ramming the metal bar with his hip. It flew open and in the same instant the world exploded in a silent detonation of light so bright Leah had to squeeze her eyes shut and cover them with her arms as she stumbled into John's back.

Despite not being able to see, she knew immediately that they were outside. Warm, fresh air enveloped her, wonderfully welcome after the stale, air-conditioned atmosphere of the building. The ground was hard under her feet, and she risked peering through squinted eyes to see where they were.

And if anyone was waiting to kill them.

Through tears that made everything look like she was seeing through someone else's glasses, she saw they'd ended up in a parking lot. Only a few scattered cars were present, at least directly in front of them.

"Head for the woods," John said, putting an arm around her waist. "It's our only chance."

Her eyes still half-closed because of the bright sun riding high overhead, Leah looked in the direction where John was now leading them.

Past the parking lot was a green, empty field that appeared larger than her entire neighborhood. And beyond that a fence. And then woods.

He wants to cross all that without being seen? We're as good as dead. They don't even have to chase us. Snipers will pick us off before we get halfway there.

Despite her fear, Leah ran alongside John, her head ducked and her shoulders tight, expecting a bullet to hit her at any moment. It didn't matter that she'd been shot before and suffered no injury; her brain still hadn't come to terms with being at least partially invulnerable.

Besides, that had happened before, when she'd been different. Now there was no telling how her body would react to a bullet tearing through her, shattering bone and ripping organs to shreds...

Stop it! She forced away the image of her death and concentrated on running faster.

The change from blacktop to grass happened sooner than she expected and filled her with equal parts hope that they would make it and certainty that they'd be gunned down any second. John must have felt something similar, because he put his head down and somehow increased his speed even more. Leah kept up with him, her habit of jogging on weekends making up for her shorter stride. Even so, she was already breathing heavily and had the first hints of muscle exhaustion starting up in her ribs and legs as lactic acids began collecting faster than her body could break them down.

At one point she glanced up and saw that they'd covered half the distance to the fence. Spurred on by the sight of it, she tried to quicken her pace even more. Instead, all that happened was she stumbled for a second before regaining her balance, and then had a cramp ignite in her calf.

"Shi—!" the curse got lost as she gasped for air, but it was enough to make John turn around.

"What?" His breathing was just as labored, his face flushed to the point where you couldn't see his eyebrows against his red, sweating skin.

"C-cramp," she said, her gait now more of a hop than a true run as she tried not to put weight on her protesting leg.

"Can't stop, we're almost there." He put his arm around her back to support her. Without waiting for an answer, he started running again.

Leah gritted her teeth and willed her legs to move. The first few steps were pure agony; each time her foot landed on the ground, fire raced up her calf and her leg buckled.

Then a miracle happened.

The pain disappeared, washed away by a cool, energizing wave that flowed through her, leaving her feeling like she could run another ten miles. At the same time, John stumbled and she had to support him. She glanced down and saw a faint green glow around his right calf.

In the next instant it disappeared, simultaneous with her experiencing a sudden loss of energy. Not to the point where she couldn't run, but enough to know she wasn't going to be sprinting for two miles, let alone ten.

What the hell just happened? she wondered as John picked up the pace again.

It was almost as if...I shared my Power with John. Used his life force to Cure myself and then gave him back some of my energy, balanced it between us so neither of us would collapse.

All without even thinking about it.

More changes in her Powers? It was getting so she couldn't keep up with them.

Then there was no time to even think about what had happened as they reached the fence separating the field from the beckoning safety of the woods.

"Wait." John held out a trembling arm to stop her from moving forward. His breath came in huge, wheezing gasps. "Let me...test it...first."

Leah didn't even respond; she let him search for a stick while she bent over, her hands on her thighs, and tried to get enough air into her lungs to put out the fire in her chest.

John tossed a branch against the fence and it bounced off.

"Not...electrified," he said. "I'll...help you...over."

She didn't think either of them would have the strength to climb the ten-foot wire mesh, but somehow they made it to the other side without falling. After taking cover behind a tree and catching their breath, a fifteen-minute walk took them to a highway. They followed it to the nearest town, which turned out to be the Upstate New York village of Liberty, where John called a friend to come pick them up.

Leah slept the entire two-hour ride home.

Not once did she think about how easy their escape was.

Chapter Eight

Agent Michael Smith smiled as he watched the video of Leah DeGarmo and John Carrera scaling the security fence surrounding the secret base he'd set up. He'd been afraid one or both of them would get hurt during their escape earlier in the week. It'd been tricky enough guiding them to the exit without their realizing it. An injury would mean resorting to a desperation plan of having two of his men disguised as civilians "accidentally" stumbling across the escaping pair and helping them into town.

Another monitor showed General Moore in the infirmary. His condition had deteriorated over the past two days, to the point where he needed life support to maintain him. Smith felt no regret at the man's loss. He'd done what they needed him to—served as the command figurehead for the soldiers, all of whom would have been hesitant about taking orders from a "spook."

And when Moore became a liability, there'd been no choice but to stop him before he told DeGarmo more than she needed to know.

He'd had a moment of near panic when DeGarmo brought the general back to life, but luckily healing memories was beyond even her power.

Power. The word echoed in Smith's head. DeGarmo was an untapped source of limitless possibilities. And other than her boyfriend and a double handful of soldiers—all of whom would be assigned to his special ops team before the end of the day—only two people in the world knew about her.

And it was time to call the other one.

Smith tapped one of three contact numbers in his phone. It answered on the second ring.

"Hello." The voice on the other end knew exactly who was calling.

"Plan B is a go," Smith said, "as we both expected. I have to thank you. She's everything you said and more. I'll be in touch soon regarding the next steps. For now, just keep doing what you've been doing. Help her, support her, be everything she needs you to be. I'll be in touch soon." He hung up before the other man could respond.

On the monitor, General Moore coded and died.

Tapping a few keys, Smith backed the video log up to the point where DeGarmo broke out of her cell.

He had a lot of studying to do.

"Who was that?"

John closed his phone and stuck it back in his pocket. They'd been staying in a hotel in Manhattan, courtesy of Leonard Marsh, for the past three days. During that time, Marsh's security team had been watching Leah's house and office, plus John's house, to see if they were under surveillance.

"Marsh," John said. "As far as they can tell, everything's clean. No bugs, no suspicious vehicles, nothing. He thinks it's safe for us to go home."

"That would be like a miracle." Leah patted the overstuffed mattress of their bed. "Staying in a hotel is great, but I really miss my own house."

The news that they weren't being watched was just the latest in a string of good luck that had Leah feeling like life might finally be returning to something close to ordinary again. The most important thing was that physically she was perfectly normal again. What she referred to as her "dead eyes" had disappeared at some point during their escape from the military base. She believed—and John agreed with her—that it happened when she passed the general's wounds into the building's network.

Of almost equal importance was finding out they weren't on the Wanted lists of any military or government agencies. Leah had called Marsh as soon as they got to Rocky Point, and in turn he'd called some of his contacts. As far as he could tell, the names DeGarmo and Carrera weren't raising red flags anywhere.

"That doesn't mean you're safe, though," he'd told them. "From what you've told me, this sounds like more of a covert operation, something off the grid. Which means someone might still be looking for you. I think you should hide out in the city for a while until we're sure it's safe."

They'd taken Marsh up on his offer of a hotel room and checked in under his name.

Now, if what he said was true, they could finally get their lives in order again, or at least something close to it. Marsh had promised to post security guards at their houses and the clinic 24/7, which went a long way toward easing Leah's lingering fears of being taken hostage again.

That she wasn't completely terrified was something of a shock to her. She wasn't sure if it was because she'd become numbed to the danger of it all, or because the exponential growth of her Powers gave her a confidence her conscious brain hadn't processed—or accepted—yet.

What will be, will be.

A sentiment that could either be defeatist or optimistic.

Maybe it's both, she thought, getting off the bed. *Or maybe there's a third option: realistic.*

"Ready to go home?" John asked. His expression told her he already knew the answer, but she said it anyway.

"Let's start packing."

A week later, Leah opened the door to the clinic and couldn't help but smile at the sight of a completely filled waiting room. She greeted the people and pets she knew, and introduced herself to the others before heading into the back to put on her white lab coat.

John arrived an hour later with coffee and donuts, and the news that his retirement from the police force was official and he was ready to take on the role of office manager. It was something they'd discussed over the past week while reviewing applications for Leah's new assistant.

"I'll feel safer if I can keep an eye on you," he'd said, and while part of her cringed at the thought of them being together day and night, she had to admit it made her feel better too.

"Just for the first month," she'd told him. "Then you have to get a real job."

He handed her the coffee, gave her a kiss and then grabbed his keys.

"I'll get out of your hair for a while. Bank and then post office. I'll be back in an hour."

He paused at the door to her office.

"Try to stay out of trouble while I'm gone."

"Yes, Dad." She rolled her eyes at him. "Don't worry. This place is as safe as Fort Knox."

He started to say something, then shook his head and left.

A month of working together? Leah, what were you thinking?

Still, it was nice to have him around. Security details or not, it was John who'd kept her safe longer than anyone. And at least he was a visible presence.

There was no sign of Marsh's team but she knew it was out there, thanks to the daily email reports she received. That, plus the new video security systems at the house and clinic, provided the kind of security only rock stars and dignitaries merited. There were only two rooms with no camera coverage.

The examination room and the operating theater.

It was into the former where she led her first patient of the day, a six-year-old boxer with a massive growth on the side of its neck. Based on the pulsing green glow surrounding it, Leah was pretty certain the cancer was reaching the critical point.

"We'll have to keep him overnight, Mrs. Weston," she told the dog's distraught owner. "It may be a tumor, but it might also be nothing more than a fatty deposit or a cyst that needs to be drained. I'll do an ultrasound and a biopsy this afternoon, and most likely you can pick him up tomorrow."

Once out of sight, she guided the dog up onto an examination table and placed her hand on the tumor. There was the familiar electric shock and the dog gave a startled *yip*.

When she took her hand away, the lump was gone.

"Definitely cancer," she whispered as a throbbing pain started in her neck. She gave the dog a treat and then opened a nearby closet. Inside were four dozen portable radios John had picked up from various discount stores. She took one and placed it in the sink. Holding it with both hands, she concentrated on transferring the pain in her throat to the radio.

A second later there was a sound like bacon frying and a shower of sparks exploded out from the casing, leaving melted plastic in their wake.

Tossing the radio in the garbage, Leah looked at the dog and smiled.

"Congratulations. You're my first guilt-free Cure."

As she led the dog away, she marveled at how the road of her life could go from hell to heaven in only two weeks.

For the first time in far too long, she was looking forward to seeing what lay down that road.

Chapter Nine

"So, that's all you're going to do is watch her?"

Michael Smith jumped inwardly at the sound of Tom Niagara's voice. He'd been so engrossed with the live feed of DeGarmo curing a cat with a mangled back leg that he hadn't heard his boss enter the room.

Careless. That's the kind of thing that can get you demoted.

Or killed.

"For now, yes," he said in a casual tone, as if he hadn't been caught unawares. "The idea is to give her a lot of rope. Let her think she's safe so she returns to a normal routine. Think of it as a primate study. We're observing her in her natural habitat so she won't be hiding anything from us. We'll learn a lot more this way. Gradually, we'll step things up. Put her in potentially dangerous situations and see how she reacts."

"Won't that make her suspicious?"

"A random mugging in the mall parking lot? A dog or cat that suddenly goes berserk in the exam room? I don't think so. And if they do, we've got our man on the inside to smooth things over."

"You mean the man who almost ruined everything," Niagara said, his voice filled with scorn.

Smith turned in his chair.

"None of us could have foreseen the unexpected events we had to deal with. A rogue employee? Religious fanatics? Kidnappers? DeGarmo becoming some kind of Grim Reaper? All things considered, our man's done a damn fine job of staying in DeGarmo's good graces."

"Speak of the devil." Niagara pointed past Smith to the video monitor where John Carrera and Leonard Marsh were entering the clinic through the back door.

"See?" Smith didn't try to hide the satisfaction in his voice as Leah greeted them. "The more trust he builds now, the easier it will be for him to manipulate her later."

"And what about the other one?"

Smith smiled. "Carrera has no idea he's a walking surveillance unit. We have teams watching him twenty-four seven. Trackers and bugs in all his clothes. Cameras in his office, car and house. We hear everything he hears, and we see practically everything he sees."

"Let's hope so." Niagara turned and headed for the door. "There's a lot riding on this. More than you can imagine."

Smith waited until he was sure Niagara was gone before getting up and closing the door. He didn't want to be surprised again. He had a pretty good idea just how much was riding on Leah DeGarmo. Someone like her was worth more than any top-secret weapons research. Certainly worth more than the lives of a few spies.

Which was why he had his own plans for the veterinarian. And why he was keeping an ace up his sleeve. Having a man on the inside was a good idea.

Having two was even better.

Especially if one of them didn't even know it.

He watched Leah talking with the only two people in the world she trusted, and he allowed himself a smile.

Soon, Ms. DeGarmo. Soon the entire world will know about your powers.

And I'll be the one controlling them.

About the Author

A life-long resident of New York's haunted Hudson Valley, JG Faherty has been a finalist for the Bram Stoker Award® (Ghosts of Coronado Bay, The Cure) and ITW Thriller Award (The Burning Time), and he is the author of five novels, nine novellas, and more than 50 short stories. He writes adult and YA dark fiction/sci-fi/fantasy, and his works range from quiet suspense to over-the-top comic gruesomeness. He enjoys urban exploring, photography, classic B-movies, good wine, and pumpkin beer. As a child, his favorite playground was a 17th-century cemetery, which many people feel explains a lot.

He is also a member of the Horror Writers Associations' Board of Trustees as well as the head of the HWA's Library & Literacy program, and an active member of the Science Fiction Writers of America, Mystery Writers of America, International Thriller Writers, and Romance Writers of America. You can follow him at www.twitter.com/jgfaherty, www.facebook.com/jgfaherty, http://about.me/jgfaherty, and www.jgfaherty.com.

Other Books By JG Faherty

Novels
The Burning Time
Cemetery Club
Ghosts of Coronado Bay
Carnival of Fear

Novellas
Death Do Us Part
Winterwood
Cult of the Black Jaguar
Legacy
Thief of Souls
Fatal Consequences
Castle by the Sea
He Waits
The Cold Spot

Made in the USA
Middletown, DE
16 January 2023

22281457R00166